Praise for *We*

"A twisted campus novel told in the third person, which collectively expresses the perspective of three ambitious, brilliant students. . . . It's a rollicking read that offers a sharp take on the creative process, revenge, and envy." —*Elle*

"Elegant and enthralling." —*Newsweek*

"[*We Wish You Luck*] does not disappoint. . . . The story explores inspiration, aspiration, and good, old-fashioned literary thievery." —*Vanity Fair*

"A classic tale of revenge and redemption, as well as love and friendship, and success and ambition. . . . Zancan adeptly describes the naked wanting, aspirations, and work that are part of the MFA experience, but she also shows how devastating cruelty or even mere criticism can be depending on how it is received and the recipient's mindset. The novel's characters are multi-dimensional." —*BUST*

"[An] elaborate revenge plot, which I just had to see through to the last dark deed." —*Goop*

"Zancan does a wonderful job of describing the characters who populate this program, with excellent pacing and a momentum that turns the MFA life into a gripping story of professional and personal revenge." —*The Millions*

"Immersive and atmospheric, easy to stick with. . . . *We Wish You Luck* is a clever take down of the systems and privileges of writing programs and the academicification of creative writing." —*BookRiot*

"So unbelievably satisfying." —*HelloGiggles*

"Literary catnip . . . young writers, bad teachers, revenge, poetry. A Eugenides-esque chorus of students narrate the events of their time at a low residency MFA program in Vermont." —*Lit Hub*

"[I]nventive, addictive. . . . Zancan excels at portraying the claustrophobia and competitiveness that can arise when someone is near others who share the same goals. This ambitious novel about love and revenge reads like a thriller, while asking probing questions about what it means to make art and how artists influence each other, for better or worse." —*Publishers Weekly*

"Captures the fraught environment of almost-grown-ups on campus in sharp, unsparing detail and with lyrical momentum. . . . Asks intriguing questions about power, complicity, and the urge to tell someone else's story." —*Kirkus Reviews*

"Zancan weaves together an extraordinary story peopled by fascinating characters who are not easily forgotten. She explores the communal process of literary production and creates a palpable tension between creation and destruction that will keep readers engaged." —*Booklist*

"Caroline Zancan's wizardry is difficult to summarize: her prose is precise, deft, cutting—summing up a glance, an intent, a person's inner weather with perfect efficiency, and making it look easy. *We Wish You Luck* is a book for anyone who's ever had literature change their life. It makes the undeniable case for the power of words on a page—their power to make us, and to break us apart completely."
—Rachel Khong, author of *Goodbye, Vitamin*

"A seductive and tightly controlled literary revenge story. With a dash of *The Secret History*, *We Wish You Luck* is a wonderful, hypnotic novel about craft, narrative, and the stakes of literary production." —Lydia Kiesling, author of *The Golden State*

"A coming-of-age story filled with fascinating, richly imagined characters, Zancan tells the story of writers and their intricate, at times darkly ruinous desires. It's rare to describe a book about writing as 'addictive,' but that's exactly what Zancan has done here." —Hala Alyan, author of *Salt Houses*

"*We Wish You Luck* is a thrilling tale, a puzzle that isn't so much assembled as revealed by its crafty chorus of We. I loved watching the story unfold, and I loved never knowing if the collective impulse was to create or destroy. A smart, fun read."
—Lindsay Hunter, author of *Eat Only When You're Hungry* and *Ugly Girls*

ALSO BY CAROLINE ZANCAN

Local Girls

We
Wish
You
Luck

CAROLINE ZANCAN

Riverhead Books · New York

RIVERHEAD BOOKS
An imprint of Penguin Random House LLC
penguinrandomhouse.com

The Library of Congress has catalogued the Riverhead hardcover edition as follows:

Names: Zancan, Caroline, author.
Title: We wish you luck : a novel / Caroline Zancan.
Description: New York : Riverhead Books, an imprint of
Penguin Random House LLC, 2020.
Identifiers: LCCN 2018050040 (print) | LCCN 2018051481 (ebook) |
ISBN 9780525534952 (ebook) | ISBN 9780525534938 (hardcover)
Classification: LCC PS3626.A6293 (ebook) |
LCC PS3626.A6293 W4 2019 (print) | DDC 813/.6--dc23
LC record available at https://lccn.loc.gov/2018050040
LC ebook record available at https://lccn.loc.gov/2018051481

First Riverhead hardcover edition: January 2020
First Riverhead trade paperback edition: January 2021
Riverhead trade paperback ISBN: 9780525534945

Printed in the United States of America
1   3   5   7   9   10   8   6   4   2

BOOK DESIGN BY LUCIA BERNARD

For Louie and Mirabel,
who came along and made everything better

The truth will set you free.
But not until it is finished with you.

—*David Foster Wallace*, Infinite Jest

AUTHORS' NOTE

There are a million different versions of this story. We were all so desperate for material back then that we turned taco night in the cafeteria into an event. If one of us told a story about the cruelest way we had ever been broken up with, or the contents of the note that got our best friend suspended junior year, the rest of us would lean in, just in case the punch line or reveal could be borrowed for first drafts currently in progress. We had twenty different words for the shade of milk that Bridget Jameson threw at Jamie Brigham when he told her that her fiction read like fiction. There is no place where your life is less your own than at a gathering of writers.

We were all there to get our MFA in creative writing. Because ours was a low residency program we were only on campus for ten-day residencies twice a year, in June and again in January. What happened across the three residencies we're about to cover—a January sandwiched by two Junes—would be worth telling even by much higher narrative standards than ours, but the sweeping scope of the story grew even larger in our minds over time, in our open, unnamed Word documents. There are those of us who would call this an underdog story, but we can't agree on which of the characters would really, technically qualify as an underdog. Hannah and Leslie were confident in the unfussy, understated way that girls who have the great fortune of being pretty both before and after puberty often are, and Jimmy was the best writer the school had ever seen. The less subtle among us might stretch for the word *evil* when it comes to themes, though there is no strong consensus on whether to use it for the girls themselves or for the thing that made them do what they did—if it was the act or the reaction. In some versions of the story, Simone first joined the faculty during the summer residency that Hannah and Leslie and the rest of us started the program, while others are adamant that it was the January before. This might sound like a small detail, but when you are in northern Vermont on a cloistered, remote campus for ten days, the weather is more than a detail.

Maybe it was because Hannah, Leslie, and Jimmy's story was more interesting, always and finally, than the unfinished novels we kept in drawers after we graduated and the chap books we self-published, that it always drew us back in.

Maybe it was because we missed one another, and making sure we had every detail of the story right—that every turn in the version we were currently working with happened at just the right moment and in just the right way—was as good an excuse as any to call one another up at impolite hours of the night when we couldn't sleep. Whatever the reason, it's as much our story, in the end, as it is theirs. Maybe more.

Maybe we need to move on. Maybe this story that doesn't truly belong to any of us is blocking the stories we could otherwise write, each of us on our own. Maybe the details matter less than we think they do, or they're as sharp and true as we'll ever get them. Maybe even the best stories need to be retired at some point, even if you think you could tell it better if you had another try.

But we'll tell it one last time.

June

There is no train ride in the world prettier than the one from New York's Penn Station to Albany. Ten of the seventeen people in our class took that train up to the first June residency. The solemn, solitary appreciation that those of us on the train had for the violent ripples of the Hudson River, which ran along the tracks, and the eerie, radioactive-orange just-after-sunset light is one of the few things we all had in common. We sat in separate rows—separate cars where possible—pretending not to see one another when we passed each other in the aisles, knowing these three hours would be the last we'd have completely to ourselves for the next ten days.

It was half camp, half graduate program we were headed to. Half vacation—at least, it used up all our vacation days—half second job. We sometimes hated telling people we only had to be on campus for two short residencies a year, because it made it seem like a part-time program, when in reality we had to mail our professors packets with twenty pages of new work and two critical papers every month, which was considerably harder than drinking wine on campus during the stretches we were technically "in school." In between residencies, we didn't have the luxury of writing all day, and had to set alarms an hour earlier than we would have for our paying work alone, and we scribbled good lines on napkins during lunch breaks. But we graduated without all the debt. There are fewer than ten low-residency MFA programs in the country, and the classes tend to be small, but that only makes it a more exclusive club. Fielding's program was set up so that its students had minimal interaction with the liberal arts undergrads—our residencies were held during their summer and winter breaks. The undergrads had not yet tasted the tedium and burnt coffee that best characterizes most entry-level office jobs, which we felt certain kept them from fully appreciating the beauty of a campus we loved at first sight.

We all had secret lives back home. We were doctors and judges and waitresses. Baristas and teachers and marketing managers. We had children and grandchildren, boyfriends, wives, and pets, pictures and anecdotes about whom, it was silently and mutually agreed, would come out for sharing only once, in the beginning of the first residency. They were the tools of our procrastination, interrupting the stories we were working on to ask for a warm cup of milk or the name of the new neighbor, just when those stories were starting to get good. This was our time—time for which we had given up tropical cruises, family reunions, and exotic destination weddings. We had shown up tired and droopy to our jobs the mornings after all-nighters pulled to make packet deadlines, and typed dialogue on our cell phones in the middle of our children's dance recitals. And so, during the ten-day stretch when our part-time campus beckoned and kept us, we guarded our time vigilantly, careful of the omniscient threat of home and all its comforts.

The program's students generally fell into three categories. The first was the married accountants. Or married ad-copy writers. Or married drug reps. People who had jobs that no one's practical father had ever warned against. Monotonous, reliable, well-paying work that came with benefits and retirement plans and that nobody ever dreamed about doing when they were young. These holders of practical jobs were almost always men, but it was not their practical jobs or their gender that really defined this first kind of student. It was their boredom. When they were off campus they fought their boredom in the small, suburban towns they lived in by writing gratuitously violent stories in clunky, showy prose that always felt like a version of somebody else's writing, but less sure of itself, less effortless. It was prose you could feel working. The rest of us almost felt bad for them, because it was clear that their overwritten Westerns and Brooklyn crime novels had been written by someone who had never seen the desert or ridden a subway, but also that these stories had been labored over, redrafted again and again, and were loved. We didn't, though—feel that bad for them—because during the ten days they were *on* campus this group of students fought their boredom by flirting with the twentysomething female students who had not been out of school long enough to realize that the beers these men bought for them, and the men's willingness to laugh at their jokes or encourage their latest novel ideas, were all bad clichés. The only people more convinced than the rest of us that these men would never do anything with their lackluster, after-hours writing ambition and their time in the program except maybe strain their marriages even further than they already were, were the men themselves. They didn't have the stacks of rejections the rest of us did, because they hadn't bothered to submit their work anywhere.

We all secretly took pride in having Lucas White and Robbie Myers as our class representatives to the larger married-accountant body of students, because they took the art of revelry to a new level. Noticing, on the first night of our first residency, that our informal semicircle of first-years drinking wine out of plastic Solo cups dispersed earlier than it might have if the grass hadn't been so itchy, they drove into town to get those bouncy balls that double as chairs. They eventually incorporated the balls into the literary drinking games they created, which had surprisingly thoughtful and complex rules. During our last residency Lucas threw Robbie a surprise thirty-seventh birthday party that featured a homemade cake with Lucas's face on it. Though we all laughed when he uncovered the cake, we had to admit that the homemade buttercream frosting was as delicious as any we'd ever tasted. It was only years after we left campus for the last time that we realized these flourishes had been as inspired as the sturdiest, most well-crafted lines of prose any of us could point to in our own work—we can still recall the surprising way the vanilla of the frosting and the coconut of the cake took turns arriving on our tongues. We feel bad, remembering that cake now, about how we assumed their games and jokes and general good natures made them less serious writers than the rest of us, even as we played the games and laughed at the jokes, and retreated to our dorm rooms feeling less alone in this strange place because of them.

Though each of us could point to plenty of times we'd been on the receiving end of Robbie's cutting humor, Lucas was the one who was truly gifted at pushing boundaries and buttons. A bad case of septic arthritis as a child had left him with a pronounced limp. His four older brothers had taken it as their duty to teach him that the most effective way to avoid jokes at his expense was to think up the cleverest, most stinging insults before anyone else could, so that by lobbing the biggest stones at himself he would leave only pebbles for bullies. He took this habit of his as permission to point out the blemishes and soft spots the rest of us tried to hide about ourselves. And though none of us really minded, given that he never focused too much on any one target, some of us swore his limp was more pronounced just before or after his most savage ribbing, reminding us why these liberties were his to take. More important, though, his limp left him with a prescription for medical marijuana, which he and Robbie smoked freely around campus. Spotting any sort of authority, even on the distant horizon, they made fast, delighted work of pointing to the massive joint between them, Lucas's *I need it for medicine* timed perfectly to Robbie's *It's for his limp.* Robbie never bothered to make up an excuse for the considerable number of hits he himself took.

The next group of people was the retirees and the babies. The former doctors and lawyers who wanted to leave some record of the careers they had just retired from, and all the strange and interesting things they had seen and the noble acts they had done in the face of them—the jury that had returned the verdict they had gone to bed praying for every night for three years but never really expected; the guilty clients they knew how to help and the innocent ones they didn't; the patient who survived a three-story fall or fourteen-hour surgery and the healthy thirtysomething who had died on the table during a routine procedure. These students were always the gentlest in workshop and rarely drank or danced in the student center. We saw them walking sometimes in the early morning, on the edge of campus, while the rest of us scrambled to the dining hall to grab something on the way to class before they stopped serving breakfast, and again during open, unscheduled chunks of time in the afternoon, heading out into the woods with their binoculars, eager to find the rare birds the Vermont woods are known for. The counterpoint to these gray-haired baby boomers were the twenty-three-year-olds who had come to the program at the very start of their postschool lives, with everything ahead of them, unsure how to fill the years to come. They didn't necessarily have a passion for writing; the problem was that they didn't really have a passion for anything—if they had done better on their LSATs they might've gone to law school. Some of them already had graduate degrees. They worked in coffee shops and volunteered on political campaigns when they weren't on campus.

Tammy had just retired from thirty years of social work for the state of Virginia. She also had a law degree she still occasionally used for pro bono work. She was the authentic version of the country protagonists so many of us tried in vain to capture on the page. She used words like *Mama* without any irony, or even any awareness that this was not how everyone addressed their mothers. Her work was cancerous with the worst things her career had shown her—the most hopeless cases and the darkest parental acts—but she had the good sense not to describe them in any detail, and instead she let them live just off the page, letting your imagination do the dirty work. The language she used to convey these things was abundantly unfussy; her words were functional, not acrobatic. That someone who knew as little as she did about verbal pyrotechnics knew that what went unsaid was more powerful than even the sharpest, most colorful language reminded us all that as useful as training was, predisposition counted for something, too.

The details of the various hells her career had taken her through were not the only things she withheld. She had introduced herself as only "Tammy" to all of us—no last name. People in her workshop confirmed that it was the only name on top of her writing sample. She was the first person in our class whose name we all knew.

The final group was the industry people—the people who worked at magazines and online journals that reviewed books, sometimes even at publishing houses. They never came right out and said that they knew things about books and writing that you didn't, but their knowing, pressed-lip smiles and their literary tote bags made it so they didn't have to. They occasionally hung out at the student center, but they mostly drank nice wines and brown liquors that they had brought up on the train from New York, in small, exclusive groups in their rooms. They judged the married accountants harder than anybody, and the accountants learned quickly not to make a romantic target out of anyone from this group.

Mimi Kim was the social media coordinator for a small press in Brooklyn and relished any opportunity to display her considerable knowledge of things that have had exactly zero effect on the course of human existence. She knew what appetizers were served at the Nobel Prize ceremony and the name of the Silver Lake speakeasy that served the strongest gin cocktails. She knew which Metro-North lines went to which long-weekend destinations and at which parties she was likely to meet people who owned houses in each of them. She knew the paint colors on the walls of Joan Didion's apartment.

Though there was some contention between the groups, there was no hierarchy. The married accountants were the ones who kept the parties going late into the night, not caring how fresh they were for the next morning's workshop, and even the most well-behaved, nondrinking retiree and most dedicated industry person needed the escape of a drink at these parties at least once a residency. Everyone knew the industry people could help you get published, or pass along the email address of an editor who would look at your short story. And the retirees could give you the Heimlich should you choke in the cafeteria, or serve as your legal representative should you get caught driving back to campus after one too many drinks or without a license, and they could spot you money for drinks at the student center—they seemed like real people in the way the rest of us, when placed alongside them, didn't. They were the adults, and the only ones who didn't define themselves by the program—who didn't necessarily bring it up when they met new people at parties and meetings in the Real World.

Occasionally there was cross-pollination between the groups, letting everyone feel a little better about themselves, writers not generally a group of people who like to think of themselves as close-minded or exclusive. Sarah Jacobs probably had less in common with Mimi than any other member of our class, even if they were both women of roughly the same age. We liked to joke that if reincarnation were real and each person had a different number of lives in their back pocket, Sarah was on her first. She was all big-eyed curiosity and guilelessness and had enough freckles to make this adorable instead of tiresome. At twenty-three, she was still living over her parents' garage and, until the June we all started at Fielding, worked as a lifeguard at her local YMCA. There was a story Sarah's family members liked to tell that Mimi reported back to us after she started vacationing with them. During a visit they made her freshman year at Wellesley, Sarah's midwestern, baseball-loving family had insisted on going to a Red Sox game. Upon entering the stadium they noticed the purposefulness of her gait and, happily deciding that this meant her time away from home had bred self-sufficiency, followed her without a word. They were dismayed to learn, upon the start of their second lap around the stadium, that she had been walking for the sake of walking, eager to explore the stadium and whatever curiosities it held. During the seventh-inning stretch, though, when a rogue baseball came directly at her little sister, Sarah batted the ball away without a sound or flinch, shattering all the bones in her right hand. She had unexpected reserves of extraordinary capability when she needed them. It's not that she wouldn't have been able to find the family's seats if she had any real desire to, it's just that she sometimes wanted to marvel at the shapes of the clouds. It wasn't so much laziness as an appreciation for the sky. Mimi knew the sky was blue only by its reputation. She found what was happening on the ground, behind doors closed in front of her, and in darkened corners of whatever Brooklyn neighborhood was in the process of gentrifying, so much more interesting than anything she could find out by looking up on a clear day. And yet despite these and other differences, by the time we graduated the girls had gone in on a time-share at the Jersey Shore together, and Sarah had spent enough nights on Mimi's couch in Brooklyn that she stopped having to tell people she still lived at home.

We have as many details about every other Fielding pair and every solo silhouette that crossed campus the four terms we were there. But even before the things we're about to tell you started to happen, no pair interested us half as much as Leslie Spencer and Hannah Arya, and eventually Jimmy Fiero, their unlikely third—the heroes of this story, *we* think, at least, and the strangest, most singular people any of us had ever met, even at the outset of all this. We'll forgive you for forgetting any of the rest of us, but it's important you remember these three. We aren't arrogant enough to consider ourselves more than the story's background at worst, its keepers at best. But there is no story without them.

Part of the reason we lingered on Leslie and Hannah from the very beginning of our time at Fielding was they were the only two people who didn't fall, even partly, even imperfectly, into one of the three groups. They rarely went to the student center, which gave us plenty of time to talk about them—and there was plenty to discuss. Both of them were well liked enough, but we couldn't figure out what they saw in each other. And we were writers, so we tried.

Leslie spoke four languages and had nine tattoos but would reveal the location of only five of them and said there were only three people who had seen the others but no one single person who had seen them all. She had lived all over the world. Not in an army brat kind of way, but in an *I got kicked out of three boarding schools* one. She said she was an orphan whose parents were still alive, which only made about as much sense as most of the other things she said.

Everyone else in the program talked about the *New York Times Book Review* and small literary presses. Leslie talked about sales and money. It was clear from her shaggy, sloppily worn designer clothing, tossed on so that the shoulders never lined up where they were supposed to and the seams always fell at a diagonal, that she already had plenty of the latter. She said that if she *actually* needed money the last thing she would do was try to become a writer, because she wasn't a *fucking idiot*, but if she was going to take the time to write something, she wanted to make sure other people would read it because otherwise, what was the *fucking point?* No one could get out of her where she lived when she wasn't on campus. When she asked Patrick Stanbury, the six-foot-three basketball player from UConn who was writing a collection of essays about playing semiprofessional basketball in Asia, to define what he meant by "where she lived" and he said "the place where her mail was sent," she told him that if he still received paper mail he was at least partly to blame for our current ecological crisis, even though in addition to being a D-1 basketball star, Patrick Stanbury also had a master's degree in environmental science from Duke, though he had never had a job that paid health benefits.

Hannah was the human embodiment of hospital corners, which we later learned was in her blood—both of her parents had been physicians, and her older sister still practiced medicine. And though she had been born and raised in Boston and still lived there most of the year, she had spent a lifetime of holidays visiting family in Mumbai, which she had fallen so completely in love with that by the time we met her, she spent her summers there working for an urban planning firm that had offices in both Mumbai and Boston. After decades of American teachers and classmates butchering her given name of Aahana, she introduced herself to us with the closest American equivalent. Privately acknowledging how unnaturally her real name sat on our own tongues was one of many things that made us feel like bumbling, sunburnt cowboys next to her.

Hannah wore her hair in a tidy, low-hanging ponytail every day, and while she wore the ripped jeans and secondhand T-shirts the rest of us did on campus, she usually paired hers with a black or gray blazer that was best characterized the way we suspected a lot of her wardrobe in the Real World was—well made by a well-known, dependable brand but never trendy or overtly stylish. While she was generous in workshop and friendly in downtime, she was often too committed to whatever was at hand, whether it was a fellow student's story or a ranking of every film Paul Thomas Anderson had ever made, to smile, but when she did it was the part of the class or conversation you were most likely to remember. Her smile was as unexpected and magical as seeing your kindergarten teacher at the grocery store when you were five, the kind of pure embodiment of joy most human faces lose the capacity for at puberty.

Hannah's poetry had been published in *The Paris Review* and *Tin House*. She had done her undergrad at Oxford and could recite most of the soliloquies that Shakespeare had ever written. It sometimes felt, in fact, like she naturally spoke in iambic pentameter. She had a beautiful face—the kind of face you couldn't help but stare at, sometimes unconsciously, and had to force yourself to look away from—but it felt like she tried to keep this a secret, lest it would make anyone take her less seriously.

Leslie always looked like she was on her way back from a rave at dawn, no matter what time it was: smudged mascara and purple bra straps peeking out from sleeve holes. While we couldn't imagine, and never dared to fictionalize, what Leslie and Hannah talked about in their private conversations, we became well acquainted, that first term, with the sight of the two of them making their way across campus, heads drawn in close, arms linked, mouths open in conversation that required the entire body—flailing limbs and wide eyes. Everywhere they went they were always laughing.

Both women were too able and worldly to count as babies, too cultured and bohemian to be married accountants, and though Leslie had never said anything that confirmed she wasn't an industry person, she seemed to be amused at the exclusivity that the group was known for, reflecting their insider smiles back at them in a way that clearly rattled the professionals, even if they wouldn't admit it.

We didn't know any of this on that first train ride up, which neither girl was on. Hannah had carpooled to campus with a third-year from Boston, and *wherever* Leslie lived it was somewhere you had to travel to and from by plane, because she was on the second airport shuttle, getting onto campus two hours before the last train of the night stopped in its tracks in Albany. We were all first-term students that June— five long residencies away from a degree. Each of our first four residencies would commence a term of off-site work with our professors. We'd come to campus for one final residency after that, but only to deliver our graduate lectures and readings and then walk in the graduation ceremony that would culminate the residency, with plenty of revelry in between.

Jimmy was one of the ten first-termers on that train, though, probably tucked into the last seat of the last car somewhere in the back, the most nondescript person any of us had ever met, from his five-eight height to his 172 pounds. From his dirt-brown eyes and hair and completely unreadable complexion to his name. No one in our program ever would've given a character—protagonist or peripheral—a name like Jimmy. It was too ordinary. Too forgettable. Too obviously everyman. Not that there weren't stories full of everymen. All of us had read workshop stories about woodcutters named Rex and factory men named Simeon. But a name like Jimmy was way too on the nose.

He was probably sleeping on the train, something he did in just about every building and outdoor landmark of campus during the only residency he attended. He was a greedy, desperate sleeper, adjectives we would never have paired with sleep if we hadn't met Jimmy. It was like he had gone his entire life before campus without closing his eyes for more than a moment or two, and had to spend the rest of his life making up for it. When any of us spotted him curled into the fetal position on a bench at the back of an empty lecture hall or slumped against a tree out on the main lawn, it was impossible not to notice how active he made what seemed dormant and passive when anyone else did it. He slept like a screaming baby heading openmouthed toward a nipple, or a runner sucking water down at the end of a long race.

As strange as it was, his habit of impromptu naps is not what we remember when we think about him now. It's that whenever he was awake, he was writing. Not doodling or taking notes about the lectures or a novel he was reading that he thought he might learn something from, but *writing*. Like he had just then come up with some million-dollar-story idea. He wrote even more urgently than he slept. None of us could understand it, watching him. The next six months would be filled with deadlines and late and early hours spent making them. Those days on campus were supposed to be spent girding yourself, giving you the tools you would need to make the stories you submitted at those deadlines better, worth something. If he only wanted time to write, he should've just applied for a MacDowell fellowship.

We were jealous, of course. Because even as we nudged one another, passing him nose-deep in a cracked faux-leather journal that never seemed to run out of pages, we knew that, for all our undergrad awards and Pushcart Prize nominations and contest honorable mentions, the way he spent his time meant that Jimmy was the only one among us who could call himself a real writer across those ten days that we knew him.

Though none of us could figure out the elements at work in the chemistry between Hannah and Leslie, the story of how they met was legendary. It was on the first day of workshop, the morning after Jimmy woke up on the train ten minutes after it had stopped, the interior lights already dimmed, having made himself into so tiny a human ball that even the conductor didn't notice him. And he saw for the first time that dark at the top of New England is completely different from dark in rural Michigan.

After all three of the airport and train shuttles had landed safely on campus and all the students who had driven, carpoolers and solo missions alike, were accounted for. After Jimmy had managed to convince the ticket booth operator to let him use the back-office phone to call a local cab to take him to campus, having missed the shuttle and not being in possession of a cell phone. After all eighty-seven of us from all four active classes, including all seventeen of us first-years, plus the fifth, graduating class, had checked in and collected the keys that would unlock our square, stuffy dorm rooms, which were sticky with an uncountable number of paint jobs and lit by bare lightbulbs that stank of 1960s mental institutions. After syrupy wine and limp vegetables dipped in runny ranch dressing at the welcome reception at the student center. After late-night *I made it* calls to loved ones, conducted by pacing silhouettes outside the dorm buildings with imperfect reception, and the fitful sleep of people who have traveled all day only to end up in unfamiliar surroundings and scratchy, starched bedding intended for much younger people. After morning showers in communal bathrooms so grimy they required flip-flops, and too-hot coffee that was already stale even as it steamed out of the steel industrial thermoses, and chewy tater tots and flabby pancakes. It was finally time for the first workshop of the first day and, more important, time to put faces with stories and the names that had been written across the top of them.

Six weeks before the start of each residency we were supposed to send eleven hard copies of the story we wanted workshopped to the MFA office on campus—one for each of the other nine students in our workshop and one for each of the two teachers leading it. About three weeks before everyone was due on campus, when just enough time had passed since we had sent copies of our stories off that the anxiety and uncertainty about them had dimmed to a manageable level, we each got a package in return, filled with copies of the nine stories that the other students in our workshop had sent in. Some of us tore into the stories right away—as eager to engage with others' work as we were to improve our own—and some of us didn't read each story until the night before it was workshopped. What was uniform across the arrival of these packages was that they reminded us that our own work was arriving on *other* doorsteps across the country, the closest most of us had ever come to being published.

Normally there were two teachers for each workshop of ten students. Each student had one designated professor for the semester that followed the on-campus residency, with whom they would establish a reading list before leaving campus and to whom, on the first of each month, they would send twenty pages of new fiction, twenty pages of revised fiction, and annotations on two of the five books they'd read that month. Each professor had five students per semester, and because you can't do a workshop with only five writers, each professor and his five students was paired with a second writerly cell, for a combined workshop of ten students and two professors. Though it wasn't stated in any of the promotional literature on the program or acknowledged in any formal way, it seemed clear to anyone beyond their second residency that teachers were paired because of how in or out of sync their teaching philosophies were. And the more extreme or prescriptive a teacher's philosophy was, the likelier it would be that their partner's philosophy would be the complete and utter opposite of their own. You can't have two highly esteemed adults telling you with any sort of authority that adverbs and exclamation points are strictly forbidden, because there is no such thing as a rule that fiction cannot transcend. But you *can* have two adults at the front of the classroom agreeing that if you break chronology, there should be a good reason for it, and it should add a narrative element, and that stakes are generally a good thing to have in a story if you want readers to keep turning pages. The students who were in workshops with harmonious professors almost always became frustrated by the extent to which their professors ganged up against them, creating a combined authority it was impossible to overrule. They loved hearing about the sometimes acrimonious sidebars that teachers in disagreement had to take. Meanwhile, students in the workshops with warring teachers often grew tired of leaving each class totally confused, after two of their favorite writers had offered completely contradictory advice on how to better their work. We all loved the idea that there might be one perfect answer to the problems in our stories, and made the students in the workshops with simpatico teachers tell us more about the consensuses that had been reached.

Lucas White enjoyed a brief period of campus-wide notoriety just after our second residency when he illustrated a series of celebrity death matches between professors on campus based on the rules or maxims they were known for. The outcome of each match was determined by the number of master works the application of each professor's rules could be found in. Though brilliant, the graphic novel that the matches amounted to was far too controversial to publish, but lived online and as attachments in our emails for years after we graduated.

Leslie and Hannah's workshop was the first of its kind at Fielding, because it was the first ten-student workshop led by only one instructor, Professor Sam Pearl, who, with a name like that, could never have been anything but a writer or actor. This hadn't been planned. Professor Pearl was originally paired with Johanna Green, a short story writer twenty years his junior, but her widowed mother had died suddenly two weeks before residency and, being an only child, she had no one to pawn the estate-settling responsibilities off on, and pulled out of the term.

While it was generally understood that even six students would have been too many for a single thinking mind to attend with any rigor, it was also understood that if there was one person who could manage it, it was Professor Pearl. The long-standing director of the program, he had written one novel in the seventies to such great acclaim that it was still in print. Originally published in Spanish, the English translation, *Cactus and Dust*, was required reading in high schools across the country. It was impossible to read the final lines without tears blurring the words, and many of us could still remember the first time we had. A good half of us who had taken Spanish in college to fulfill a language requirement had done so in the vain, naïve hope that we could learn enough Spanish in a single semester to read the book in its original language. It was set in Mexico, where Pearl was from.

He had never published a single other piece of fiction—not even a short story—but there were rumors that he had written a second masterpiece, which he kept in the top drawer of his desk and took out only when he was completely alone. Some sources said he had actually finished it years ago but, too afraid to let it go, combed through it endlessly, changing just a word or two at a time or maybe the placement of a few commas. Others said it was incoherent.

The irony of Pearl's name had been delighting readers and reviewers for nearly as long as *Cactus and Dust* had been making them cry. While he wasn't carrying a loaded rifle in his author photo, people usually remember him having one. His picture promised that he was the kind of man who killed his own dinner but didn't take any joy from the killing; he always did it as quickly and humanely as possible. He had a somber, prematurely gray mustache in the picture that had only grown grayer since. There was a longstanding debate among Fielding students on whether a Republican could create great art, and it is no coincidence that the people who said they could are people who had been in Professor Pearl's class. Not because he had professed affiliation with any political party or candidate, or even because of that gun he surely owned even if it wasn't in his photo, but because he had the air of a small-town mayor or sheriff. Not in a power-hungry way, but in the sense that he believed people took care of their own and didn't need any larger, more formal mandate to do so. People who swept in from far away generally only brought trouble. You got the sense he didn't like suits. If the apocalypse hit, you'd want him around.

Pearl had been married when his book was published, to an equally celebrated novelist name Joan Pasquale, who, unlike her husband, kept writing after her first success. She had been a finalist for the National Book Award twice, once for her debut novel and once for a collection of essays about a random group of women who happened to get their chemotherapy at the same time and place that tracked the members of the group long after their treatments. Though she had lost both times, her almost maniacal following couldn't have loved her more if she had won. Even at the peak of their combined fame, the couple had apparently been wary of any sort of exposure or literary celebrity. The one interview we could find with either of them was a joint profile *Life* had done the year after *Cactus and Dust* came out. In the picture we all remember most vividly, one as iconic as his author photo, Pearl looks up at the camera from a mahogany desk in front of which a four-year-old girl with enviably shaggy locks and the lingering effects of a late-afternoon nap sits playing. The couple divorced a year later, after which Joan and their daughter relocated to California. We couldn't find any evidence that Professor Pearl kept in touch with either woman—his office walls were notoriously bare of personal photos of any sort—but this seemed out of character for him, and we wanted all our characters consistent back then, both on the page and in life, not having yet considered that this was not only uninteresting, it was inaccurate.

We know better now, though: good men falter all the time.

While the details of Pearl's personal life and the status of his second novel were in dispute, we could all agree that he was not the kind of person you disrespected by whispering to someone else while he was addressing the group, which is why what Leslie did on the first day of workshop was even more surprising than if she had done it in any other professor's classroom.

She and Hannah were the only two first-years in the class. Like most of us first-years, unfamiliar with the campus and hoping to make a good first impression, Hannah had arrived at Sunset Cottage ten minutes early. Leslie was three and a half minutes late, and not because she was lost. She pulled her hot pink ear buds out of her ears only after she had shut the door behind her, so everyone in the room got a few chords of Robyn's demand that her new boyfriend call his girlfriend. The circle of students around the long table in front of her was small enough to appear informal, but the look her classmates gave her when they turned made it clear just how sacred they considered the ritual she was interrupting.

"Sorry," she said in a way that insulted the word.

The look Professor Pearl gave her was direct but empty at once, a look as meaningless as her sorry.

"Sit," he said.

And she did, but not in the chair he had nodded to, which was the one closest to the door. She directed her winking hips toward the table's only other empty chair, right next to Hannah, which she had to pass most of the circle to get to. Four students had to scoot their chairs forward to make enough room for her to pass. The collective squeal of metal chair legs on the linoleum floor was more offensive than even the Robyn, but still he did not kick her out. He had already diverted his attention back to the rest of the class by the time he slid a copy of the one-page syllabus to her across the table, the graceful glide of his forearm totally divorced from the rest of his body. It finished its apathetic arc right as she finally landed in the chair.

One of the few ways in which Professor Pearl's workshop did *not* depart from those in adjacent classrooms was the first-day agenda. Even he used it as a throwaway day, dispensing the rules under which the workshop would be conducted and determining the order in which students would be workshopped. It was a soggy curriculum better suited for the first day of high school English, usually capped by the professor handing out a page or two of prose that was universally understood to be perfect. It was academic small talk, and Leslie had little patience for small talk of any sort.

To be fair, Professor Pearl *did* try to curtail the condescension implicit in so basic a class by not insisting all the students go around the room reading a paragraph of his selection aloud. Instead, he had everyone take a Xeroxed copy of Alice Munro's "Fits" to read quietly to themselves. Most of the other students in the class were still on the first page when Leslie bent over and unzipped her backpack to retrieve a pencil case—she didn't even have the sense to be ginger in her unzipping or her case opening.

She inspected each of the half dozen colored pencils she took out of the case before lining them up in front of her. She didn't appear to put the colors in any particular order, but she did stop to make sure they were laid out evenly, so that their admirably pointy tips formed a perfect line, before she picked up the green pencil closest to her. Once she began working, she stopped only to change colors, so focused on her creation that she didn't look up to note which color she was picking up in favor of the one she had just discarded, making everyone think there might have been some premeditation to the order she had put them in after all.

With each new letter, she drew the attention of more of the students in the room. By the time she got to the second *n,* everyone had abandoned the story, their heads up in some mix of curiosity and outrage, including Professor Pearl's. That Leslie had created a spectacle sufficient enough to distract from their reading would mean more to you if you'd ever read "Fits."

"Are you not going to read the story?" Professor Pearl asked, more amused than we would have been. "I think you'll like it. It's one of her best."

"Yeah, I know," Leslie said, pausing only briefly in her exchange of a blue pencil for an orange one. "I've already read it. I've read all of her selected stories."

For a second or two the only sound in the room was the scratch of pencil on recycled paper.

"Wellllll," said Professor Pearl, leaning back on two chair legs, still considering how to proceed even as he spoke. "I suppose that makes sense. Just try to keep it down, all right?"

Leslie nodded but wasn't any less rigorous in whatever she was doing with the orange pencil.

The students in the class who liked to see other people get in trouble exchanged *What the fuck* looks, but most people who know Professor Pearl wouldn't be surprised. He was a man of logic, and Leslie's was a logical explanation. He didn't believe in wasting time or doing something just for the sake of doing it, like rereading a familiar story just because someone told you to.

The students closest to Leslie had made out the six letters in Hannah's name—from which several stars were now shooting, against a plaid backdrop—just before Leslie ripped her creation from the corner of the syllabus sheet she had written it on. She tried to be coy—her smile was small—but her manic, childish excitement was unmistakable. She slid the scrap of paper over to Hannah, who was the only person in the classroom still reading at that point, offering her friendship the only way she knew how, by trying to startle or scare or impress her intended into it.

Instead of being impressed, or flattered, or nervously cowering into her seat, hoping not to get blamed for this further interruption, since her name was now at the center of it, Hannah turned to Leslie—with her entire upper body, not just her head—and said, in a voice that wasn't loud but wasn't entirely a whisper, either, "You're being rude." Without giving Leslie or anyone else a chance to react, she turned back to the page in front of her, and the story even Leslie couldn't distract her from.

After that, Leslie was completely in love. The kind of absolute, all-consuming love that distracts you from the tenets of life as basic as three meals a day, and conquers even the bleakest, most devastating strands of loneliness. Which was a good thing, because even before Hannah chastised Leslie, the eight other students in the class had marked Leslie as someone to be wary of, and promised themselves they'd avoid starting up with her the sort of instant close friendship that happens only at summer camps, freshman year of college, rehab, and low-residency MFA programs.

What the other people in the workshop didn't know, and

couldn't tell the rest of us when they recounted the story later, was that Leslie hadn't chosen Hannah at random. She hadn't written out Hannah's name in her too-big, childish scrawl because she liked Hannah's blazer, or the "bad spellers must untie" sweatshirt she was wearing underneath it, so dorky it was almost cool. She did it because she loved that first story Hannah had sent to the class the way she loved very few things— truly and purely, without satirical comment or a joke to distance herself from it. She had read it long before she arrived on campus and several times since. She had reread it just that morning—it was part of why she had been late—and would read it again before the story was workshopped. She loved it the way you can love only a certain number of arrangements of words across the span of a life. If we had known this then, we might not have been so quick to judge, and the rest of the students in the workshop might not have told everyone else what happened quite as quickly as they did or in quite such condescending terms. Because we had all loved something—some poem or passage or cluster of words—as much as Leslie loved Hannah's story.

It was the reason we were all there.

The first person Leslie made an impression on *outside* of class was Margaret Jibs. Everyone got their own room on campus, but the bathrooms were communal. Margaret's and Leslie's rooms were adjacent. On the way back from that first work-shop, Leslie passed Margaret reading Mark Strand's *Collected Poems* in the bay window at the end of the hall their rooms were on—probably getting an early start on her reading list for the residency, fully intending to include the book on her list of twenty-five titles for the term even though she was al-ready halfway through and she and her adviser hadn't met to set their list. Leslie didn't hesitate before interrupting Marga-ret's reading to ask about the duration of her morning bath-room routine.

"Excuse me?" Later, Margaret claimed she had asked po-litely, as in *I didn't hear you*, not *What did you just say to me?* But by then we'd all known Margaret long enough to know better.

"You know, like, how long does it take you to put that eye makeup on?" Leslie said, allegedly nodding at Margaret's face like an angry cabdriver when she said it. "Or, more impor-tantly, are you regular?"

"I have no idea what you're asking me."

"You've seriously never heard that expression?"

"I mean, I've heard the word *regular* before."

"Well, my system's like clockwork. So every morning at about five after nine I'm going to need the bathroom for about ten minutes. And you'll probably want to let it sit for a good five minutes after that."

The expression on Margaret's face as she registered what Leslie was telling her is a detail she left out, but we could all picture it well enough, and understand why Leslie felt compelled to make some sort of peace after having been on the receiving end of it.

"Sorry. I guess I'm not as shy as most people when it comes to things like this. Probably because I write erotica."

This is the first time any of us can remember Leslie naming this as her specialty, though it certainly wouldn't be the last.

"The program doesn't really *do* genre fiction," Margaret said, probably now wearing the look she would've had had she walked into that communal bathroom at a quarter after nine, a look she used in response to all sorts of things.

"Oh, well, I don't really need help with the sex part. I have all that down. *Practice*, you know." There would've been a wink here, probably.

"I need help with the story *around* it. I have notebooks full of sex scenes and only a handful of names and jobs and backgrounds for all the characters, you know, *engaging*. I'm gonna need a lot more for the series I have planned."

Though Leslie talked about her explicit sex scenes as easily as she did her morning bathroom routine, Margaret took this first mention of them as some sort of dirty little secret that Leslie had let her in on. Because it was Margaret, this only increased the speed and enthusiasm with which she relayed the conversation to other people. The news quickly looped around campus, merging mightily with Leslie's appearance and wardrobe, and the uncontested story of what she had done in the first workshop, the start of a reputation she would never fully shed, even after everything else she would go on to do. If it had been someone other than Margaret reporting on the exchange, we might've been skeptical, but Margaret didn't have the creativity to make up something like that and we all knew it. Her imagery and language were flawless, but she lacked imagination. She could never write about anything she hadn't actually seen or experienced.

"If you don't know how to write, how did you get into the program?" Margaret asked.

Knowing what we do about Leslie, it feels safe to say she winked again after telling Margaret, "Everyone knows erotica writers give good head," right before turning and walking away.

In other corners of the campus, other introductions were being made.

Bridget Jameson went down to the laundry room in the basement of her building after lunch without even stopping at her room first. Though she generally didn't rely on expensive or ostentatious clothing, being the type who looked better with hair that's been left to dry on its own and no makeup, she had worn a pair of red velvet leggings to dress up the ordinary denim shift she wore to meet the rest of us that morning. When she had thrown the milk at Jamie Brigham after his comment about her fiction at lunch, just after their first workshop, she had gotten some of it on herself, as we usually do when we sling something at someone else, and she was on just the wrong side of desperate to get the milk out of the leggings before it had time to set.

Given that it was the first full day of the residency—too early for anyone's clean laundry to have gone dirty—Bridget had counted on being the only person in the laundry room, so she was delighted to see that Hannah was leaning against one of the dryers. The afternoon's desperation wasn't solely on account of the milk, as much as she loved those leggings. Bridget didn't have nearly as many friends as a person of her caliber deserved, we were all on our way to discovering. While most people make their close friends in high school or college, she had missed her window at both for reasons not entirely within her control—a work transfer for her father in her junior year of high school, and an 8:10 a.m. Latin class in her freshman year of college that kept her from staying to the end of the early-morning parties where friendships in progress were cemented with bad decision making and incurable hangovers. So while she was justifiably secure in herself on most fronts, and would've made a perfectly solid, reliable friend, she was a little too eager in new group situations like this, which explained not only the velvet leggings but also why she had thrown the milk. Seeing Hannah felt like the promise of an immediate do-over.

Bridget had just taken a step forward with an open mouth, ready to say hello too loudly, when she saw that Hannah was talking to someone who had been out of Bridget's view until that step. We would be sad about the way she closed her mouth in defeat, sensing that the conversation in progress was an intimate one, designed for two, if the person Hannah was talking to had been anyone other than Jimmy, who was even less well acquainted with friendship than Bridget was.

Instead of going back upstairs, Bridget picked a washer close enough that she could hear Hannah and Jimmy's conversation but far enough away not to interrupt it. This wasn't only because, having identified Hannah as a particularly strong candidate for friendship the moment she realized their dorm rooms sat side by side, Bridget wasn't ready to give up on some sort of friendly exchange before going back upstairs. She was also as curious as the rest of us about Jimmy, the boy from nowhere.

We had all received a first-year directory in the welcome packet that arrived just a few weeks before the residency. It included our street and email addresses, cell phone numbers and the occasional landline, and full names with a second line designated for any nickname we might prefer. Leslie's was the only missing entry. Having found a way to be delinquent even before arriving on campus, she had failed to send the information in on time or at all. For Jimmy there was only a name and a PO box. After we all checked to make sure our own entries were correct, and to see what they looked like in this new context, trying to imagine how eyes that had never seen the information would process it, and what our street names and email addresses said about us, we set to work studying one another's entries, looking up how close various zip codes were to big cities, and trying to guess how old people were based on the email servers they used. We all stopped at Jimmy's entry, as intrigued by his lack of information as we were by even the most exotic and moneyed zip codes and the cleverest Gmail addresses.

We had thought the PO box might be ironic, the closely cultivated understatement of a hipster who had gone so far to one extreme of ostentation that the only thing left to do was circle all the way back to the bare beginning. But once we saw that he was completely free of ironic facial hair, with no flannel in his wardrobe, we realized the mystery was real. He was earnestness incarnate, more incapable of irony than even the squarest of our parents. No one had heard him speak, so geographical colloquialisms were no help, and we hadn't been able to listen for an accent. His last name made it just as likely that he was Latino as Italian. Just as Hannah and Leslie eventually became a source of interest because of how they were always together, Jimmy was a curiosity because of how often he was alone. While the rest of us clumped off with other members of the class according to age and geography and, though we would never admit it, the caliber of our writing, no one had seen Jimmy outside of mandatory orientations and classes—not awake, at least, though his sleeping figure became something of a campus Where's Waldo. He always arrived at and departed from the things he did attend by himself. He seemed to have more interaction with the service staff—the cafeteria workers and security guards—but even these were brief, nonverbal correspondences, a nod to say hello or thank you.

Then there were the whispers that had already started to trickle down to us from the people in his workshop, about how remarkable his poetry was.

If Bridget was hoping to learn something about Jimmy that day in the laundry room to report back to the rest of us, she would've been even more disappointed than when she realized Hannah wasn't alone. Because Hannah was doing almost all the talking.

"I know it's kind of weird to be down in the basement on a day as nice as this, but I've never been one of those people who can write or work or do *anything* that requires any real attention when I'm outside in a place as pretty as this. I get so consumed by the grass and the trees and the view that it's kind of just what I'm doing, you know? There's not much to distract a person down here."

When Jimmy didn't say anything Bridget looked away long enough to scan the room, which was, in fact, desolate. It was the kind of grim, cobwebby place that would've depressed her if she didn't go on to associate it with Hannah for the rest of the residency.

"Don't be fooled by the dryer," Hannah went on, nodding over her shoulder at the machine humming gently behind her. "There's nothing in it. Some people like to listen to music when they work, but I like white noise. And none of that over-the-top rain forest, ocean stuff. I like the pure, empty buzz of a dryer. The more high-powered, the better. These are pretty good for a campus laundry room, don't you think?"

One of the things we would all learn about Bridget was that she was an excellent conversationalist, something close to a wizard at small talk. When Jimmy didn't answer right away, she opened her mouth a second time, to save Hannah the embarrassment of pure, deafening silence in the face of her friendly overture, but Jimmy finally spoke before she could think of what to say.

"I don't know," he said, not looking at either girl. "I've never had a dryer before."

Bridget might've been disappointed one final time that afternoon. Hannah didn't follow up with a question about what Jimmy was doing down there. Bridget worried the question might've already been asked, before she arrived. But her disappointment was stayed, because just before Hannah turned to go back up the stairs, her empty dryer still running, she gave Bridget one little crumb to bring back to us after all. Hannah laughed at Jimmy's answer, happy at such an odd, unlikely response rather than befuddled by it the way we might have been.

For this, Jimmy rewarded her with a smile. The first and only smile any of us would ever see on him.

After that first day of workshop, after people put faces with stories and sniffed out how gentle or not their professors were going to be. And heads were poked into dormitory neighbors' rooms, and suitcases were either unpacked or shoved under beds. After Jibs had searched for and found the next closest bathroom, to avoid Leslie's morning movements altogether, and Bridget had hung her red leggings across the back of her desk chair to let them dry, we finally had a few hours to ourselves.

We first-years used this time to explore campus while the rest of the student body sought out their favorite corners. Mimi Kim and Sarah Jacobs picked wildflowers in the field in front of the music building, which, from the outside, looked more like the sort of crumbling mansion that survives wars and keeps secrets better than even the best, most discreet humans can. Lucas White and Robbie Myers got stoned in the lobby of the ultramodern campus apartments that were reserved for undergraduate seniors and MFA students in their graduating term. They sat there exhaling languidly and talking around the girl they had met earlier that day and both thought they were in love with, a second-term student whose name eludes us all now. Penny Stanley, who was already trying unsubtly to win the unofficial role of class leader, even though we had already given it to Jordan Marcum by then, met Professor Salter at the student center to finalize the movie lineup for the film night they had planned for the one free evening of the residency. She hadn't realized yet that, because the program didn't give letter grades, and there was no honors program or valedictorian, her extra efforts and extracurriculars and all the tasks she invented for herself would culminate in nothing but less free time, which she wouldn't have known what to do with anyway.

Walking alone, or clumped in twos or threes, it was easier to notice the eerie, abandoned quality of the campus and the side streets around it. Mimi noted that the mom-and-pop stores that lined these streets looked a lot like the barbershops and general stores and pharmacies that were always opening in Brooklyn and Portland and Austin, but with more dust and frumpier owners—authentic relics that the new stores were throwing back to. It felt like a place time forgot, even as the school brought the most of-the-moment writers and artists to campus. There was a Great Lawn, at the edge of which Adirondack chairs sat around a fire pit. There was a steep drop-off just after the chairs, and sitting in them, you could see all the way to the highway you turned off to get to campus, a lonely, cement-colored vein. The patch of grass the chairs sat on was called The End of the World for several reasons, not least the simple one that that's what it felt like, sitting there.

It wasn't just the vast, open stretches of campus that we graduate students—fewer in number than even the notoriously small undergraduate student body that had fled for the summer—could never fill that made the campus feel empty and apart from the rest of the world, and maybe a little strange. There was always a haunted quality about the place, even before anything bad happened. The hallways always felt as if someone had just passed through them, even when you were blowing off a lecture or reading everyone else was attending, so that you knew you were the only one in the building. It wasn't a very well-lit place, electricity being no match for the advantages natural elements had on so remote a campus, and the sensor lights they did use went on only when someone walked directly in front of them except for the stray times they popped on or off when we were clear on the other side of the room. Often one of us would assume we were alone only to have the "gotcha" pop of a sensor light make us jump, even if we'd been the one to set it off.

The infrequency of our interactions with the locals made us pay more attention to them—the cafeteria workers and the bartenders who set up giant plastic bowls of stale ice and cheap lite beers mixed like confetti with stronger local brews each night in the commons room beneath the dining hall, for predinner cocktail hour. The program, we all quickly learned, ran on routine and tradition. We had workshop every morning at ten, craft lectures at two, faculty readings at seven, and, the prize for each day's work: the five o'clock cocktail hour before six o'clock dinner. There was a different bartender each night, serving the same nearly tasteless but somehow irresistible trail mix. We could never find the mix in any store off campus—even the massive wholesale places and the upscale specialty shops—leaving us with the distinct but doubtful impression that it was prepared each night by the bartender who sat behind it, who never did manage to look comfortable in the ties they were made to wear. These bartenders were always robotically polite and efficient in their work—friendly but noncommittal—but almost graceful in the speed and agility with which they took the caps off beers and held them out to us before we even had time to open our wallets. They were professionals. And though they were almost entirely immune to chatter or small talk, you could see in their eyes that they knew things. They could've shown us the houses where the worst things had happened—the house Shirley Jackson died in, or where Mary Rogers, the last woman legally executed by the state of Vermont, had lived when she rolled her husband's body into the river a few miles from campus just before composing his suicide note. Their benign indifference to us made it clear that while we might have an education, they thought it sweet, all the things we didn't know about this place. Which cafeteria workers sold drugs, or which quaint little blue cabin's owner was building an arsenal for whatever postapocalyptic event would finally do the rest of us in. They were almost all young—younger even than the babies among us—but they had the placid air of someone who has already resigned themselves to being wherever they are for a very long time, even though there are a million other places that might suit them better, and nothing will age you quicker. They never gave us a single indication that they took our myriad differences personally, but if we're being entirely honest, we feel a kernel of discomfort when we think of them now. Maybe because all of us loved to talk about how poor we were—it was a common exercise among us, to list all the things we couldn't afford

because of the money we spent on the program, on our art—
and the bartenders and cafeteria workers, like the security
team and the janitors who were their neighbors off campus,
made it clear again and again, each night at the same time, that
there are many different kinds of poor, not all of them equal in
nobility or arrogance or actual hardship entailed.

The people who worked in the cafeteria tended to be a few
years older than the bartenders, by our rough and often inaccurate eyeball estimations, and were split more evenly down
the gender line. They made the hipster foodie bent of the
meals the cafeteria served feel even stranger and more out of
place than they would have anyway. There were corn and feta
pancakes and sweet potato tater tots. Baked, not fried, so always a little limp. There was homemade red pepper hummus
and crawfish benedict. Each meal's contents read like the
menu of an alternative CSA cruise, or a new Brooklyn bistro
in the first floor of a Park Slope brownstone, but it all tasted
the same, and was all served at the same five-minutes-too-
cool temperature. The food was laid out in massive, trough-
like quantities, and almost everyone gained a few pounds
across each residency, even the people who opted for the salad
with toasted pumpkin seeds and watermelon tossed in homemade raspberry lemon vinaigrette dressing. This could have
just been because the food left everyone constipated, so se-
verely that we all had to wonder how regular even Leslie
ended up being. We never heard her utter a word on the subject after her initial warning, and bowel movements were so

prized on campus that it seemed the kind of thing she would brag about.

That first night, after we had taken the trail through the woods into town, to buy cheap and surprisingly smooth wine, and after the third-years had drawn out maps for the first- and second-years that would lead them to the swimming hole a few miles off campus, we sat down for the first dinner.

Dinners at Fielding were part high school cafeteria, part extended family Thanksgiving. It was the only time the entire student body and faculty were in the same place without having to be quiet to listen to the lecturer or speaker. People dropped into breakfast and lunch on the way to or from the day's events, so while you might pass someone you were looking for on your way in or out of the cafeteria, if you really needed to find them you'd look for them at dinner. It was the only time when we were all present but free to converse openly, and after all the hours spent listening, and taking notes, and living among our own thoughts and responses to the ideas and writing samples put before us, we always had a lot to say. Even though the days were long, the energy in the dining hall was always high during these final meals. The talk was animated and boisterous. If they could have captured it in a picture, it would've been perfect for the brochure—proof of how stimulating your time here would be, and how much it would evoke from you. There never were any pictures of the dining hall in the brochures, though, because it was the ugliest room on campus. All of the buildings on Fielding's campus were different—different styles of architecture, different ages, and different sizes—and the dining hall felt like the one where they had finally run out of ideas. The one that seemed functional above anything else. The ceiling was one giant skylight, the room's one nod to beauty or aesthetic, but that was another thing that couldn't really be captured by a photo, which was maybe the other reason the cafeteria felt so safe. It was a secret—a place only people who'd spent enough time there would know to love.

Though there were more than a dozen tables in the main room of the dining hall, spread far enough apart that interacting from one table to another would've required shouting, there was often a shared topic across the tables' conversations. Fielding was a lively campus, but it was also a small one that rarely saw more than one noteworthy event or development in a day. Sometimes the item of interest was that night's fluke crostini, and how good or terrible it was, and sometimes it was a debate on whether the visiting octogenarian, Pulitzer Prize–winning poet who was going to read after dinner really was a misogynist or just being read out of context. Sometimes it was the pompous student whose work had been lacerated at that afternoon's workshop.

That first dinner that first night of our first residency, it was Simone Babbot, the final star of our story.

Simone was the biggest deal the faculty had ever seen, in both the size of her profile and critical acclaim, making the more hopeful among us believe that her arrival signaled a spike in the program's prestige. Six months before accepting a position on the faculty, she had landed a glowing cover review in the *NYTBR* for her first novel, *Girls with Outdoor Voices*, a nearly impossible feat for a debut. She was the kind of celebrity novelist that we had all come to accept had died in the eighties—the kind your best friend's mom had heard of, was maybe even reading for book club, but who was also shortlisted for all the biggest awards. Brad Pitt had optioned her novel, but it was also required reading for freshmen at Princeton. No one could figure out how she landed at Fielding. She had the cheekbones of a Tom Ford model and she had just moved in with the sort of New York restaurateur who usually dated them, or so we had heard. Though only a fraction of us had actually read her novel, it was easy to claim we had, because a compilation of the death scenes in the film adaptation of the book, which had come out that spring, had gone viral a few months before we arrived on campus. The book was narrated by a group of dead girls who had all been victims of the same killer, and haunted the small town where they had died. Though the book had allegedly kept the grisly murders tastefully off the page, the film had not. A lot of flowy white dresses and blond hair were involved.

We'd had only one workshop by that first dinner, during which she'd remained disappointingly quiet, nodding brightly in agreement with the things that Gene, her teaching partner, said. Gene had begun his career as a memoirist who wrote in turns about falling off and getting back on the wagon, essays full of sad-funny anecdotes about rehab stints and the dark things that inevitably happened in between them, and had evolved, by then, into a marquee name in the narrative poetry world. Though Simone was a fiction writer and Gene was one of the five faculty members who made up the program's poetry department, they were co-teaching a single workshop not because of an oversight by the administrative staff we all knew to be diligent but because together they were leading the program's first ever mixed-genre workshop. The thinking being that reading and studying poetry would lend a natural rhythm to the prose writer's work, and that while not necessary, narrative and theme weren't terrible things to incorporate into a poem. It was the first mixed-genre workshop in *any* program, as far as any of us knew, and it was only another reason we were all secretly glad Simone had joined the faculty, however withholding we were of an official verdict on how helpful a teacher she was or wasn't, and how much she would contribute to the program outside of reputation.

We hadn't had time, by that first night, to learn much outside of these biographical, on-paper statistics about her, but that only made the details we had been able to pick up feel more significant. She was overly nice in public—using the kind of verbal exclamation points she would never use on the page. She was silent and distant until directly engaged, and then almost embarrassingly effusive. She overenunciated, which we attributed to her failed acting career—we had spent the night before clustered in dorm rooms, searching for her *Law & Order* cameos and tampon commercials online.

Even if she hadn't done what she eventually did, Leslie would have hated Simone. Because even though there was no one thing she had said you could point to as evidence of it, Simone's words oozed condescension—Leslie's kryptonite— and the certainty that while your work might be charming or thoughtful, it would never be any of the adjectives that had been used to describe Simone's work. *Masterful* or *blisteringly original*.

It would take us only a few more days to learn that Simone always sat in the same seat in the rafters of the auditorium where we met for lectures and readings, the seat closest to the stage but farthest away from the students, as if she were afraid we might contaminate her, though she would have scoffed at the suggestion. Perched there, she loomed over the student body like some sort of modern, intellectual king. We also quickly learned that she was the biggest offender of the *mmm, aah* response to points that a speaker made, a verbal head nod, and an MFA affect we were almost all guilty of, a sin akin to laughing harder when you're watching something funny with someone else than you would if you were watching alone. When she did it, it was half the noise you made when you were eating something delicious and half sex noise, which, given those cheekbones, wasn't entirely unpleasant. Her X-rated *ohs* and *aah*s sounded even louder from where she sat. It was the first seat the speaker would notice when they looked up after finishing their lecture or their reading, so she was often the first person called on when it came time for the Q&A part of each session, and she always had a question—the sort of question it was impossible to answer, but that sounded smart when you asked it.

We would learn all this soon enough, but that first dinner was the first time we had all been in a room with her, and it felt a little like a dinner held in her honor, not least because she'd chosen a seat at the head of the table at the very center of the room.

By the middle of the next afternoon, most of us first-years were finally starting to relax a little. We knew where our classes were, and we could make our way back to our dorm rooms without the hand-drawn maps that had been distributed to us at check-in, even in the dark, even after a few glasses of wine at the student center. We knew the names and faces of most of the people in our workshop and the people in our class, and we had the day and time that our own stories would be workshopped committed to memory. Those of us whose stories were scheduled for the end of the week worried less than we had upon arriving on campus, when our workshop felt like it could happen at any minute and so felt like it was happening at *every* minute, and those scheduled to go in the next day or two felt grateful to be getting it over with.

We're not sure if Penny's email—which came at 12:13 that afternoon, when most of us were shoveling a second plate of caramelized Brussels sprouts into our mouths—was annoying because it arrived just when we thought we had a grasp on all the responsibilities we were going to have to manage, and it added to that list, or if it was because she sent it to us on such a nice day. It was one of those days of long shadows so perfect it looked like the sky had been painted. The kind of day so bright that even as the hours collected toward dinner, you didn't really believe night would fall until it was all around you, already fallen. Most of us read the email in the hour window between lunch and the two o'clock craft lecture, checking only to make sure there was no crucial news in our in-boxes, and eager to get outside to the front lawn for the hour before we had to start walking toward the auditorium. Maybe it was just that she had used an exclamation point in the subject line, which most of us considered ourselves too serious to ever do.

From: Penny Stanley
To: First-Years
Subject: Ideas!

Hi guys,

I hope you've all been enjoying these first few days as much as I have been. The one thing all the third- and fourth-years seem to agree on is that these residencies fly by, and I for one am trying to savor every second! The other thing that has really stuck with me is that we're the smallest class Fielding has seen in a few years, and not for lack of applications. They've maintained their selective status by only admitting students whose work reflects a certain caliber, regardless of the number of applicants they receive. I think our size presents a real opportunity both to make ourselves stand out, and to become a really tight unit, in a lot of different senses of the word. I don't know about you guys, but having a group of people to be accountable to was a big part of why I decided to come here. What if we got together tomorrow after workshop for just a few minutes, to talk about some of the things we might do to make the most of our next four terms here, and each other? Say noon, at the cluster of Adirondack chairs just before The End of the World? I have some ideas. . . .

Yours,

PS

We could all agree, after reading the email, that the ellipsis at the end was the least enticing promise of something to come in the history of ellipses, and that even though it had taken only thirty seconds to read, it made the window of time we had until the afternoon lecture feel dramatically smaller. And there were very few of us who would've listed accountability to our classmates as a reason we had borrowed or emptied our savings accounts of the money we had to pay for the program. But the heights to which we rolled our eyes at the meeting she was proposing varied across our group, because it was made up of both joiners and drifters. Or maybe we were all a little of both—we all considered ourselves *writers*, the most solitary calling there ever was, but none of us was ready to go completely off map, with just a notebook and a story idea and a point of view, in true Cormac McCarthy or Jack Kerouac style, because there we all were, getting ready to gather at a preappointed time and place. We were reading other people's twenty-page writing samples while Ernest Hemingway had been hunting elephants. It was the uncomfortable-making tension, many of us would realize across Penny's committee meetings, at the center of a formal degree in creative writing.

MFA programs have trained authors who went on to create some of the past century's greatest novels, from *Infinite Jest* to *Fates and Furies*. We liked to think it was the programs' deadlines and rewriting assignments that bred in these writers the discipline and stamina it would take them to achieve what they did, to say nothing of the contacts that would get their first, fledgling works into the hands that would shape them into what they became. These programs, we had to believe, had instilled in countless famous writers the confidence and determination it takes to get from a half-formed idea to a standing-room-only crowd at a book launch. But the very idea of these programs ignores the fundamental, inescapable fact that writing always has been and always will be a lonely pursuit, most often engaged in in dimly lit rooms. True writers are best pinpointed from space, little glowing orbs of desk light under which the typing of keys is the only sound against the hum of empty night or very early morning.

Our practical fathers had hinted at this when asking us to explain what, exactly, the point of the program was when we called to tell them we had been accepted. To boost our résumés? To get published? We thought their questions made them shortsighted, our logic-loving fathers who knew how to fix things and how things worked, who had gone to trade schools for jobs that didn't have business cards, and fancy colleges and law schools for jobs that did. We thought we knew things they couldn't understand but the truth was, of all the things we disagreed with them about—the best candidate in the next election; the names it was acceptable to give a child—this was one issue on which we had to concede, although maybe not to them, that they had a point.

English majors and book nerds and almost everyone in the program knew that a piece of literature can be the perfect antidote to loneliness, but the truth is that creating that antidote often makes the writer more vulnerable to the thing it's fighting. Some writers—the good ones—accept their lot, and the mood swings and the depression, the frustration and the isolation and the strain on their most intimate relationships that creating something of any substance will almost always entail. Many find their way through this forest using creative writing programs like ours. But these programs are also filled with people who want the validation that comes with telling people they're pursuing their MFA, as if that alone ever made anyone a real writer. They do it for the transcript and the sweatshirt and the cocktail party conversation. Getting an MFA is part luxury and part necessity and we were all hoping our own experience would be heavier on the latter than the former, for both our practical fathers' sakes and the sake of the stories we wanted to tell.

If she was being honest, Jenny Ritter, whose daughters were two and five that June, knew that she would've been happy to pursue an advanced degree in balloon animal making if it guaranteed her a few days away from her family twice a year, but most master's programs were full-time commitments. Though he had always saved some of his weekly allowance for his school's annual book fair as a child, and had always gotten his easiest As in English, Patrick Stanbury knew, on some level, that he had started looking up MFA programs online because the completion of one would hold the perfect weight to balance his science degree.

Penny's email made Jenny and Patrick and all the rest of us uncomfortable, not only because of the punctuation, and the time obligation, but because it reinforced the possibility that we were here to pledge allegiance to the tribe of aspirants, rather than to make something.

We were all still polite with one another at that point,

though, so outside of Leslie writing back "Unsubscribe" to everyone and then, two minutes later, "JK I'll obviously be there but I'm not missing lunch, is it just me or are you guys ALWAYS HUNGRY here?" to which nobody replied, we all simply added the time and place Penny had suggested to the schedules that we had assumed, until we'd gotton her email, were final.

Jude Morgan's comments in the workshop just before Penny's meeting the next day surely helped Leslie and Hannah's friendship evolve past their first, terse workshop exchange at the speed that it did. Like fights between Red Sox and Yankees fans in sports bars, and tattoos in Saturday morning yoga classes in Austin, the Jude Morgans of the world are an inevitable fixture in writing workshops across the country. Some workshops are friendlier than others, and some have more rigorous course loads or longer reading lists, and they range in size, but there's always that one guy. Who had a lot of sisters where a brother or two might've served him better. Who thought the sun rose to hear his writing. Who loved to cite Nabokov or David Foster Wallace when trashing perfectly fine stories, stories that bore no obvious similarities to the works he compared them to, and were also better than his own. It quickly became clear that his knowledge of these authors came from their Wikipedia pages or excerpts from their biographies or an undergrad lecture rather than anything the men themselves had written (and they were always men). The Jude Morgans of the world might have read the novels themselves in high school or college, and even underlined a paragraph or passage that touched something in him that his video games and sports huddles and garage band practices had not, but he cited them now out of laziness or hubris rather than nostalgia or love. It never occurred to him that these citations, and the points they were in support of, might offend anybody, because this type of boy is used to being adored.

This guy's work was almost always in the distant third person, and he used uncomfortable synonyms for his male protagonists' genitals, which almost always made their way into his stories. And while his protagonists were often kinder or nobler or did more interesting work than he did, it was clear that the writer was mostly just talking about himself. He almost always started writing later in life than everyone else had, and went around telling people that fact like it was a fancy alma mater, like it meant that writing was a calling that you had to listen to eventually, no matter how many years you tried to ignore it, as if the rest of us didn't know by now that it almost never was. It was really just hard work and, like so many other things in life, wanting it more than the next person. And this guy couldn't want it, because he assumed he already had it.

While there might be a temptation to attach a privileged-white-boy bias against this workshop menace, and he usually *is* white, and almost always male, all the other white boys in the workshop hated him, too. Even the professors stepped around his annoying habits, never criticizing his work to the extent they did the others', not wanting to hear a dissertation on which portions of the canon proved wrong whatever helpful suggestions the professor had for him. But of course this restraint encouraged the problem behavior.

The only way to victor over this particular breed of workshop menace is to outlast him. To be as blatantly terrible as him. To send out empty, meaningless gusts of wind to meet his own. Filling this role was deterred by the amount of time and effort it would take to engage.

But Leslie didn't have much else to do. At least not yet, anyway.

It wasn't *just* a time issue. Though she could tell you every word of every album that the Strokes had ever written, picked up references to every movie from *Citizen Kane* to *Harold & Kumar Go to White Castle*, and had read social satires from every century of America's existence, Leslie was totally oblivious when it came to the predictable and time-honored types that human beings fall into, and the empty gestures and routines they perform every day. She had never said or done anything she didn't feel or believe completely, and couldn't fathom that anyone else might. *Decorum* was not a word she spoke in any of her four languages. When skinny girls made references to their bulging thighs she asked them how much they weighed and how tall they were instead of dismissing their claim out of hand, not knowing it was just something insecure people who needed a compliment said. It wasn't difficult for us to imagine that when her teachers in junior high and high school pleaded a complete lack of understanding as to why one student would slander another so viciously or spread a malicious bit of news, true or false, Leslie would have politely raised her hand to explain that it was so that other people would like them more, never thinking for a second that even teachers had once wanted to be liked more, and had to plant themselves firmly on the slippery slope between mean girl and Pollyanna. So while the rest of us telegraphed rolling eyes to one another without actually looking skyward whenever Jude Morgan spoke, Leslie responded to each of his claims and questions and suggestions as if any sane person had said them, instead of taking his idiocy for granted and looking politely away.

She might simply have continued to engage him on the low, ambient level she had during their first two workshops, if Jude hadn't reacted to Hannah's story the way he did during the third.

To be fair to Leslie, while no one liked the story as much as she did, we all certainly liked it more than Jude did. We *respected* it. It was narrated by a nameless young woman who works at the local grocery store in the small town she returned home to after graduating from college. She gives nightly dispatches from the graveyard shift. She's generally miserable, but there was a magical passage at the end about all the dented cans and broken eggs employees got to take home for free, and how determined she was to use every last broken egg and not let a single one go to waste. It was imperfect, yes, but it had heart without sentimentality. The language was clean, and the voice didn't try too hard to seduce or impress you, but it did. The protagonist's pain at the recent death of her mother was quiet and fierce, and filled the pages as mightily as any story line could without a single darling or exclamation point. And you had to stop whatever you were doing when you got to the final line.

It was short, and it was called "Broken Eggs."

As usual, Hannah was asked to read a paragraph of her choosing before the workshop conversation began about the strengths of her story, and the ways it might be strengthened further (we were not to call them weaknesses). There were a good twenty minutes between the moment Hannah finished reading the final paragraph and the moment Jude started talking. During that time there was a five-minute discussion of whether the broken eggs of the title were a reference to the broken eggs in the opening of Joan Didion's essay "The Women's Movement" in *The White Album*, and the temptation to give a feminist reading of the narrator's pain on account of the possibility that it was. One student professed sympathy for the narrator's father, which got a few nods, and another student said she would've liked to know more about the store manager, which got even more nods. When no one responded to Professor Pearl's question about what kind of insight into the narrator's life and story this additional information might contribute, he changed the question to "Does anyone have any further suggestions?" and Jude saw his opening. He raised his hand and started speaking before he even got the go-ahead nod.

"There's no plot," he said. "No scene."

"Well, Jude, that's not really a suggestion," said Professor Pearl, doing a remarkable job of withholding *you asshole* from the end of his sentence, though it was implied.

"You know what I mean."

"These rules of discussion are here for a reason, Jude."

"Okay. I think the story would feel more intimate and immediate and alive if there were scenes for us to witness firsthand, and a story for us to follow."

"Uh, yeah, that doesn't even really *mean* anything," said Leslie. Professor Pearl's considerable eyebrows seemed to sit a few millimeters higher above his eyes than they had before she'd said this, eagle alert, but he didn't stop her right away. "How is a story *alive* or not? That sounds like bullshit to me."

Though Leslie had disagreed with pretty much everything Jude had said in class up to that point, her voice hadn't had nearly so severe a *fuck you* quality until now. Feeling the assault of it even as bystanders, the rest of the class later reported surprise that Jude continued with no pause, without withering or stumbling even a little.

"It's like Henry James said, 'Characters must be real and such as might be met with in actual life.'"

"Look, let's not pretend this is a Henry James thing,"

Leslie said, not addressing the content of Henry's message. "I'm sure you watch a lot of Bravo. I mean, that's pretty clear to anyone who's spent more than ten minutes with you. And that's fine. Some of those shows are funny. But everything in a story doesn't have to reside right there on the surface. And someone doesn't have to fuck someone's husband or pull someone's weave off their head for it to be a good story."

Years later, when the *New York Times* did a profile on Leslie after a novel she published with a tiny press became a bestseller, we would understand, a little more, why she'd reacted the way she did. Why she loved the story so rabidly. Because, like Hannah and the unnamed narrator of "Broken Eggs," she had lost her mother at a young age. That was the way the *Times* piece worded it. "She *lost* her," the way you might lose a favorite sweater. And she didn't only love the story, she loved Hannah, and not only because she had written it but because motherless girls are like white dresses and red wine, or mustard—they inevitably find each other, and will not be separated once they do. We didn't know any of this then; Leslie was only an oversharer when it came to the present and recent past. We knew how many pairs of underwear she had ruined in the last year from not tracking her period, but we couldn't have told you how many siblings she had. (From the same *Times* piece we would learn that she was an only child.) We must have smelled something feral and broken and searing to the touch in what she said, though, instead of just her normal bravado, because of all the things we might be tempted to hold against Leslie, both as individuals and as a group, this workshop isn't one of them. Like the plan she eventually set in motion—one so daring and foolish and bold we still hardly believe it now—it was an unthinkable overreaction that somehow felt just right.

For all their absurdities and lack of awareness, writers can also be very sensitive and kind, and Professor Pearl, who has likely seen more severe outbursts than even rumor or legend can spin, still didn't cut Leslie off, though he did sit up a bit straighter, that much more ready to intervene if he needed to.

"If you're going to quote someone, quote someone interesting, whose stuff people still read and actually *enjoy* instead of only saying they do," Leslie continued. "Someone who makes you *feel* things. He can still be old and dead and white. Like Hemingway. Do what Hemingway said and write like the iceberg."

"An iceberg?" Jude looked confused, and a little bewildered, but he didn't look angry, and we still remember feeling something very close to sorry for him when reports of this exchange first made their way to us. He was a nuisance on par with gas on a long coveted third date, but he wasn't mean, only clueless, and he looked a little sad. He wasn't challenging her, everyone who was there agreed, he just really didn't know.

"'The dignity of movement of an iceberg is due to only one-eighth of it being above water.' He said that. Like, that's a direct quote, I'm not paraphrasing. Most of an iceberg—the majority of the mass that makes it able to sink a ship like the

Titanic—is underwater. You don't see it, but it's there. And if you write really well, like, *really* well, a lot of the story is off the page, under water, but the person reading it feels it as strongly as if it wasn't. Stronger, maybe. No not maybe, *definitely*."

"*Death in the Afternoon,*" said Professor Pearl, turning up the edges of his mouth just enough to make it clear that he was impressed, or maybe pleased. "That's good. I think that's relevant here. So what do the rest of you know or feel that isn't on the page? That the author isn't telling you directly here?"

The rest of the workshop was friendly enough, as far as workshops go. Leslie didn't say anything else. At the end of class, Pearl asked her to stay after, as wholly without emotion or affect as he said everything else, so Leslie and Hannah didn't walk out together the way it might have gone in Leslie's dream version of the day. But everyone who was in the room noticed that on her way out, Hannah went the long way around the table, so that she passed right by Leslie, and that the smile she gave her was direct, fierce but warm, the kind of smile you feel in the same place where that last line of her story gets you.

Professor Pearl is a gentleman and Leslie, impossible to embarrass though she was, was in no rush to disclose information people wanted just because they wanted it, so no one has even a seedling of how that conversation bloomed. If he chastised her, or comforted her, or asked her if everything was okay. If that was the start of their long, now legendary friendship, or something they had to overcome to build it. Whatever he said, though, he took his time saying it, because Leslie was fifteen minutes late for Penny's meeting.

By the time she arrived, making no more effort to be quiet when arranging herself and her belongings than she had when she was late for workshop that first day, the rest of us had already realized that the "ideas" Penny had in mind was mainly a T-shirt with our class motto on it. The challenging part about this was that we didn't *have* a class motto, writers being wary of mottoes in general, often seeking to overturn or poke holes in the most familiar of them. While none of us would have even voted for a class shirt, given the option, none of us was going to have words we less than fully believed and stood behind printed above our names for all the family and friends of the seventeen people who would be receiving these T-shirts to see. And this was a problem, because Penny was proposing that all our names go on the back, right under whatever slogan we finally landed on.

Leslie had finally reclined herself against her backpack at an angle sufficiently comfortable after a good five minutes of leaning forward and back, testing out various possibilities, just as Penny decided it was time to open up her grassy semicircle of authority to suggestions from the class, which was when she lost the scraps of control she had been grasping at since the meeting began.

"I got it," said Patrick Stanbury, whose six feet and three inches were arranged awkwardly on the grass in an as-compact-as-possible cross-legged position. "Just write it."

We all burst into robust laughter at the same time, which we had to bottle before it ran its natural course once we realized from Patrick's wounded face that he had been serious.

"What about that Pablo Picasso quote?" Jenny Ritter asked. Jenny had told us that part of the deal she made with her husband when she quit her job as a real estate agent to be a stay-at-home mom was that she got a home office to write in, and she seemed like the kind of person who would have one of those quote-of-the-day pull-off calendars on her desk. "Oh, how does it go? 'Inspiration exists, but it has to find you working.' You know, like we're here, doing the work, not just assuming becoming a serious writer is some lucky fluke, or happens overnight."

"I mean, yeah, I guess that's true," said Margaret Jibs, "but shouldn't we also do the *work* of coming up with our own motto instead of using someone else's?"

We all liked Jenny more than Margaret, even if we thought those quote-of-the-day calendars were a little cheesy and kind of a cliché, so we all worked hard not to laugh at this.

"I know I know I know," said Lucas White, who seemed stoned even though he had just gotten out of workshop and hadn't had the chance to smoke anything. "Real writers do it better."

"Seconded!" said Robbie Myers, looking at his friend

admiringly, even though his suggestion had been as uninteresting and predictable as most of the other things he said.

Sarah Jacobs and Mimi Kim giggled, earning them a *seriously?* look from Bridget Jameson, who seemed uptight only when she interacted with Sarah Jacobs and Mimi Kim. The girls had an effect on Bridget that made us forget that she wore her third glass of wine more elegantly than many of us did our second, and had hiked the same trail Cheryl Strayed did in *Wild*. She wasn't jealous, exactly, being self-aware and thoughtful enough to realize that she wasn't suited for either Sarah or Mimi the way they were suited for each other. But their instant close friendship was exactly the kind of thing her life had, until that point, been missing.

"Can't we just, like, write these all down and you can type them up and we can vote anonymously, or something?" asked Jibs, who managed to make this suggestion seem annoying and whiny even though the rest of us had been thinking the same thing.

"I think I have something," said Jordan Marcum, filling us, for the first time that meeting, with hope. Jordan had the good looks and youthful spirit of the most attractive married accountants despite being old enough to be their father and, as a district attorney in Chicago, career credentials beyond even the married accountants' boyhood ambitions. They might've gone ahead and considered him a father figure, given the advice he was always happy to dispense when they came seeking it after two too many drinks, but his actual children were well on career trajectories almost as impressive as his own that dissuaded the married accountants from lining themselves up for comparison. Jordan had never shown us a picture of his wife, but we liked to think that she was pretty enough to explain why he never stayed late enough at any of the campus parties to give us anything to talk about. He was the most presidential member of our class, or any class at Fielding, with hair that made a career in politics seem inevitable. We suspected he might still have dreams—realistic ones, at that—of running for higher office, but his age made most of us designate him a retiree. His most annoying habit was making sure everyone's attention was on him before speaking, but when he smiled directly at us we could forgive him for this. Sometimes a lifetime of being adored breeds bad habits, we understood.

He paused long enough to give us time to anticipate whatever it was he had to say, wanting to make sure he was at the center of the stage before the Jordan Marcum Show began. It had already become one of our favorite shows, but the grass was really starting to itch.

"Write your ass off," he finally said, when all thirty-two of our eyeballs were on him. "Fierce and irreverent, but inspiring and motivational, too, right?"

We were trying to convince ourselves that this idea was as good as the way Jordan's features had arranged themselves on his face when Jibs groaned.

"Dude, *The Rumpus* sells mugs that say that," she said.

We were surprised at how averse Jibs was to this meeting.

We would've assumed she was the hand-raising type, but we had started to understand that while they both aligned themselves with authority and never broke the rules, she and Penny were on opposite sides of the same too-bright coin. Jibs maintained law and order only because it made it easier to tattle on people who *weren't* following the rules, while the whole reason that Penny took that third AP class in high school and started all those clubs was the nodding heads and approving smiles of the teachers who sponsored them. There were plenty of faculty members who could applaud whatever apparel Penny's efforts eventually yielded, but there was nobody at this meeting with enough authority to discipline anyone who got out of line. We used this observation as a distraction from Jordan's mistake, which only reminded us that, as good as it was, there was something familiar about his first workshop story. Not in a plagiaristic way, more in a sitcom one. Once we had filed all this away, we all started talking at once, and Penny's face tightened the way human faces do just before they start to cry.

"Hey!" said a voice from the back of our semicircle, which was both a relief and a bother. Because we knew we were going to have to do whatever Tammy said, but also that it would probably be the right thing anyway. We can see the appropriateness, looking back, that she was the one who made sure Penny got the chance to advocate for her slogans and spirit wear. Because while Jordan was our class president and Penny was our square, Jibs our whiny little tattletale sister, in addition to being our favorite retiree, Tammy was the closest thing to a mascot that we would ever have.

"Now, I hope y'all will excuse me for sayin' so, but y'all are being rude. Whether you like other people's ideas or not, Penny's taken some considerable time to get us all organized, and is probably gonna have to spend more time getting these T-shirts made and paid for. And despite all this time and extra work, she's given y'all a say on what we put on the T-shirts. I think the appropriate response to that is a thank-you, not a bunch of bellyachin'."

Though we didn't disagree with her, this only led to another round of everybody talking at once, which was no less annoying now that what everybody was saying was meant to be helpful instead of combative.

"*Here's* what we're gonna do," Tammy said, once again winning our attention over the other contenders for it with the depth and heft of her voice, which you felt physically as much as you heard it. Despite its magnitude it was clearly female, which was the magic at its center.

"We're all gonna turn our mouths off and our minds on and give this a little thought over the next day or two, and when we meet again, we're gonna be more prepared."

This, of course, created another gust of seventeen overlapping voices, most of them complaining about the possibility of a second meeting, or listing free periods already accounted for.

"*Penny* will decide when we're gonna meet again, so if there's a time that's not gonna work for you, email it to her. All right?"

Our unprecedented silence in the beat after this question was both its answer and an opening for Penny to take the floor back. "All right, guys, I'll email you! Thanks to everybody who pitched an idea. In addition to sending me schedule conflicts, send me mottoes! I'll organize them all, and have them ready for our next meeting!"

We had all trickled past her by the time she'd finished this final thought. The meeting had ended when Tammy stopped talking, even Penny knew. Though we left disheartened at our failure to avoid getting roped into further commitment to this nonsense, we had to walk past Tammy to get to the dorms, and the commons, where most of us were headed, and it was hard not to notice that she looked like the runty neighborhood kid who had just caught the biggest fish by five pounds, and not even because she had been the star of the meeting, but because she was happy to have reinforced for herself the fact that not all things were beyond consensus.

And even now, it gives us comfort to report that there are parts of this story that have a happy ending, even if other, more important parts of it do not.

───────

Jimmy and Hannah gave no indication that they understood the meeting was over—they stayed in exactly the same positions they had been in throughout the meeting as the rest of us migrated away. Somehow it was clear that they were together even though they didn't exchange a single word and Hannah's eyes were closed. When Leslie saw them lying in the grass, faces to the sun, she threw her body down next to theirs and said something that made Hannah laugh. Hannah's laugh was like outdoor seating in front of sidewalk cafés on the first real day of spring—a call impossible to ignore.

Tanner Conover and Melissa Raymond—the last two members of our class whose names you need to learn—were on their way to her dorm room to "read silently to themselves over a bottle of wine." They had yet to begin the ferocious it's-on-it's-off affair that would last two full years beyond our final residency, even though she lived in Washington and he lived in Milwaukee, and she would be married to someone else by the time the last hushed midnight call had been placed.

Hearing Hannah's laugh as they passed, they reconsidered their plan and sat down right there, giving up the possibility of sex for the certainty of the sun, and that laugh, and the promise of the day itself, air too pleasant, too perfectly suited to the human body's temperature to feel.

"Jesus, that meeting almost killed my Pearl buzz," Leslie said.

"I'm not entirely sure what you mean about Pearl," said Hannah, not opening her eyes, "but I agree that meeting could've been about twenty minutes shorter."

"Oh my God, *that mustache*," Leslie said. "It's so fucking rad. I don't know how I'm going to sit through four more workshops with it without watching *Super Troopers*, though, am I right?"

Hannah and Jimmy finally looked directly at her, committing to the conversation. They didn't say anything, but Hannah smiled and Jimmy shook his head pleasantly, both of them pleading ignorance.

"Nooo! How are you guys gonna come in here and try to tell stories without watching the greatest story ever told? Like, *ever*?"

"Jimmy's not really a storyteller," Hannah said, tapping the sole of his shoe lightly with the toe of her duck boot. "He's a poet."

"Ahhhh," said Leslie, as if this revealed some secret fact about Jimmy, and explained a lot. "I'm familiar with the art. That's smart. It's easier to sound smart in poetry."

Hannah couldn't help herself—she laughed again. Not because it was funny, but because it was absurd. Of course it was.

"I think some people would argue that it's harder," Hannah said, looking at Jimmy, who was twisting blades of grass at his feet.

"No," said Leslie. "You just use certain words and structures and syntaxes, and banal thoughts become poetry. You know, you just fance shit up."

"Did you just use *fancy* as a verb?" Jimmy asked. Not challenging her, but genuinely intrigued enough by the possibility to emerge from the silence that the rest of us had already started to take for granted.

"I have no patience for people who speak of ennui—my experience was always wonder," Leslie said instead of answering him, looking somewhere off into the middle distance dramatically.

"Who said that?" Jimmy asked.

Asking two questions in a row is so out of character for the Jimmy the rest of us remember that we made Melissa and Tanner confirm it twice, but they didn't hesitate either time.

"No one," Leslie said. "I just made it up."

"That's not no one. That's you," said Jimmy. "And I like that. Wonder."

This is the first and only thing we ever knew Jimmy to hold an opinion on, a first and last as memorable and important-feeling as that lone laundry room smile. It feels strange to tie such a bright, shiny, three-dimensional word around a boy like Jimmy, but there it is. We do.

Wonder.

None of this gave Leslie any reason to pause. "It's essentially just saying people who get bored are assholes, or maybe idiots, given how small a time we're here, and how much there is to see while we are, which everyone already knows is true," she said. "That's what poetry is—it's reflecting people's experiences and observations back to them, making them seem cooler or more astute than they were."

Jimmy laughed, a timid little field mouse of a laugh that

might not have qualified as a laugh for anyone else. For someone who laughed more often. We had only known Jimmy for four of the ten days we would know him by then, and we still didn't know as much about him as we might've liked to, but it was clear he was no more a laugher than he was a smiler. Not because of any foul humor, but because he was too busy worrying, too alert to possible threats that needed his attention, even here, in what was perhaps one of the most coddled environments in the world. He had the kind of shrunken posture that promised something terrible had happened to him. Even though there wasn't a single line in Jimmy's work to point to as evidence of some troubled past or accumulated cruelties, you could smell it. From the way he kept his head down to the world, and how infrequently he laughed.

When you kick a dog a certain number of times, one of two things happens—it becomes mean, and goes on the attack, or it becomes afraid, and keeps its head down from the world, hoping the world won't notice it, shrinking into itself as far as possible.

"I think people in all genres do that—look for meaning in the everyday and the banal," he said, the field mouse laugh having scurried away. "But I don't think you're wrong."

No one is surprised that this was Jimmy's answer, or that he didn't take offense to Leslie's critique of his genre, his mild manner aside. Among writers, having thick skin often just means you're really good, and we all knew, by then, just how good he was. The whispers that had been trickling down from his workshop classmates had become shouts. He was good not in a polished, fourth-term kind of way, consensus had it, but good in an *I would be good even if I lived in a cave* kind of way. The kind of good you can't teach.

There is no way of knowing which moments any of us will remember as they're happening. We've all hotly anticipated some event or meeting or date or celebration that passes pleasantly enough, but without any one part that you could grab on to and save somewhere safe for later. And then there are moments like this: ordinary, empty afternoons that present themselves with no warning that you'll turn over again and again for years to come. We all thought of the first residency as a beginning, the start of something that would always hold some importance in the stories of our lives if only because it was something we were doing for ourselves, however good or bad our reasons were for doing it. And however many doubts or delusions we had about the quality of our own work, and where it might take us, there was no question about the caliber of Jimmy's. He was talented, maybe exceptionally so, and because life still seemed simple to us then, or simpler than it does now, we thought that guaranteed him something, however small—some publication or piece of public praise—and that good things were ahead for him.

The moment was a nothing conversation typical of school lawns, so standard, outside Leslie's unconventional thoughts on poetry, that Tanner and Melissa stopped listening and gave themselves more fully to each other. But when we look back, we see now how important it was, this ordinary summit of theirs. If personalities had sizes, Jimmy's was David to Leslie's Goliath, and Jimmy had spent his entire life dodging Goliaths, knowing that while that was a nice story, for every fallen Goliath there were at least a hundred fallen Davids.

Leslie was terrifying to most of *us*, who met the workshops and the lectures and the student center dance parties with pointed eye contact, ready for all of it, eager for it, even. Maybe it was because Leslie never had a thought that didn't become a statement, and you didn't have to guess even for a second where you stood with her, and after a lifetime of trying to figure out whom to trust—who would hurt him and who would not—Jimmy was more tired of guessing than anything else. Maybe it is because after a lifetime spent in the company of truly hard people, he knew that Leslie, for all her brass and candor, also had heart. Maybe Leslie was just one of the first people to start a conversation with him, unable to see that he was perfectly content in his silence the way the rest of us did. That he wasn't alone because he hadn't been able to find friends, but because he didn't trust anyone enough to want to. Or maybe she saw and just didn't care, just blazed ahead anyway. Maybe they both just loved Hannah enough to make it work. Whatever it was that bent in these two lone wolves to make them animals of the same Hannah pack—and it was bent by the time they had this conversation, or maybe during it—it was crucial.

Because none of what happened later could have happened without all three of them.

Tanner and Melissa knew, by the time they looked up and saw only three patches of flattened grass where Leslie, Jimmy, and Hannah had been, that they wouldn't see them at any more committee meetings, though they didn't talk or even refer to that hour in the sun until years later, during the third, or maybe fourth, to last of those hushed calls. Melissa had just had a baby, and was standing over a crib in a nursery already dark at a quarter to five, looking out at the first snowfall of the year. Out of nowhere, and without thinking about it first, half delirious from exhaustion and half genuinely happy in a way so few things before this had made her, she said "Wonder" right out loud, without even worrying that it might wake the baby she had spent the better part of the day getting to sleep. And it made her want to call Tanner, even though she had sworn she was through with all that. And even though she hadn't slept more than three consecutive hours since the spring before, and her husband was late again, she felt it, and when she did call Tanner to ask him if he remembered that day, he said yes right away—simply "Yes," knowing no expounding was necessary—without having to think about it, and none of us is surprised, because that's the kind of effect this place and these people had on us.

We know it might seem, from the amount of time and close attention we spent studying Hannah and Jimmy and Leslie, that we didn't take the program very seriously, or were easily distracted, or that we were wasting our time. But none of those assumptions could be further from the truth. We wanted so badly to be good. To *write* something good. Maybe even a little bit great. We wanted it more than anything else eight thousand dollars could buy us. Four months of mortgage payments. A weeklong trip to Paris for two, to usher new, promisingly electric relationships to higher ground or to try to strengthen delicate marriages. New parts for cars that ran poorly, time-shares on the shore, and braces for our children.

There were a million different things that had drawn us to the pursuit and there were a million different motivations that kept us writing, but the one thing that we all had in common besides this wanting was that there was some arrangement of words in each of our pasts that had done something to us or for us that we weren't yet good enough writers to explain, or put into words of our own. Those arrangements had made us miss subway stops and humbled us even as they gave us power. They made us switch majors in our junior year of college and inspired us to seek out other arrangements with similar effect. Each of our collections of words varied in length and tone and style, and we often judged one another on them. But we could agree that the effect of these arrangements was powerful enough to rationalize teeth that stayed crooked, or a long stretch of years without a real, proper vacation.

Even the novices among us, and the doubters—the Patrick Stanburys and the Jenny Ritters, who worried that they were there for the wrong reasons—could still remember the way they felt, reading the passages that had first made them decide to try to assemble their own clusters of words. Every time they reread those passages (which they did often), it reaffirmed that they had made the right decision, coming here.

And though we never talked about it, one thing we all could have agreed on is that the only thing more powerful or desirable than stumbling on an arrangement that felt like it was written just for you was writing one yourself.

Maybe the creepiest detail of a campus that felt almost designed for a horror film set were the nooks that seemed to have been installed solely for spying on people. There were dormer windows with lonely, retro 1970 school desks built into the floor in front of them, and dusty benches below some of the country's oldest stained-glass windows. These creaky seats often looked out onto green pockets of campus that felt, when you were in them, entirely private. The perfect place for an illicit affair or private phone call home. The night after Jimmy and Hannah and Leslie's campus lawn summit, Jimmy was sitting in perhaps the most claustrophobic of these hidden stations, a tiny computer cubby set apart by a thin half wall from the student commons, where the predinner cocktail hour was held. The wall made anyone in the cubby invisible to commons dwellers, but it was open at the bottom, giving the cubby occupant full access to any conversation or event conducted in the commons.

It was 6:05 when Simone walked into the commons, five minutes past the end of cocktail hour.

Sarah Jacobs, whose parents were funding her time at Fielding, and doing so without a lot of consideration for flourishes like cash bars on a weekday, had already done her evening lap around the room for any half-finished drinks that had been abandoned. Having seen her do this the night before, Jamie Brigham had bought an extra glass of Chardonnay that he left out for her, and not for any of the reasons Robbie or Lucas would have. Those of us who saw him do it forgave him for what he had said to Bridget about her fiction. Melissa Raymond and Tanner Conover had just walked up to dinner from the commons arm in arm—the first public physical gesture between them that any of us remembers—that bottle of wine in Melissa's room apparently having been drunk after all.

Carter was manning the drinks station that night. He was everyone's favorite bartender, and the oldest son of one of the few black families in Fielding, a town that is 96 percent white. He was the only bartender whose name we all knew, and one of the few Fielding employees on whom we had managed to form a consensus, positive or not. By the time Simone walked in he was packing the unopened beers back into the red cooler and corking the half-finished bottles of wine.

"Can I get a glass of Chardonnay?" Simone asked his back when he didn't immediately turn around.

"Oh, I'm sorry," he said, looking over his shoulder to at least do her the courtesy of saying no to her face. "It's after six."

We all knew by then that Vermont's liquor licenses came with arcane rules about when, exactly, alcohol could be served in certain locations. It would've been illegal for Carter to serve her. By that point we had all been told no for this very same reason, an answer that sat unmoving even when we offered to pay cash, or turn our watches back five minutes. For show. We had learned not to take it personally. The kids who held these jobs knew which rules they could break and which ones they couldn't, and Carter, of all people, would've looked the other way if he could have. He smiled more than the other bartenders, and always said "Ah, my favorite" whenever anyone ordered the local Vermont IPA, which made it more popular on his shifts.

"You can't be serious," she said, completely serious herself when she said it.

"I'm afraid so. I'll get in trouble if I do it. The student center opens in less than an hour, though, so you don't have long to wait. They have a better selection there anyway."

"Yeah, well, I don't care about selection. You have the wine I want right here. Can't you just look away for a second? I'll get it myself and be gone before you turn around."

He wrinkled his nose as if he had smelled something unsavory and shook his head, making it clear that, as unpleasant as his answer was, there was nothing he could do to change it.

"Oh, Jesus, what is it with you people?"

"Come again?" Carter asked, any traces of playfulness gone now.

"See, that's the thing. I really don't have time to. Some people have jobs they care enough about to do more than the bare minimum, and you'd be surprised how time consuming that is."

"I'm afraid I don't follow," Carter said in a new, hard voice that we hoped made clear just how clearly he did.

"Oh, I think you do."

It's hard not to wonder what would've happened if Jimmy hadn't coughed just then. Simone might never have seen him, and who knows how the rest of the term would've gone then.

There are certain writers whom the program favored—Jo Ann Beard and Rick Moody were two of them, Anne Sexton another—and the result was that there were a lot of books that had sold fewer than ten thousand copies that all of us had read. We were all fond of Anne Sexton's claim that "Love and a cough cannot be concealed," and repeated it often.

So maybe we should've known that there was never any real hope of Jimmy staying hidden for the entirety of this exchange. Maybe he was just so honest he thought it wrong not to let her know he was there, something akin to eavesdropping, even though he was there first. Maybe it was a small but noble gesture on Carter's behalf, the closest Jimmy could get to defending him. We don't really know enough about Jimmy, even now, to say.

Accident or not, the cough made Simone twirl on her expensive, cobbler-made clogs to face the half wall and whoever was behind it. She stared at Jimmy's feet, visible beneath the partition, for a moment before filling the uneasy silence that had fallen, giving him time to stand and face her instead of cowering in the cubby, or making her come in to confront him.

"You're in my workshop, aren't you?" she said once he was fully in front of her.

Jimmy coughed again before speaking. "Uh, yes, that's right. I'm being workshopped the day after tomorrow."

This would have been more consecutive words than any of us can remember Jimmy saying, outside of the lawn conversation, which is maybe the thing that makes us feel the worst about all this. He wanted badly enough to end the exchange favorably that he was willing to go against every instinct his body had. It sometimes felt, when we did hear him speak, that each word cost Jimmy something, or physically pained him. Even though the conversation was a small one, we know the experience of it was not.

"Yeah, okay. That's fine. But I care less about our workshop schedule than why you're skulking around down here, inserting yourself in conversations that have nothing to do with you when you should be up at dinner with everybody else."

"Yes, of course. I mean, no, I wasn't—"

"It's really rude, and I think you'll find in my class that I'm a real stickler for manners." She didn't quite brush his shoulder with her own as she passed him on her way up to the cafeteria like a proper villain, but she came pretty close.

As desolate as the lounge was for this exchange, there was, of course, one other person not only close enough to hear it all and repeat it later but right there in the middle of it. It makes us uncomfortable to think that we might never have learned this crucial piece of the story—five lonely little lines of dialogue that set everything else in motion—if it wasn't for a game almost none of us watched, never mind played.

Carter had been a high school basketball star so talented that the sports section of the local paper ran his stats every Sunday. When he shattered his left shinbone in a car accident six weeks before the start of his senior year, he lost any chance of a basketball scholarship when he otherwise would have had his pick of them. Though the crash had happened late at night, and on the way back from a party where minors were drinking beyond the limits of the law or common sense, neither Carter nor the teammate of his who was driving had had anything to drink, which somehow made the whole thing feel that much worse. The deer they had swerved to avoid hitting was fine, though, and the only part of the story anyone could ever get Carter to talk about.

Carter took all this a lot better than most of us would have. Maybe it was because deli ladies and bartenders in town always gave him an extra pickle or topped his glass off without asking, but he seemed happy enough, or at least not tormented by the other life that had wandered off just behind the deer. Though people around town still caught sight of him playing basketball at the court at the Y, and sometimes in the Fielding athletic center, it was almost always alone— layups and distant three-point shots—nothing that came close to the glory of the game played all out, chaos and heart and the occasional defiance of gravity.

But when Patrick Stanbury arrived on campus, Carter finally found someone good enough to play with. Carter kept up, despite the three years Patrick had spent playing semiprofessionally in countries he would probably never see again, and the countless assists he'd had to teammates who went on to play with the Knicks. It was only catching sight of the two lone figures, one of them usually suspended in air, both of them still beautiful in that way that only young people are, that it was clear how much Carter must have missed the game. You would've thought Carter had lost that beauty years ago, watching him bartend, but when he played it was impossible not to see.

The night after Simone was denied her drink was the first of many over four residencies that Patrick and Carter snuck into the school's athletic facility after hours, Patrick skipping the last of this residency's student readings once he realized that Carter's employee key card got him just about everywhere on campus. After going several rounds, they might have smoked a little bit of the pot Patrick had managed to buy on campus, during which, in the haze of friendly, random observations and general inquiry, Carter asked what the hell Simone's problem was. Patrick's confusion at the question prompted Carter to tell the whole story. Carter might've taken one last hit after he finished and let it really settle in his lungs before he exhaled and said that maybe Simone had accidentally let Jimmy see a part of her she didn't like people to know about, and wanted to scare him out of making too big a fuss about it, or telling anybody else, which seemed about as close to the truth as any of us is likely to get. Neither Patrick nor the rest of us were surprised to learn that Simone wasn't the first person of respectable standing who had spoken to Carter the way she had, and it was almost always when he was alone with them. None of them were as subtle as they imagined.

What Carter and Patrick had no way of figuring out that night to report it back to us was that the problem wasn't just that Jimmy had seen a piece of Simone she never intended to show anybody. Worked actively, in fact, to hide. Though that was certainly part of it. There was something in Jimmy's poetry—some wild, living thing—that scared people. Jimmy's writing was everything he wasn't. It was graceful and confident. Effortless. It grabbed people's attention immediately and wouldn't let go. Maybe the problem Simone had with him was that he was *too* good. Or maybe it was the kind of good he was. It wasn't just that the rhythm and flow of the language felt as natural and effortless as waves breaking on sand, or that each word he chose was just the right amount fresh, unexpected, but not so strange that you couldn't picture or feel right away what he was talking about. It was the moment of realizing some private little thought that had always made you lonely—the kind that seems to fall from empty air on hungover, rainy Sundays spent in bed, or in the middle of the night, when you wake up running through the list of people you love the most, ticking off all the ways they might be in trouble—was actually as common as speeding tickets and spring allergies. He put a finger on all the things that you had spent your entire life discovering were true but were only just starting to try to find the words for. There was power in writing that good, and authority in being able to feel your way through the world like that, even if it was the only authority he had. It was one of the few great equalizers in life, a kind of authority or ability that doesn't correlate with how attractive you are or how much money you have or even how smart you are otherwise. The problem is that the people whose power is derived from those other sources, the impeccably fashionable, connected, pedigreed Simone among them, want to keep that power for themselves, not realizing that there has never been less of a zero sum game than storytelling, or someone you have never met reading your own brain and heart back to you. There are as many different stories and feelings and thoughts and ways to tell them as there are freckles on all the redheads who have ever lived.

And someone like Simone Babbot should have known that.

We understood this part of why Simone reacted to Jimmy's cough the way she did because it's something every writer, at every level, every aspirant and every National Book Award winner, rubs up against at some point. Just after a perfect page of prose catches your breath in admiration and changes the way you see the world for one bright, blistering second, it makes you want to write one yourself, to re-create the world for someone else.

It's not that we wanted our colleagues or classmates to fail, or that our professors wanted their students to—we liked one another for reasons outside of proximity and shared interest, enough to send the occasional email in between residencies, or even grab a drink if one of us was passing through another's hometown on a business trip or college reunion. When Tammy's father died at ninety-seven, a month after our third residency, and Lucas and Robbie caravaned to Virginia for the funeral, meeting at a rest stop in Ohio, Tammy almost didn't recognize them when they stepped into the vestibule of the church, eyes freshly Visine'd, unnatural looking in their ill-fitting accountant suits, even if they wore them every day in the Real World. We like to think that at least some of the patrons of the midtown Starbucks where Mimi and Jordan met when he was in town on business so he could look over her prenup the fall before her wedding speculated that they might be a couple. When we pointed out to Mimi that prenups aren't exactly what district attorneys *do*, she scoffed at how little we knew.

There were also more selfish considerations to take into account, outside of friendship or loyalty. Any one of Fielding's students or faculty landing a glossy book deal or prestigious award made us all look good. Not to mention the simple, selfish fact that it's more pleasant to read good writing than bad, and we spent at least as many program hours reading one another's work as we did our own. It's just that to be the best— which we all wanted, on some level, to be—someone else had to be the *worst*. Not to mention all the people who would have to be *worse*, and there was no applying either of those adjectives to Jimmy's work, no matter what you thought of him otherwise, or how deeply his silent demeanor unsettled you.

Or how badly you wanted him not to have heard what he had.

Simone didn't hesitate long before acting on whatever reservations or regrets she had about her interaction with Carter, and what Jimmy might've made of it. Two nights later at dinner, the conversational thread that weaved itself through all the tables in the cafeteria was not the stray dog two third-years were trying to domesticate in their dorm rooms, or the keg that the graduating married accountants had apparently ordered for the evening's festivities. It wasn't even the peanut-allergy scare that lunch had witnessed, a close enough call to make even Lucas and Robbie go quiet. It was the poor first-term student who had been completely eviscerated in that day's new mixed-genre workshop.

Gabe Marcus said that not only the student in question but all nine of the other students in the workshop had gone directly to their rooms, forgoing lunch entirely, too rattled by the class for massive, salad bar portions of poorly prepared luxury foods. Sally Windsor said that she saw Gene Witter, Simone's co-teacher, shaking his head and talking to himself on the way back from class, and that it looked like he needed a drink. What we all knew for certain without anyone having to confirm it for us was that the professor had been Simone and the student had been Jimmy.

According to the stories the cafeteria told, it was the most substantial and fiercely held opinion Simone had ever contributed to the class. She waited until the exact moment the last of the ten students in her workshop took their seat around the table and the door had been shut to begin. When she did, she didn't even make any pretense about wanting the workshop on the pieces Jimmy had submitted to be a discussion or a conversation. It was a lecture, if you wanted to be generous; a takedown, if you didn't. The strange thing was, Jimmy was a poetry student, and Simone was the fiction expert in the class. It almost seemed rude to poor Gene, who everyone knew was due for a relapse, to take the authority on his form away from him.

Despite the number of reasons she listed for why "the poet" should put his poems in a drawer and never take them out again, and the intensity of her dislike for his poems, she had clearly read them a number of times—her critiques were very specific. Somehow the fact that she kept calling him "the poet" instead of by his name made it seem crueler and more brutal—like he wasn't even a person to her—even if she was only following the rules. She was very efficient in her work, almost cheerful in the confidence with which she listed off point after point that she wanted to make, like a flight attendant going through a safety checklist before takeoff.

Apparently she was smiling the whole time.

Maybe it's the smile that makes some of us think that this is where it all began, instead of with that cough. Like maybe Simone enjoyed reestablishing who had the advantage in this fight. Or felt emboldened by how easy it was to do. Maybe the horror in the ten little faces in front of her—eleven, counting Gene's—was no match for the satisfying, if fleeting, confirmation that whatever Jimmy had discovered about what kind of person she was underneath all the poise, and whatever he was or wasn't capable of on the page, she was still the one in charge, and her voice was still the one that mattered.

None of us has ever spoken to Simone about any of this, and probably never will, so we'll never know for sure. And while all fourteen of us did our part in cobbling together the bits of the workshop we do know, Jimmy was the only first-term student who was actually there. We can't be sure how much of what the cafeteria had to say to each of us was true and what was merely speculation or hyperbole, but we do know that this was the only term the school offered the mixed-genre workshop it had hyped so proudly in all the program literature leading up to that term, and no one disputes that the Jimmy debacle is the reason why.

Mimi Kim had carpooled to campus from Brooklyn with a second-year named Danny, resourceful enough to avoid public transport even as a first-termer. Danny was the only person in Jimmy's workshop any of us knew, even slightly. When he stopped by Mimi's room after the now infamous workshop to pick up the snacks she had been squirreling away from the cafeteria for their journey home in two days, he said it was because he wanted to get a jump on packing, but Mimi said his hands were shaking. She ushered him in and discovered he was more rattled by what Simone had said *after* Jimmy's turn at workshop ended, at which point the critique of a short story by a fourth-term fiction writer began.

The short story had a happy ending, Danny reported. It was all tied up in a neat little bow, so that the insufferable, controlling boyfriend of the protagonist not only lost the breakup, he lost his job and most of his friends because of what a dick he had been to his girlfriend. All this happened in the nice, tidy span of a week, even though he'd presumably been a dick his whole life, and certainly for the three years the couple had been dating. While Simone liked the story considerably more than she had liked Jimmy's poems, she had a problem with the ending.

"Look," she had said, "we all like a happy ending. Something that might lead us to believe that we'll all get what we have coming to us, and that things tend to work out in the end. But unfortunately, that's not always the way life works, is it?"

It had seemed, Danny said, like she actually wanted them to confirm this for her here, but she went on before they could.

"Life is *messy*," she continued. "Life is *complicated*. And while it might feel good, in the moment, to have things work out in the tidy way they so rarely do in life, you have to trust that your readers can handle more nuance than that. More complications. More *honesty*. Some people hate ambiguous endings, or stories left open-ended, or downright tragic endings, but a truly honest story will find its readers. People want the truth, not a lesson."

She stopped here to survey her work and evaluate from the looks on the faces in front of her if her point had been sufficiently made. She must've decided it hadn't been, because she hit her note again, as certain in what she was saying as ever.

"Fiction is meant to capture the reality of what it means to be a human being, which as we know entails all kinds of contradictions and complications. There are no true villains or heroes. The villains in novels don't know they're the villains, or don't think they are. Readers want the gray area and all the uncomfortable questions that live there and the fact that things almost never work out the way we want them to. Sometimes the good guys do lose, or realize they weren't as good as they thought they were. Sometimes the evil corporation wins the lawsuit. They don't catch the whale at the end of

Moby-Dick. The Great Gatsby dies and the people who kill him go on with their lives as if nothing happened. And we know all too well what happens to poor Lenny."

She gave the class a second here to recall it themselves.

"There's a reason why these endings strike such a chord in readers, and why these books have lasted. Because people recognize the truth in them, however much we might wish we didn't. And capturing that truth is what real, literary fiction is about. That's what good fiction is meant to *achieve*."

By then their faces must've reflected back how befuddled they still were, Danny said, but she didn't give up on convincing them even then.

"If there's one thing I want all of you to remember, it's this. Not how to create a lasting, memorable image or the importance of striking every hint of cliché from your work. But this: achieving what fiction can achieve at its best sometimes means embracing an unhappy truth over a happy, naïve lie."

And in this way, Simone got what she wanted. Because none of us has ever forgotten that she said this.

Mimi had the same distant fondness for Jimmy that the rest of us did, and asked, as soon as Danny's tale ended, his hands still too unsteady to successfully arrange the considerable number of bags Mimi had for him, what *Jimmy's* reaction to all this had been.

To this, Danny shook his head. Jimmy had stopped listening. His eyes never left the table immediately in front of him after Simone had given her final word on his poems. It was clear to everyone in the class that he had had his fill of program wisdom by then. Which is too bad. Because of all the pieces of this story that we've put together after the fact, the easiest detail to pin down was that it was clear that even during that second half of the workshop, Simone was still speaking mostly to him.

That first dinner after Jimmy's workshop, we didn't recap the nastiest, most horrifying bits of the debacle again and again out of gossipy instincts, or at least not *only* on account of them. Our own work was implicated in it, too. If Jimmy's poems weren't good enough to be above this sort of public humiliation—every writer's worst nightmare—none of our work was. So while we exchanged the pieces of information we had each managed to gather, since that's what people do with information of this sort, given enough time, it was also a sort of unconscious search for some detail about the exchange that made it feel less personal to the rest of us. No one was surprised when Robbie, who didn't bother to swallow the bite of truffle meatball in his mouth before speaking, was the first one to say out loud what everybody else was thinking, if in somewhat less delicate terms than we had been thinking it.

"Well, look, I mean, as brutal as this all sounds, and as bad as I feel for the guy, isn't this just how things go here?"

Robbie always seemed five degrees harsher when Lucas wasn't around, as if trying to compensate for his absence, and Lucas was missing from dinner.

We were all tempted to nod our heads even if we never would've said it ourselves—*yes, yes, everything is fine, the workshop process is working as it should.* If what had happened to Jimmy was simply standard operating procedure, rather than a personal attack, it meant that the fact that we had been spared similar fates was a credit to our work. It meant we didn't have to think about it anymore, or consider the darker, unspoken implications of the whispers, or even acknowledge just how subjective this art form we were all sacrificing our time to really was, or the fact that, even if we did work hard enough to become as good as Jimmy, there might be someone around to deny us our accolades. Most of us were ready to let Robbie's words be the final, accepted consensus on the matter, but Jenny Ritter, who was in the habit of asking her two- and five-year-olds what they meant by the vague or nonsensical things they said, aware, by then, of the habit young children have of repeating things they've heard in a totally different context, pushed Robbie.

"What do you mean, *That's how things go?* I don't know about the rest of you, but this sounds like it was a hell of a lot more intense than anything that's happened in my workshop."

This was not the first time Jenny asked Robbie to clarify what he meant, and you could hear his impatience when he answered: "Like, that's what workshop is—a critique of your work. You know, if you can't take the heat . . . right?"

It was clear even to Jenny, who almost always had a follow-up question, that when Robbie said this he meant it rhetorically. With the exception of Jenny, we all tended to nod our heads blandly at the empty or throwaway things he said, which was generally good enough for Robbie. And there was still the fact that we wanted him to be right, and for Jimmy's problem to be his alone and something the rest of us didn't have to worry about. But instead of the nod Robbie would have settled for, Jamie Brigham, who had been less vocal at meals since Bridget threw her milk at him, said something that struck us as strange as he was saying it, but seems like the only thing that could have been said by now.

"Well," he said, "this seems to me like a case of rain."

It was the first of many times he would say just the right thing at just the right time, an ongoing attempt to make up for his initial misstep with Bridget, who he quickly learned was smarter and more interesting than his first impression of her had measured. It sounded right even when he said it, even though we had no idea what he meant by it at the time. We sometimes remember him being part of conversations that he wasn't present for, because we wish he had been. None of us can remember now what he did or where in the Real World he lived, though he wasn't brooding enough to try to keep this sort of information from anyone, or to try to make the answers to those questions sound more glamorous or novel than they were. He's the only one besides the girls and Jimmy not to graduate with our class, so he's not around to ask. We figure he must've been one of the married accountants who actually liked his job—was good at it, and took satisfaction from the order and sense of the numbers he worked with.

Robbie looked over at Jenny Ritter to see if she was going to hold Jamie to the same standard of clarity she had held him to. When it was clear she wasn't going to, he only shook his head and did it himself. "Okay, how do you figure that?"

"Well," Jamie said, not bothering to stop oversalting his sunflower-seed-encrusted cod, like it was a routine answer to a routine question that he had been expecting, "like most people, I love rain when I don't have to go out into it, but hate it when I do."

Robbie didn't even wait for Jenny or anyone else to rescue him this time, probably sorely missing Lucas by now.

"What the hell does *that* mean?"

"People only seem to think something's a problem when it's a problem for them."

At the exact moment that Jamie was delivering his philosophy on rain, Linda Marcum's 1994 Honda Accord was pulling up in front of the dorm the first-term men had been assigned to. Linda was the fifty-year-old program secretary, the top of whose head was far more familiar to us than her face, on account of the number of hours she sat cross-stitching pillows for her family in between her duties and shifts instead of making small talk the way the rest of the administrative staff did. Most of us would've identified her more quickly by name than by face anyway, since one of her main jobs was to send us emails about the state that the classrooms were left in after workshop, and the items that had been left there, or gone missing. We remember the emails even years later, not because they reunited any one of us with any valuable missing item, or even because we're still not exactly sure about the extent of Linda's role in the final act of this story, or how much she knew when, but because the emails hinted at a rich, playful inner life that was completely at odds with the drawn, humorless *I'd rather not* face she put on at anyone's approach. Robbie and Lucas were later convinced that she wasn't actually the one composing the emails and spent a considerable amount of time they could've spent writing trying to uncover the emails' true author. One of Linda's most notorious and memorable pieces of work was about a jar of mustard that had been found on one of the classroom bookshelves wedged in between the collected stories of Chekhov and Cheever. She attached a photo of the mustard, and in the line where she usually reminded us where these items could be claimed she wrote, "Not available for pick-up because it was nine months expired."

Lucas White was sitting on the front steps of the building when Linda's car pulled up. We all know Lucas White is prone to exaggeration in addition to biting humor, but we also know that he sat on the same step of that front stoop every night at exactly the same time, even across future residencies, when he was assigned a room clear across campus, because it was one of the few places on campus that got perfect cell phone reception.

We had all heard him on the phone with his wife enough times to know that she was not the person he was talking to there each night. When Tammy finally just asked him who it was in our final graduation term two Junes later, probably suspecting a long-distance affair, he said it was his mother, who'd been losing another piece of her mind to dementia every day for years, but was always strangely, suddenly more aware during that witching hour just before dusk. Even this was not somber or sacred enough material to keep Lucas from making a joke about it—he told us how he and his four older brothers had been manipulating the situation into later curfews and extra spending money for years. While the idea of five Lucas Whites was something we wanted to forget, we had known long before Tammy asked that whomever Lucas was talking to, it was someone he loved, and that a little piece of his mother's mind was not the only thing that was lost each day. He never missed a single night's call, and it was only when Jenny Ritter saw Robbie Myers carrying a peanut butter sandwich out of the cafeteria one night that we would later see Lucas eat that we realized that his mother's hour happened to coincide with Fielding's dinner. Seeing him on that stoop, once we knew who he was talking to, made us more inclined to forgive his most savage barbs than even spotting his limp half-way across campus, the only way to identify him from that far away.

Because he was on the stoop that night, Lucas was there to see Linda get out of the car and walk around to the passenger side to open the door for Jimmy. Lucas said she left her door open so that it made that annoying pinging sound open car doors make, which, when he told us, seemed like a detail that only Lucas would remember—his stories were always bulky with backdrop and props that never went off, too much mood and context and not enough story. But by now all of us hear that pinging when we replay the conversation that followed. Lucas didn't have much of a view of Jimmy—Linda was blocking his door—but from what he could see, Lucas said Jimmy was totally empty of agency or intent, a dummy of surprisingly realistic coloring and warmth.

After she opened his door Linda didn't make any effort to get Jimmy out of the car. She just leaned against the side of it and waited, as if she had asked him a question he was formulating an answer to. Lucas said she waited a good five minutes—which is longer than it sounds when it's being filled by empty country air and that pinging door noise—before she said anything.

"I may not know much about the books you people read here, but I've been alive long enough to know a few things."

She tried to make eye contact with him to see how receptive Jimmy was or wasn't to the idea that she might know something he didn't. Lucas said she seemed to take the fact that he was still mostly just an empty human body at this point as an indication that Jimmy didn't mind being spoken to.

"One thing I've seen time and time again is that most people who succeed in anything, whether it's books or, I don't know, *Olympic horseback riding*, seem to be a little different from the people around them, either by birth or by determination. I like to watch biography specials on the History Channel when I'm cross-stitching. You can just listen without watching and still get the gist of it. And that's what the people around successful or famous people always say: *You could tell from when they were very young that they were a little different.* And while the fact that you didn't come from the same schools as some of these people or haven't had the same opportunities might make it seem like you don't know as much as they do, or like they have a head start, it might be just the thing that makes you different. Or to make you see the world differently enough than the way they do that you might have something new to say about it."

When Lucas first told us about this part of what Linda said to Jimmy, we occupied whole days and email chains trying to figure out how they knew each other well enough for her to know anything about where he came from. It was only long after that we realized some of the things that happened in this story can be explained by the simplest answer, and that Jimmy was probably just another lost item left behind in a classroom Linda was tasked with clearing. He was in her car not because of any prior relationship they had, but because when she went to tidy Simone's classroom and found Jimmy still slumped forward in his chair, she knew that if she didn't get him back to his room, nobody else would. And she probably gathered her insight into what Jimmy had or hadn't had in life up to this point the way we all did—from a single look at him. She had been working here long enough to know what happened in the classrooms she managed, and why someone might feel the way Jimmy looked after class.

Linda gave him another minute or so to either contribute to the conversation or indicate that he didn't want any part of it before she continued.

"And if anybody makes you feel bad about who you are or where you come from, it may be because they already know what I'm telling you. As proud as they may be of the lives they're living, they know there are only so many snapshots you can take of a path as well traveled as the one they're on. And maybe I'm overstepping here, but it feels to me like the forest you're trying to make your way through isn't on a map, never mind a path to guide you through it."

Lucas said that by this point it was dark enough that the little light in between the driver and passenger seats that comes on when the door is open illuminated half of Jimmy's face. He still didn't say anything, but he turned to Linda just enough that Lucas is confident he didn't imagine it, which Linda seemed to take as a question about how she knew all this. Because the last thing Lucas heard Linda say before

Jimmy finally got out of the car like it was nothing and walked right up the steps Lucas was sitting on just as he and probably Linda had given up on Jimmy ever moving again was, "Like recognizes like, son. And even if you're the only one in the forest you're in, the world is full of lonely forests not on any map, and none of them are empty."

Jimmy was in hiding for a full nineteen hours before anyone realized he was missing. Leslie and Hannah went looking for him after lunch instead of going to the 2:30 faculty lecture, and found him in the first spot they looked, his room. They had half expected him to have disappeared off the face of the earth entirely, without any evidence that he had ever been there, but also knew that when a person like Jimmy, who already spent most of his days hiding in plain sight, really wanted to get away, he'd do it in a place with a lock that only he had a key to.

His face was as mangled as accident wreckage so twisted and broken that you knew it contained at least one fatality—swollen with tears and panic and resignation at the same time. That's the way Leslie would describe it later, at least, defending what they eventually did. You'd think that having lived a life like the one Jimmy had, it would take a lot more cruelty than a one-hit-wonder novelist like Simone was capable of to create that kind of anguish. But that would be true only if

Jimmy was the kind of dog who became mean after all those kicks, instead of the kind that keeps its head down, pulling a little farther away every time it's hit.

When we picture him coming to the door to answer the girls' knocks, his head is down, as if he were too ashamed to look at them, or couldn't face the terrible news he had to tell them.

"Ummmmmm, can we come in?" Leslie asked, trying to look around him for clues to what was happening behind him, deeper in the room, which smelled like clean sweat and clothes that had been in storage for more than one season.

He held the door open but still wouldn't look at them. Hannah probably would have had to stop herself from hugging him—what she would've wanted from him if their places had been reversed. It was probably only because she already loved him by then that she was able to resist the impulse, and give him what he needed instead of what she wanted to give.

"Whatever happened, it's going to be okay," she said instead. "I promise. I don't know what's going on, but I promise you that."

"Yeah, if somebody died I'm sure they'll let you outta here. They'd probably refund your money, too," Leslie said. "And then you'd be up a few dozen meals, so you'd be ahead, minus the dead person."

"I screwed up," he said, hitting his forehead with his open palm more than once, a caustic, echoing series of smacks. "It's no one else, it's *me*. I did something terrible."

"Do tell," said Leslie at the same time that Hannah said, "I'm sure it can't be that bad."

When he recounted what had happened, Hannah, at least, probably tried to seem concerned and reflect the gravity that Jimmy seemed to think the situation held, while Leslie probably didn't even try to not seem confused, and maybe a little disappointed, the interest in her eyes shrinking with every word until she started waving him off before he even finished. We're pretty sure that only both reactions at once was the exact right thing.

"Duuuude," said Leslie, cutting anything Hannah might have had to say about it right off. "You're seriously surprised that the fancy New York lady is a gaping cunt? Everyone here knows you're smarter than that, Jimmy-o. We've all read your work. And having someone like that come for you is a badge of honor—it means you have completely opposing world-views, which is a *good* thing."

"I can't believe she said that to Carter," said Hannah, probably sounding genuinely sad. "What a—"

"Gaping cunt?" Leslie asked. "Yeah, we covered this already. Let's move on. Who has *time* for her? Let's go *do* something."

"But, I mean, she's a *teacher*. She's *my* teacher. She's not going to forget this."

"Um, I'm pretty sure she already has, and so should you," Leslie said. "Plus, she's a teacher at a low-residency MFA program, not *Oxford* or something. Like, let's keep it all in perspective."

"No offense intended, though, right?" Hannah asked, taking a break from comforting Jimmy to scold Leslie with her eyes, even though, as the only one in the room and probably the entire campus who had actually gone to Oxford, she was the only one outside of the insult.

"Let's get out of here," Leslie said. "This place is claustrophobic. There are not enough windows in the world to air it out right now."

We don't know what they did when they left campus. The high school junior who sold Patrick the weed he and Carter smoked at the athletic center that night (and the rest of that residency and probably every other residency) also worked on the horse farm fifteen miles off campus, and said he had seen the girls there once that June. We can't think of any other time they were unaccounted for long enough to go. He doesn't remember Jimmy, but that doesn't really mean anything.

When he gets stoned, the junior likes to talk about the cats on the farm. There's the one that catches half a dozen mice a day and plays with them before he kills them. Not with any evident malice—it really looks like he just wants to play. There's the three-legged one, and the one that's entirely black—black eyes, black fur, black little lizard tongue. Best, though, is the cat who thinks it's a horse, who lines up when all the other trail horses do, and never drops pace or falls out of line, no matter how far they ride. He apparently had the other horses convinced that he was one of them. He even had his own stall. The cats practically run the place, the junior insists, so it's safe to say they were roaming freely that day, hard to miss. Leslie probably had some showdown with at least one of them. The fifteen miles you go to get to the farm are pretty much straight north, so though it's hard to picture, the farm is closer to falling off the edge of the earth than even the campus is, and the sun rises there earlier and sets later, so the light was probably something, that day, two days from the longest day of the year.

The funny thing is, the junior says Professor Pearl was there that day, too. He was as much an honest-to-God townie by then as he was an acclaimed novelist, so it doesn't feel like a stretch to think of him engaging with the small local businesses—maybe he even had a horse or two of his own that he kept at the stables. What we can't figure out is what he was doing with three students off campus during the exact hour and a half they were supposed to be in a faculty lecture about postmodernism in the wake of David Foster Wallace. Rebel though Pearl is, it feels like a stretch to think he would have aided and abetted such wanton disregard for the sched-ule. Our best guess is that when he saw them there, where they weren't supposed to be, he saw some remnant of the di-saster on Jimmy's face and left, abandoning whatever business he had gone to the farm to conduct, not wanting to have to yell at them, and not wanting to condone what they were do-ing by letting it go unremarked upon. In some ways Professor Pearl is as much a mystery to us as the others—Simone and Hannah and Leslie and Jimmy—but we feel we know him well enough to say that he would have understood. He was the sort of man who loved and respected the books he taught, which he reread every time he taught them, knowing there would be some new thing every time. He loved them enough that he knew the things these books could teach a person, and the way they could shape and improve a life, but also all the things and ways they couldn't, which would have to be shaped and improved by other things, like the sun, and strange little half-wild cats, and people who would break the rules for you. To really love something, you have to know its shortcomings and dull bits.

He probably knew from the way that Jimmy was sagging into his horse, and the fact that Leslie and Hannah put him in the middle of their own horses, sandwiched between them as if to keep him on the trail, even though most of the talking they were doing was to each other, and from their overcompensatory laughter, which felt too bright, like canned studio laughter, that although this was a rebel mission, it was also a desperate one. He was the kind of man who knew that, mandatory or not, there were some things in life more important than classes, and some virtues—like kindness and spontaneity and loyalty and escape—that can't be taught from a book.

Jimmy wasn't the only person who saw something that June residency that he wasn't meant to see. And Hannah and

Jimmy and Leslie weren't the only ones who had blown off the late-afternoon lecture on poor DFW. Margaret Jibs was spread out in the strangely secular pew on the second floor of the "barn," where most of the workshops were held, which looked out over the quad all the way to The End of the World. The barn was a giant, cheerful red building that greeted visitors as soon as they arrived on campus. Its architecture was one part old schoolhouse, one part old firehouse, one part actual barn. The pew was often where people met to discuss the workshop they had just finished on their way out of it—a place for impromptu teacher-student conferences, and conversations that began "That thing you said about x reminded me of this essay I once read by y." It could fit half a dozen people, but Jibs is an only child and doesn't have a great sense of space, never having had to share it, so her things had probably filled the entire area that her reclining body didn't. She always brought too much with her wherever she went, in order to maximize her comfort—she was a carrier of tissues and eye masks and extra layers of clothing, which would've made her handy to have around if she ever shared those things. She had just looked down at her watch and realized that the lecture was probably close to finished, and that if she started packing up her considerable pile of things now she might get the first drink at cocktail hour, when she looked up to see two tiny people meet at the very last patch of grass before the drop-off at the end of the lawn. They looked like the last two people on earth, and probably felt like it, too, given that everyone else had circled that lecture in their schedule as something not to miss, mandatory or not.

When she told us about what she saw, Margaret would say that she was sick, which is the only reason she would ever dream of missing a lecture, but we all saw her drinking her Chardonnay spritzers at the student center that night, made with seltzer she brought with her since the student center was not the sort of place that sold drinks with more than one ingredient. She was too much of a hypochondriac to drink if she truly suspected there was something wrong with her. And we had all heard her talk about how she couldn't stand writers, or anyone, really, who got attention just for being strange, or different from everyone else. Like, if you had to try that hard, what was the point. Normal was underrated, she thought, even in fiction. She was a classicist, and if any of us had ever asked her, we feel confident she would have told us that her favorite book was something that even people who never take a single English class after high school have read, like *Pride and Prejudice* or *The Great Gatsby*. So if there was a lecture she was going to dodge for no other reason than pure lack of interest, "Postmodernism in the Wake of David Foster Wallace" feels like a pretty safe bet.

If we're being fair, though, she was probably also tired by then. We all were. It was the second-to-last day of classes and lectures that term, and there was no small amount of information we had been asked to take in and process and turn into a measurable improvement in our writing. Maybe *tired* is the

wrong word. Maybe *small* is better. Our heads had been filled
with the thoughts and rules and revelations of the most brilliant writers in history, across numerous decades, and it wasn't
until we had them all put in front of us, side by side like that
and in so short a chunk of time, that we realized how many of
them there were. Even the great ones bled into a sea of other
great ones, and it made us feel inconsequential, even if we were
destined for some little bit of greatness ourselves. We had arrived on campus feeling closer to real writers than we ever had
before, and now we saw how much work still lay ahead of us,
and how much we still had to learn and how hard we would
have to work. *Small* may be an okay word for it, but *lonely*
might be even better, since the people in our normal lives who
often made us feel bigger were still miles away, and considered
us on some sort of low-glam vacation that we would have to
make up for later with extra garbage duty or matrimonial
attentiveness.

Poor Jibs's loneliness was probably only made worse when
she saw the two people out on the lawn lean into each other
for a kiss that melted them into one lone figure, a silhouette
cut out of the horizon. The room the pew sits in is so stuffy,
so completely shut off from any fresh air, the windows around
it having been painted shut for decades, or never meant to
open in the first place, that you could see the particles moving
in the air around you. The space felt like such a vacuum that
it probably made what she was watching feel even farther
away, on another planet or in a dream she once had instead of

across only a hundred yards or so. She said she wasn't sure if it was just that time moved slowly during the late-afternoon march toward dinner and the clink of ice in glasses, but it felt like they stayed that way for a while. Even after the kiss, their faces lingered just millimeters away from each other, she said, so that it was impossible to say where one of them ended and the other began. Neither half of the pair was ready to separate from the other, even if discretion or bashfulness or time kept them from giving that first kiss a twin.

Whatever else you want to say about Margaret's writing, she knows how to hold a story. That night in the student center, she waited until the exact moment we thought she had told us everything there was to know before telling us that it was remarkable, how clearly she saw the two faces bent toward each other just after they finally pulled themselves apart. A true testament to just how powerful the light in Vermont is in the summer, without too many things to bend or break it or get in its way. She said the distance and the height did nothing to diminish the happiness on their faces or the weightlessness of their gaits as Jimmy and Hannah separated, and walked to their opposite ends of the campus.

Probably the only thing that could have distracted us from further speculation on both the confetti Simone had made of Jimmy's work and what Jibs had seen was the graduation dance that was scheduled for the next night, the last night of the residency. Even we first-years knew that the last night was the best. There had been so much talk about it from the upper classes that we knew to anticipate the event without having experienced it. Finally getting to drink and listen and see firsthand all the things they had been telling us about made the night ahead of us and its events feel like some sort of milestone, instead of just another gathering of bookish nerds, which we all surely were, despite the many things that set us apart from one another. We took pleasure in ticking off all the customs and traditions we had been told to expect, because it made them ours, too, from the jam band that played the new graduates out to the kitschy, ironic tokens each student bestowed upon their favorite professor—one year it had been leis, another pinwheels.

After the graduation ceremony in the big, more formal auditorium you had to cross that field of wildflowers to get to, which was lit up with fireflies by the time you crossed back. After the speeches given by the visiting emcee—an NBCC-winning transgender essayist—and a student speaker elected by their classmates, this residency a poet who wore mismatched Converse sneakers in bold colors and had an arm sleeve of *Sesame Street* tattoos. After the last plate of a chocolate mousse far more traditional and far more edible than anything that had been served in the cafeteria all residency had been cleared, we all streamed back across campus to the student center for the farewell party.

We took up the spot in the student center our class had been occupying all residency, a lonely island of plastic booths in between the pool tables and the snack machines that over-charged. We weren't sure if it was the spot first-years always got, or if it would be ours until we graduated and left it open for the incoming first-years, but we realized, settling into it that night, that we'd know soon, because we were almost done being the new guys.

We were feeling pretty good by the first sip of our four-dollar student center beers. A little wistful that we had to leave, but excited to see our families and roommates and lovers in the Real World, who were starting to feel like characters in a short story we had once read. The last workshop was the following morning, earlier than we might've liked, but after the wine we'd had at the graduation dinner, we were feeling confident about the opinions we had formed on the stories being workshopped, and those of us who were being work-shopped were feeling so generous and warm toward our class-mates, nestled into one another in formal wear that made us feel as if we had all just gone to prom with one another after ten days of fleeces and jeans and college T-shirts, that we weren't even that concerned about what these friends might have to say about our work. We trusted them with it. Mostly, we were thinking we had made it. One residency down.

By the time Jimmy, Leslie, and Hannah walked into the student center we had given up on them ever arriving. We wouldn't have blamed Jimmy for staying away. If his workshop had been even half as brutal as we'd heard, we might've stayed away ourselves. We were feeling so benevolent to this place and its people by then, and so optimistic about the things we would achieve before we left it for good, that we didn't even hold their exclusivity against them, realizing only as the resentment dissipated that we'd had it in the first place.

The impenetrable borders of the triangle they formed suddenly felt like another tic of our class that we would think about when we were off campus, like Tammy's stories about the strangest, drunkest client she had ever represented and Tanner and Melissa's clumsy public flirtation, which still seemed sweet to us then. It felt like something that we were a part of, instead of something we were forced to stand outside of. More than anything, we admired Jimmy in that moment he appeared in the student center's doorway, and are sorry we never got the chance to tell him. None of us said anything to or about him when the trio joined the fringes of our group. We told ourselves later that it was only because we didn't want to scare him away.

Penny took their arrival as her cue to start her speech about the brown box of T-shirts at her feet. Patrick Stanbury and Jamie Brigham started drumroll pounding on the table, making us forget the irritation we'd felt at the undertaking's first email and meeting. Sarah Jacobs and Mimi Kim wahooed with their arms raised above their heads, the closest thing to cheerleaders any graduate program has ever had, making Robbie look over. Even in the dim student center lighting we saw him blush when his gaze lingered on Sarah a beat too long. Penny had less wine at dinner than the rest of us, but her too-alert eyes looked comfortable in her face for once, and strands of hair were starting to fall from her normally very-crisp braid. She looked prettier in the late-June student center light than she would when we pictured her later—she was the kind of woman memory wasn't kind to. Leslie put two fingers in her mouth and whistled so loudly that some of the wildly drunk graduates turned around, and we felt the warmth of a hundred draft beers for her.

"Thanks, guys, thank you," Penny began. "I don't know about you all, but I find being on this campus inspiring."

Lucas and Robbie whistled as if she had just taken her shirt off.

"There are so many people here who care about the same things you do, things that seem maybe a little indulgent, because they don't always make money, or serve a practical purpose, or because the purpose they do serve is hard to measure. It makes it easy to forget about these things off campus, in Real Life. And being around other people who feel as committed to these things as you reminds you that these things really do matter, no matter how easy it is to lose sight of them when you go back home, to other responsibilities. And I know I don't want to forget that in between now and next residency. And I'm hoping that maybe these T-shirts will help. To remind us why we came here and what we're hoping to get out of being here."

She took a T-shirt out of the box and held it up like some sort of flag as she scooted the box to the next person in the clumsy half circle we formed. On the back of the T-shirt, we saw, as we each grabbed a shirt out of the box, all of our names were listed. Tammy was just plain Tammy, even there. Penny's name was first. Hannah's and Leslie's names were last. There was no ostensible criteria for the order of the names in between. The box had made it halfway around the group before anyone realized that Jimmy's name had been left off entirely. Those of us who realized it looked back at Jimmy, who already had a T-shirt in his hand.

Leslie grabbed hers and Hannah's and Jimmy's T-shirts before Hannah had time even to put her hand on Jimmy's left shoulder, the most intimate physical contact we can remember anyone having with him, other than the kiss, which only Jibs can verify. No one said anything as Leslie walked to the kitchen in the corner of the student center without looking back, though Penny kept looking over her shoulder nervously, as if Leslie were there collecting weapons. We felt a little sorry for Penny, horrified though we were at her oversight. None of us held it against her, even if we wouldn't look at her while we waited for whatever Leslie was doing. The truth is that, if you'd never read Jimmy's work, he was utterly forgettable, a boy destined to be left off rosters and T-shirts.

Leslie came back wearing her T-shirt, and tossed Jimmy's and Hannah's to them as soon as they were in range. When they turned to leave we saw the three neat rectangular holes on the back of all three T-shirts in exactly the same place on each one. They were neater than we would've thought Leslie capable of, so uniform across each shirt in size and location that they looked like computer em dashes. Two of them were where Leslie's and Hannah's names used to be, the third was where Jimmy's should've been.

We can't remember now the design we landed on for the front of the T-shirt, what motto we all finally decided we could live with, or even what color it was. Not realizing at the time how distinctly we would want to remember our time on campus, none of us saved our shirt, not even Penny, who probably no more wanted a reminder of her mistake than the rest of us. When we think about the shirt now, we see the three floating absences that, like Jimmy and Leslie and Hannah themselves, were somehow more vivid and undeniable than the presences they had replaced.

The floating absences got smaller as the three of them walked out of the student center to some lonely campus spot that only they know, but the image of their retreating backs still hasn't left us. We don't even have any guesses about where they went this time, and not even the high school junior, who had an opinion on everything, or Patrick Stanbury, who was so gregarious that he usually tracked down whatever detail or piece of information we were after just from breezy casual conversation with the maximum number of people possible, could say. And yet for all that we don't know and probably never will, that moment of watching them leave and the absences that floated just after them, waving good-bye, is the only moment that all of us remember exactly the same.

Leslie's story was workshopped the next morning. Every residency, there was one last workshop the Sunday morning after the postgraduation party. It went until noon, giving students two hours until the two o'clock deadline, by which everyone had to be off campus and pointed toward home, so the school could flip the dorms and get them ready for the undergrads again, wiping out any trace that we had ever been there. The hangovers alone made it nearly impossible for anyone to concentrate that morning, never mind the lists of things to pack and good-byes to make that we were all building in our heads and in the margins of almost-full-by-now notebooks. Some people thought it was lucky to go on the last day, because no one had the energy to be mean, or attack with any rigor. Others thought it meant your work got less real feedback.

Leslie was pretty much the only person who could've held our attention at that point, and not just because of how strange and dark her story was. All eight other students in the workshop arrived early, steaming coffees in hand, hoping to be there when she and Hannah arrived. We thought they'd wear the evidence of however they'd spent the night before. We thought they'd sit even closer than they normally did, chairs scooted in close, thighs touching under the table, whispering throughout class, lest anyone forget the degree to which they were more powerful than the sum of their parts. But when Blake Bowlin, a likable enough third-year in their workshop, walked into Sunset Cottage five minutes before class, Hannah was already there, marking up a copy of Leslie's story with the cold, discerning eye she might've shown the work of a complete stranger. Leslie was the last to arrive, at ten o'clock exactly, which, to be fair, was early for her. She sat four chairs away from Hannah even though there was a seat empty next to her. Though we can't say why, this complete lack of intimacy or even acknowledgment didn't feel like a sign of any trouble between them—it felt aimed more outward, toward us, than at each other. Whatever had happened after they left last night, it was theirs alone.

This public estrangement wasn't the only thing that had everyone sitting up straighter than the number of hours of sleep they'd had should've made possible. Most of the other people in the class had read Leslie's story before it became an accepted fact that she wrote erotica. And it was only when they went to reread it that last, early morning of workshop that they knew enough to be surprised when no one got laid. It was as edgy and unsettling as anyone expected, but no one got naked. Her writing was unblinking and unsentimental. We were shocked, when we finally read the story ourselves, at how much it made us feel.

The story was about two American doctors in Africa,

fighting the Ebola crisis. The female doctor is in love with the male doctor, and the male doctor is in love with the heroics of his being there in the first place. He does some unnamed thing to piss her off—the thing was referred to as "The Thing," two capped *T*s throughout—but what it *is* was never said. Every day, they're in charge of zipping each other's Hazmat suits before they go into buildings full of affected patients, and in the last scene the female doctor intentionally leaves the male doctor's suit partially undone, leaving him completely vulnerable to the disease. The last line is her watching him disappear through the doorway into a roomful of very sick people.

While the class waited for Professor Pearl to call everyone to order, Leslie wouldn't look at anyone, but it didn't stop everyone else in the room from looking at her. Her hair was so greasy it almost looked wet, gathered onto the top of her head in stringy clumps that met in a giant topknot and in between which you could see parts of her scalp so white they made her look vulnerable. Hygiene wasn't much of a priority for any of us while we were on campus—you could get away with showering about as often as you did on a camping trip. We realized, looking at Leslie's hair that morning, that none of us had seen it freshly shampooed, and we wondered if she had gone the entire residency without showering.

Maybe it was the hair, which made her seem downtrodden and small in a way that undermined her usual vibrancy, or the patches of scalp that had never seen the sun. Maybe it was that we still had no idea where she had spent the rest of the night before. Maybe it was that, reading her story that morning, it was better than anyone remembered from their initial read-throughs. Upon first read the other people in the class had admired it, they told us—it was unique without trying too hard to be strange—but it had confused them. But reading it after ten days with her, it made complete sense.

Reading it that first time, Leslie's story hadn't reminded them of anything or felt derivative of anything, but now it reminded them of her.

Maybe it was that we had all thought them complimentary, those times our professors told us that our short, less narrative stories reminded them of Lydia Davis, or that our violent Westerns had something of Cormac McCarthy in them. But her classmates understood, rereading Leslie's story, that the only thing better than writing the next *Varieties of Disturbance* or *The Road* was to write the first of something else, and that our professors hadn't meant we were cut from genius mold, but that we were writing by number. Whatever the reason, everyone in the room realized, as Leslie sauntered in with a swagger that felt so much less empty, after that second read-through of her story, how little anyone knew of her. Or maybe it's not that we knew so little, but that so many of the things we thought we knew about her were wrong.

We knew that Bridget Jameson's boyfriend was picking

her up on campus in a few hours and taking her to a bed-and-breakfast in Poughkeepsie that had been featured in national travel magazines, and we knew that Patrick Stanbury's mom would welcome him home with ten-layer dip that had three kinds of meat and no vegetables, but we couldn't have produced a state for Leslie, never mind a city or a zip code. For all the talking she did, and all the personal trivia she dropped that we wouldn't have shared with our closest friends or relatives, we knew almost nothing about her that wasn't directly related to the bubble of residency. She was a campus ghost. All the Leslie wisdom and authority the people in her workshop had found in her story that morning made them realize that, for all her Leslie blowharding, she might actually have something to say. And just when they—and we—were ready to listen, she had stopped talking.

We originally thought it was during the second residency, when we came back and learned what happened to Jimmy, but we realized on maybe the second or tenth or nine millionth telling of this story, that this was actually the moment we started to pay attention. An entire roomful of people having to turn their focus to Leslie's now-legendary story so soon after what happened at the student center demanded it in a way we're grateful for, because we realize now that 70 percent of being a good writer is paying attention.

After Professor Pearl reminded his students of the address to which their packets should be sent, and told them how much he looked forward to continuing working with them, and Leslie reluctantly pulled her pink earbuds out of her ears and read aloud the creepiest passage in her story, the second-term girl Lucas and Robbie were both in love with, whose name we still can't remember, raised her hand before Jude Morgan could. Too tired to bother with the pretense of having to say anything about the merits of the story, or not addressing the writer directly in order to treat it as a published piece of work she was encountering from some remove, she simply said: "I thought you wrote erotica." She was wearing last night's shirt, which seemed a little sad, even if there was more than one person in love with her on campus.

Though it had been firmly established that the writer being workshopped was not allowed to talk until after their session, Leslie spoke before Professor Pearl had time to reprimand Walk of Shame for not sticking to what was on the page.

"Yeah, well, she feels so guilty after he gets sick that she fucks him anyway. I'm not just gonna give you the *best* scene in the story right up front." She turned to Professor Pearl for reinforcement, not at all concerned that he would reprimand her for talking during the precise moment she was not supposed to. "Isn't that a thing you say, Professor Pearl? Make the reader want something, and then make them wait?"

His silence still didn't tip her off to the fact that he wasn't happy she was talking, it just made her angrier. "I mean, *come on*, guys. This isn't fucking *rocket science*."

And that was the last anyone remembers of Leslie until the next residency.

We can imagine your disappointment, having reached the end of our first residency without any other word on the kiss between Jimmy and Hannah, and what it might have meant. But we can only tell you things we know, or think we know, and none of us can remember a single snippet of conversation overheard that, even in our most presumptuous and far-reaching interpretations, could be configured or imagined into a conversation about the kiss. We've taken liberties and stretched truths and looked for meaning in the most routine, mundane memories and moments and conversations, and still: nothing. Though this is one part of the story we can't tell you with any authority, we have thought often, each of us to ourselves, about the conversation they might have had about that moment years later, if he had lived. Maybe just after he had finished mowing the lawn for the arrival of one of their grown children, or in those precious few minutes under the sheets, before sleep and after a three-glasses-of-wine dinner.

"Why did it take you so long?" he would ask. "Why nothing after that first kiss?"

"Why should it have been up to me?"

The excited incredulousness she would've asked this with would've been mostly for his amusement.

"You knew I was never going to make the first move."

"I was afraid." She would've waited a moment or two before admitting this.

"I can't imagine a girl like you being afraid of anything."

"Ha! Leslie was always the one acting recklessly, without thinking or worrying."

"Being reckless and being brave aren't the same thing."

They would have paused here just long enough to feel bad for exchanging words less than wholly pleasant about their friend.

"And what makes you think I'm brave, or ever was?" Hannah would ask, once an amount of time sufficient to their guilt had passed.

He wouldn't have to think about his answer for very long, because it was a moment he would've thought about often, the first time he ever saw her. It was the last meal of the first full day on campus, after an afternoon of rain so aggressive it seemed to have an agenda. The kind of rain that made everything feel quieter and smaller after it had blown through. Hannah was late to dinner that night, because she and Bridget had been leaving their rooms for the dining hall at the same time—a coincidence that had been orchestrated by Bridget, who by then wanted to be friends with Hannah more than any of the other girls she'd wanted and failed to be friends with in the past. They didn't realize how hard it was raining until they got to the door of the building, and while Hannah was ready to make a run for it, Bridget didn't want to get her hair wet, which we understood, given that she didn't own a hair dryer. Neither girl had an umbrella, and the bookstore that sold them was closed for the day. Between the delay this caused in their arrival and the fact that the storm's soggy aftermath had rendered impossible the sort of outdoor quad dining that made the June residency so pleasant, there was no table with enough space left to accommodate them both.

Realizing that she and Bridget weren't destined for best-friend-ship but sensitive to the extent to which Bridget was putting herself out there, which Hannah always found admirable, and not wanting to suggest they split their fledgling union up in so public a place, Hannah turned to her hall mate and said, "Let's just go to the yellow room."

The yellow room was a promised land of pretension—the physical manifestation of correcting someone for saying *who* instead of *whom*. The teachers all sat there while, presumably, reinforcing how accomplished one another's most recent publications had been, and how far their students' work would need to be pushed to match their own. So it was no surprise when Bridget said, with the wrinkled nose of a little girl saying *Mommy, I'd rather not*, "Um, isn't that reserved for faculty?"

"Let's be bold," Hannah had said, looking straight ahead, toward whatever horrors or rewards waited in the yellow room. "I think it'd really be better all around, if we can commit to being bold."

Jimmy—who ate as voraciously as he wrote and slept, despite his slight frame—had just gotten up for a second helping of red pepper hummus quesadilla, and was standing beside them just outside the serving area, close enough to hear her. As the girls pivoted, ably managing loaded backpacks and piled plates, his heart rose in a way completely new to him, in the way of stories he could never quite believe, having lived the life he had.

"How could a girl like that be afraid of a boy like me?" he'd ask, in the future that never happened.

She'd exhale the happy, tickled sigh that people in love exhale in bed, and maybe lie back on her pillow for a moment before answering.

"Oh, Jimmy," she'd say. "I was talking *to* you."

January

The drawback of the firm boundary we drew between campus and home was that we lost track of one another's lives between residencies. We'd come back to a solemn, snowed-in campus that we had left almost too green to believe to discover that happy marriages had crumbled since the last time we saw the half of the couple we knew. The really good short story writer who was in our workshop last term was missing, we'd notice on our second day of the ten-day stretch. At home, seven months pregnant, we'd learn. Sometimes it felt like the bulk of our relationships was the slow falling away of intimacies that usually happens to friendships only once, at their end. Each term we would ingratiate ourselves in one another's imaginations just deep enough that the absence would hurt after parting. Maybe it hurt more each time, the way a scab bleeds more each time you pick it open. We didn't know, that first January, because we had parted only once, and we were just then going through the bashful, half-affectionate, half-wooden *you again* moments with one another that felt a little like running into a rather pleasant one-night stand at the grocery store just a few hours before we were planning to call them.

Though we had been prepared for some unavoidable catching up—for weight gains we would have to pretend not to notice and impressive, unexpected losses that the married accountants would make too much of, and news of small publications and the successful completion of short stories that had been occupying their authors for years, maybe an engagement or two—we weren't prepared for the news we got that first morning, half hungover, half still drunk from all the complimentary wine at the welcome party the night before.

We know enough by now to know that the only way to avoid being overly sentimental and dramatic about the news we all sagged visibly under so simultaneously it felt choreographed is to just come out and tell you the plain facts of what happened. The fact is that two months and four days before we were scheduled to return to campus for our second residency, Jimmy hanged himself with a scrap of old rope in his sometimes-father's garage. We don't mean to seem callous or unsympathetic by telling you this way, abruptly and without the cushioning of euphemism or the familiar clichés of loss. This is the way we were told, too, so we know how it feels.

If this had been a suicide written in a first- or even a second-term student's story it would have been big and dramatic with some romantic explanation—an unrequited love affair, or a terminal diagnosis. But because it happened in life it had the quiet, nobody-noticed-for-a-while underdrama that permeates so many of the big moments you always thought would feel like more. Part of the reason nobody from the program had told us earlier, in an email or a letter, or even a small, discreet mention in one of the many pieces of mail they sent us in between residencies, was that they hadn't known about it much longer than we did. It was only when they called the last number they had on file for him to warn Jimmy that the copies of whatever writing sample he wanted to have workshopped had not arrived on campus, and that if they didn't have them within the week they would have to ask him to withdraw from the semester, that they learned why Jimmy's work hadn't arrived with the rest of ours.

And he did it not for a girl, or to finally dodge some insufferable person he owed money to, or to opt out of a stage-four cancer battle, but for the same reason that most of us do most of the dark, lonely things we do: plain old human desperation, and the certainty that there's nothing else to do.

After the 8:00 a.m. all-student orientation that followed the new-student orientation, they asked us second-termers to stay for a final announcement. They waited until we were all together, huddled in the first two rows of the auditorium, to tell us why they had asked us to stay. Professor Pearl, looking uncertain for the first and only time that we can remember, waited until we were fully quiet before saying he was sorry to have to be the one to tell us that Jimmy wouldn't be joining us on campus this residency, because he was no longer with us. He encouraged us to ask any questions we had, in the name of discouraging gossip. He and the program felt obliged to tell us as much as they knew, to the extent that we wanted to know it. What had happened was very sad, he said—maybe the only obvious, unnecessary words that he had ever spoken in his life—and we didn't need to make it any sadder by turning it into a soap opera or scandal. "So let's keep it all aboveboard," he finished. None of us thought to be suspicious of this transparency until much later, though at that point, not even Pearl could have known half the truth of it, nobody's fool though he was.

Robbie asked how he had died, and then Lucas asked how he did it, a question probably only Professor Pearl could answer with no evident horror or judgment. He answered as simply and straightforwardly as he had the first question. It was only when Jenny Ritter raised her hand to ask if Leslie and Hannah knew all this that we realized they were the only two people from our class not there, other than Jimmy. As our resident mother of two, Jenny had probably asked out of some maternal instinct, immediately stopping to consider how any piece of news, good or bad, would affect those more vulnerable to it before she finished processing it herself, rather than out of morbid curiosity, the way the question would have been asked had Lucas or Robbie asked it. In this answer, too, Pearl was concise.

"Yes, they know." For how long that had been true he didn't say.

Without any further questions to keep us there, at least not any that we were willing to ask out loud, we all walked out of the rows and then the building and into the snow, single file, without a word. In the forty-three minutes that remained of the free hour we had in between orientation and the first workshop, we wrote emails to our spouses and siblings and roommates, telling them what had happened even though it would mean less to them than it did to us. We had come to the news so long after the fact that it felt too old to acknowledge with a moment of silence or a makeshift monument; it felt like something that had slipped our vigilance, so wasn't ours to mourn. Instead we took comfort in telling someone else, the smallest form of acknowledgment, maybe, but something, even though we knew it would leave our Real Life people searching their memories for some mention of a classmate named Jimmy on and off through the rest of the day. Some of us cried, not just for Jimmy, but for the feeling—that absence of anything at all—that he must have been staring down not too long after we had seen him last, and that such a feeling lived in the world at all, right there alongside love, and sex, and happy coincidences too strange to be anything but plain magic, and Coen brothers movies, and chocolate chip cookie dough, dog parks, and the smell of spring. Some of us just looked out the windows of buildings that were even quieter and felt even older in the snow, and took comfort in the reliability of its falling that far north in January.

We never intended not to discuss it when we reconvened. We were as compelled by the feelings and motivations humans have for doing the things they do as any other group of writers. But we quickly learned how impossible it was to discuss Jimmy without descending into cliché or petty gossip, both of which we thought ourselves above. So after a few days of hushed cafeteria speculation, we silently, collectively decided that the best, only thing to do was to go back to telling stories the way we had been. Stories that, no matter how dire or depressing or tragic, had some sense of beauty or art to them, even if it was just an arresting image or moving line. Virtues that, as hard as we looked and as eager as we were to apply them, couldn't be found in what Professor Pearl had told us that first morning.

It would be difficult to overstate the difference in tone between June and January residencies. Junes were boundless and open, full of short chunks of free afternoons that felt like whole days, because the light was so full you couldn't picture it dimming. It promised to go on forever, and that there was plenty more where it came from. We were outside as often as we could be—splayed out on lawns and tromping indelicately, inexpertly through patches of forest like the suburban and city kids we mostly were.

We didn't love one another any less in January, but we did keep to ourselves more. There weren't many buildings open to us at certain hours, and our rooms weren't big enough to accommodate many more than one. There were small consolations like fires in the dorms' common room fireplaces, the occasional snowman marked as complete with someone's stolen reading glasses. But these activities were often more work than their novelty seemed worth, so we did them halfheartedly to start, and then not at all. The parts of us that had worn sundresses and not enough sunscreen and read parts of our stories out loud to one another after too much wine inevitably froze in the January windchill of a place that far north. Sarah Jacobs and Mimi Kim managed to find heavy puffer coats in colors other than black—olive green for Sarah and navyish royal blue for Mimi—and both of them cut through the snow in bright red Hunter Wellingtons that reminded us of being young. And even though these items popped against our drab wardrobes and the muddy snow, they really only reminded us how much more colorful the girls' clothes had been in the summer—handmade muumuus in every shade and palette and pattern imaginable, often times all at once, that seemed more like costumes for making flower crowns or catching fireflies than clothes.

We exchanged notes less often in January, and went to bed earlier, and even the married accountants planned their festivities with less evident relish, so that while the days felt shorter, the residency as a whole felt much longer.

It wasn't just the weather that had us down that January, of course. Even though we hadn't known Jimmy well and even though we avoided talking about him at first, we were a small community whose most commonly held value was empathy. And though we couldn't say that we missed him, since we had barely noticed him while he was there, each of us privately felt bad and befuddled about a human being we had shared patches of lawn with feeling so small and so alone that he did what he had done. And in the days following that terrible orientation announcement and our own complicity in downplaying it, we found ourselves unable to let it go, and turned our gaze—as silently and collectively as we had fallen silent on the subject—toward the only two people who might know enough to help us make sense of it.

Hannah and Leslie had always been a source of intrigue, but across that January residency their pull grew into something more, from interest to fascination, and finally obsession. Not only because of Jimmy but because in the days immediately after learning he was gone and would not be coming back, they made themselves scarcer than ever. We looked for them without meaning to, and without realizing we were.

At the times when we were almost guaranteed to see them—mandatory lectures, and walking into and out of workshops—we watched them while trying to pretend we weren't, the way New Yorkers try not to smile or do a double take at celebrities on the subway. We studied them even more closely than we had that first June. Our gazes were particularly unsparing and un-apologetically intense when they fell on Hannah. We weren't being grief whores; we just knew that to write about anything really well you had to be able to picture it. You had to know the feel of it in your hand, and the effect a setting sun's light would have on it. You had to be able to replay like a film even the parts of your story that happened just before and just after what was on the page. If it wasn't real for you, there was no hope for your reader. We also knew that a person's writing was never safe from the tragedies that inevitably find their way inside a life. That even if you never touched them, even if you wrote only of happy occasions—of first sightings of people you came to love and the exquisite poof of the sleeves of the purple dress you wore on your seventh birthday—the dizzy, disbelieving mo-ment just after hanging up the call you least want in life will mambo between the lines of your page.

We knew that everything Hannah would ever write would be at least partly about Jimmy, and we knew that sooner or later, she would have to try to picture it, to re-create the worst thing that had ever happened to her. The speed of his gait as he went first to the garage to fish out the old rope, and then to the attic, where he tied one end of it to a rafter. The color of the T-shirt he was wearing. The number of times he had gotten this far before without going through with it. If he had thought about taking the time to write a note, and if he would've stopped in his pursuit to field a call from a friend.

We had no way of knowing how often they had spoken in between the first residency and his death.

We scoured her work for him. The nine students in her workshop that term were the most popular people on campus. I'm not sure what we were expecting—a story about one lonely, unrequited kiss that haunts the rest of a life, or even something as simple and indirect as a depressed protagonist— but we never found it. He was as impossible to detect on her pages as any real evidence of whatever happened between them had been the previous June.

You could see the effects of what had happened to Jimmy in Leslie's work, but not in any of the ways we had been expecting to in Hannah's. It wasn't *him* specifically, but her stories became even darker. The nine students in her January workshop were grim in their reports on the story she had submitted for the residency. Despite the openness and irreverence with which bits of gossip were exchanged about Leslie—she had gained a level of notoriety by then that we felt entitled us to the details of her life the way a teenage girl might feel entitled to know who her favorite starlet is dating—these nine students respected the sanctity of workshop too much to actually let the rest of us *read* the story. But they would tell us that it was about a pair of terrible criminals who were either engaged or divorced but still violently in love, who tested people before breaking into their homes and robbing them, by force if necessary. They would send a mangy, sick old dog— the most hopeless one they could find at the pound, tumor ridden or blind—onto the property of their intended victims. If the owners of the house fed the dog, they would rob it after nightfall. If they didn't, they would choose another house and another set of owners. Their thinking was that anyone who would feed and otherwise take pity on such a pathetic creature surely wouldn't shoot a home invader. The story culminates in the memorable night when their theory is proven false in a very gory manner.

The only observable fact about either girl that surprised none of us was how much time they spent together. Hannah and Leslie turned in to each other more directly and more tightly than before, if possible, like they were trying to seal up the crack Jimmy had left, or to protect themselves from any further injury by turning away from the world altogether, a trick Jimmy himself might have taught them. Either way, it was a hopeless pursuit. Jimmy was a different size and shape than any of us had ever known, leaving a cutout impossible to fill, and the kind of grief they must have felt, if they felt as bad as *we* did, will find you wherever you go.

In the end, we learned more about what happened to Jimmy not from all our Hannah and Leslie recon but from the ever reliable Tammy. Hers was the only cafeteria whisper that ultimately meant anything.

On the fourth morning of the residency, Tammy, Bridget,

and Jamie decided to skip the graduate lectures that fell after breakfast and before workshop. Though they were the only lectures that weren't mandatory, we usually went to them anyway, both because we were friendly with some of the graduates and because we knew the time between now and our own final lectures would move like time travel, and we wanted to be prepared. So the three of them were three of the last people in the cafeteria that morning, making quiet, idle chitchat as the cafeteria workers cleaned up after one meal and set up for the next one. They hadn't noticed Simone reading workshop samples at the big round table in the corner of the cafeteria, though it wasn't a surprise that she was there. Since she hadn't been teaching long enough for any of her students to be graduating, and professors normally attended only the lectures of students they had worked with, Simone hadn't gone to a single graduate lecture yet.

When she walked by their table, Bridget and Jamie exchanged polite nods and small smiles with Simone, and it was only after she'd placed her tray on the conveyor belt for dirty dishes and walked out into the main serving area that they noticed Tammy hadn't done the same. Instead, she was looking down at her plate with the sort of resigned despair people normally reserve for exchanges much more significant than the one they'd just had. Bridget and Jamie both say that when Tammy finally spoke, it was like a confession at the end of an eight-hour interrogation. Because Tammy was one of the few real adults among us, there were no histrionics. There were no tears or even a raised voice. She said what she had to say to the plate, so quietly that they both had to lean in.

"She was going to fail him."

"Who?" Jamie asked, at the same time that Bridget said, "Simone?"

"He called me. Jimmy did. Three weeks before he . . . you know."

Bridget and Jamie nodded solemnly in sync, careful not to move any other part of their bodies for fear that it might scare away whatever else Tammy had to say.

"He had gotten into some more trouble with Simone after we left campus. He wasn't going to be able to finish the semester—she told him his packet work was either unsatis-factory or incomplete. I forget which word he used. I couldn't find any terminology about it in our handbook when I looked it up later."

"Meaning?" Bridget asked, hopefully, probably, knowing her the way we do now.

"She was going to fail him. Even after four months of sent packets. He called me about withdrawing from the term and coming back in January as a first-year again."

"I didn't realize you guys were close," said Bridget, in a way entirely unlike the way Margaret Jibs would've said it. As a question instead of an accusation.

"We weren't. I mean, not really. I liked him fine. He seemed like a nice kid. A little sad, but nice. He called me because he was here on an education stipend from the state of Michigan.

Former wards of the state that get into secondary education programs are eligible for funding. It's not much, a few grand per term maybe, plus some coverage of your expenses—books, that kind of thing. But it would've helped."

"So he called you to talk about funding?" Jamie asked. "That's what he was worried about?"

Bridget had been about to ask if *ward of the state* meant what she thought it did, a term she paired with foster homes and all their terrible associations and Oliver Twist tragedies. But she realized the answer to Jamie's questions were probably more important. And also that if she didn't ask, she could pretend the answer would've been no—*ward of the state* actually meant something far less sad and lonely than what she was imagining.

"He wanted to know if he could keep the money he had been given and apply it to the next semester, or if he'd have to give it back. I told him he should check with whoever had helped him get the money in the first place. Nothing I could find online said one way or the other, and these kinds of guidelines vary from state to state. Michigan might as well be the moon, as far as Virginia's concerned."

Bridget and Jamie are two of the nicest people in our class. It's part of why we felt so bad about their milk incident—we knew it was beneath them both, which somehow made it worse. We like to think that the fact that they were sitting in so small a group together means they had put it behind them by then. If Jamie hadn't already been married to his high school sweetheart at the age of twenty-seven, and Bridget hadn't just agreed to marry the boyfriend who took her to that B&B after the first term, we might've even speculated about them getting together the way we did Melissa and Tanner. It's probably because they were two such obviously good people, and because their faces probably betrayed how sad this information made them both, that Tammy felt the need to defend herself, now that she had revealed what she had and hadn't done, even though we all knew Tammy was pretty good herself.

"The thing is, those stipends are almost impossible to get, because people don't know about them, and because by the time former wards are old enough to go to secondary school, they've long lost touch with their caseworkers. Not to mention that they almost never graduate high school, never mind anything beyond that. I figured if he was still in touch enough with whoever helped him apply for the money, he was in good hands. Most caseworkers are barely available to their active clients, much less their old ones. So I assumed this was someone with a special interest. Someone who understood that he had a talent. I mean, I never read his work myself, but . . ."

Neither Bridget nor Jamie would've hesitated before nodding at the silence that Tammy's sentence trailed off into. They had heard the glowing, awestruck things that even his most cynical classmates had to say. We all had.

"I thought it was just directing the question to the right place."

"Of course," said Jamie. "That makes sense."

Bridget put her hand on Tammy's arm, but looked over at Jamie to make sure he felt the full weight of all this. He had done a remarkable job of keeping his voice light when he confirmed that Tammy's logic had been sound.

"I found out later, though, that his biological father had only let him move back in with him when he found out about the stipend, and kicked him out again when he realized there were complications with the funding. Basically that there wouldn't be any more of it to steal. He was a real monster apparently, even by industry standards, which I assure you are high. I only found that out after, though."

Bridget and Jamie disagree on what happened next. Bridget swears the girls were suddenly there, as if they'd been hiding under their table the whole time, only adding to their legendary, almost supernatural reputations, Hannah making animal noises of anger and sorrow and Leslie demanding quick answers to pointed questions. Or maybe it wasn't as late in the morning as Bridget had originally thought, and the girls were two of the flood of passing students on the way to the first graduate lecture. Jamie swears that the cafeteria was a mausoleum by then, that by the time Tammy had told them everything, even the cafeteria workers had fled to enjoy that golden slice of time in between meals. He says he remembers because he felt pressure to say something, to distract Tammy so that her guilt didn't have time to expand any further in all that empty silence. But there was nothing to say. He admits that both he and Bridget recounted the conversation to more people than they probably should have that night at the student center, after the drinks they sorely needed following so despairing a morning. So Jibs eventually got hold of it, of course, which meant everybody did, including even Hannah and Leslie, who were still slinking around the outer perimeter of the student body then, far away from the cafeteria. Maybe it's because Jamie's eventually dropping out of the program meant that we kept on talking about that morning long after he stopped being here to represent his version of what happened, or maybe it's because it makes a better story, but we tend to go with Bridget's recollection even if Jibs's big mouth rings true to all of us. It's not difficult to picture the girls appearing out of nowhere like the ghosts we half believed they were.

After Hannah regained speech long enough to say "I knew it was her" and Leslie assured Hannah and the table that "There's no way she's going to get away with this," and the pair had soared out of the cafeteria on a cloud of rage that suddenly had a target, the most dangerous kind of rage there is, Tammy and Bridget and Jamie were left with a silence even more oppressive than before.

Bridget and Jamie remember what Tammy said next exactly the same, which makes us sad enough to wish they didn't, as much as we generally prize consensus.

"I thought about inviting him to stay with me for a while but, you know, it just didn't seem like a permanent fix. Felt a little like a Band-Aid on a brain tumor, which only gives it time and cover to grow."

Bridget and Jamie were so quick to offer assurance that of course none of this was Tammy's fault, that there was nothing she could have done, that their words got all mixed up with each other, into one jumble of an invisible hand on Tammy's back.

"Ah, darlin's, that's sweet of you to say, but I know that. In my line of work, if you feel bad about the things that didn't turn out the way you wanted them to despite your best intentions, you'd just be runnin' around feelin' bad all the time."

She said it like she might've said some rehearsed line—a mantra her daddy always said, or something cross-stitched onto a pillow. Some evidently true thing that had been said so many times it didn't even mean anything anymore. So both Bridget and Jamie pretended not to notice that her eyes were flooded past the point of salvage when she said it.

We don't blame her for crying. This bit of news was hard on us, too. Both the reasons Jimmy might've had for doing what he did and the way they haunted Tammy, no matter what she said to Bridget or Jamie or herself. Tammy's reveals that day became personal in a way the rest of what had happened up to then hadn't been. They made us each think of some story or detail from our own lives that felt newly relevant to what we now understood was an unfolding story that we'd have to wait for the end of.

Some of us remembered the lonely kids who had fallen through the cracks of our own hometowns growing up, or the grand gestures we wished we'd made that we hadn't, or some terrible situation we had done nothing to improve. That we shared these pieces of our past with one another was completely at odds with our normal standards of communication, by which most of what happened outside our time on campus didn't exist.

It's Patrick's response we remember most clearly. He told us that in a case study he read about in his last master's program, they found how much more successful babies who were held regularly when they were small went on to be. How much happier they were. He said it was strange, how we were shaped by so many things we would never remember and had no control over. He said that after reading this he found a program online that let you volunteer to hold babies who had been abandoned or orphaned, or were waiting to be adopted. He said he was going to sign up—maybe he even did sign up—but never showed up to his first session, because he realized on the way to the first baby that needed holding that he had no idea how to hold a baby. We all laughed about this later, privately, because Patrick was the boy you always wanted to laugh with, but who always felt you were laughing at him. We could just picture him, too awkwardly large to hold something as tiny as a baby, all too-wide angles and good intentions left hanging unnaturally. Some of us cried about it, too, when we were finished laughing, because the fact that he hadn't gone, in the end, made us almost as sad as what Tammy told us about Jimmy, because it seemed to be Patrick's exact problem. He was a boy of many talents—he had multiple degrees from

schools we'd never have been admitted to, never mind graduated from, and we'd all seen him play basketball. And he clearly
wanted to use whatever gifts he'd been born with, because
here he was, putting in the time and work at yet another program. Yet he couldn't seem to find the best way to use any of
what he had, these degrees and his natural intelligence or his
brawn. Those of us in his workshop knew his habit of writing
terribly dull, clunky stories with brilliant, clever little endings
tacked onto the end of them. It seemed he had all these great
ideas without any idea how to execute them. His anecdote
about not holding the babies seemed to confirm that the same
was true of the rest of his life, and we wondered what the
weaknesses in our own work revealed about us.

Which we suppose is when we started thinking we might
have something to do with this story beyond witnessing it.
That we might have some role in it or that—whatever it was
that was happening, or whatever it would become—it belonged to us, too.

To be fair to them, once they learned that Simone might've
had anything to do with what Jimmy did, Leslie and Hannah
tried to handle it in a legit, on-the-books way first. They were
both on friendly terms with Professor Pearl after their semester with him, and had less hesitation than the rest of us might
have had in going right to him in his director role. They went

to his office without making an appointment first, probably the very same day that Tammy made her confession.

Joni Kleinman, Pearl's official secretary and unofficial bouncer, wasted little time reporting this back to us. Joni had graduated from the program two years before we got to campus. During her second June residency, she had fallen in love with and married an undergrad professor who had stayed on campus for the summer. Professor Pearl had created an administrative job for her as his assistant-slash-secretary, despite the fact that even those of us who have never actually been in Pearl's workshop know that he would rather watch *E! News* than have anyone do for him anything he might've done for himself, or worse, have someone meddling in his affairs. He grew to like her, though, once he learned the value of having someone hold all his calls and tell any impromptu visitors that he was unavailable.

Joni had become a familiar fixture at all our social functions on campus. She was one of those women who wasn't overweight, but had swollen fingers and wide ankles. Other women were always disappointed to learn how small a dress size Joni actually wore, thinking themselves much skinnier. She had a beautiful face, but it was from the wrong century. She would've made a great nun if she didn't say *fuck* every other word she spoke. She said everything as if it were *the best thing ever*, so even though she could be dry and cutting, everyone thought of her as bubbly, which also meant she got away with saying things other people might not have. *I fucking hate that fucking cunt* sounded a lot like "Oh, don't worry about her, you'll be *fine*" coming from her. Despite the general goodwill we felt toward Joni, it wasn't hard to see that she felt insecure about her spot as permanent student, part MFA candidate, part townie. She overcompensated for this by telling us things she probably shouldn't have, including things like the private, confidential conversations students had with the director of the program.

After ignoring Joni's bright insistence that Professor Pearl wasn't taking unscheduled calls or visitors that morning, and marching directly into his office with all the grace that the three-inch lift of Leslie's platform snow boots allowed, the girls shut the door in Joni's face before she could manage so much as a single *fuck*. Having the good sense to realize that Professor Pearl was far better equipped than she was to deal with whatever was brewing on the other side of the door that had nearly kissed her nose when it was slammed, Joni simply returned to her chair and stared at the phone, on the small chance that it might herald a distress call from Pearl.

The door did a good job of concealing the first half of the conversation. There was some muffled crying from Hannah and some cursing from Leslie, all of it mostly incoherent. There were pauses that Joni suspected were filled with Pearl's offering up a box of tissues, judging from the nose blowing that followed, and others that the girls used to compose themselves, either at Pearl's urging or at each other's. The first truly clear, unmistakable words came from Pearl, who, having spent half a career addressing classrooms full of people, was used to projecting his voice. When he sensed that the girls had said all they had come to say, and had given them the courtesy of listening to it with respectful eye contact and thoughtful posture—the only things he could really give them that day—he gave them the answer he no more wanted to give than they wanted to hear.

"Well," he said, sounding, Joni stressed, genuinely remorseful about the words he was about to say. "That wasn't anyone's intention. And I know—intentions, they're a tricky thing. They mean so much less than their results."

It was difficult, when we heard that he said this, not to call up the picture of that sleepy-looking four-year-old playing in front of him while he worked, but maybe that is unfair.

"But," he went on, "you should know there are a whole lot of people who feel as sick about this whole thing as you do."

"That's it?" Leslie asked, her voice raised now.

"I'm afraid so."

To this, Hannah only opened the door and floated by Joni with an almost eerie levity that Joni's eyes went wide at remembering when she told us. She said she looked up from the phone she was still staring at—still waiting for it to convey the missing pieces of the conversation she was already rehearsing to tell us later—just in time to see Hannah's back for one wild, frozen moment before she disappeared around a corner and out of the building. In the middle of a long, awful silence that apparently even Leslie didn't know how to fill, Joni stood and went to the doorway of the office, planning to ask Pearl if she should get coffee or water for his remaining visitor, a sort of code between them for "Do you need me to do anything?" But she was still a full step or two away from the inside of the office when she saw that Professor Pearl's unfinished manuscript was spread out on his desk, and that Leslie was staring at it without bothering to pretend that she wasn't, her etiquette gene switched completely, permanently off. She probably would've just gone on staring, unbothered by the silence, if Professor Pearl, gentleman that he was, hadn't spoken. By then, Joni was back at her chair, where she sat in openmouthed panic she didn't try to disguise, one hand that she normally used for happy, emphatic gestures over her lips to underscore it, trying to make herself as small as possible without missing a word. She said she was almost relieved when Pearl spoke, even if commenting on what was happening would make it harder to deny that it had happened later.

"I always thought it was ridiculous," he said, "this idea that just because someone writes one decent book they'll be able to write another. Every novel is a small miracle. At least one that does half of what a novel can do, at its best. To expect two in one life, well, that never quite made sense to me. It's like people who date after they lose their soul mate."

"Well," said Leslie, probably still staring at the manuscript, "maybe dating is better than sitting at home alone, watching cable news. Even if the people you go out with instead are only mildly good company. Sometimes you just need to hear your voice alongside someone else's. And I've never met a single person who isn't at least interesting, even if it's only because of how *ordinary* they are. I could spend a Ph.D.'s worth of years trying to figure out how someone turns out *ordinary*."

"Is anyone really *ordinary*?" Pearl asked, which must have surprised Joni, who, like everybody else, probably assumed there was no question the man did not already know the answer to. "I've always thought of that as a word for someone you don't know well enough to have found the strange spot in."

If what he said surprised Leslie, too, she didn't show it. She had her own answer ready.

"I mean, there's the ordinary that turns out to have a closet full of skin suits and knows the location of every missing girl in their zip code from the past twenty years, sure—like, too ordinary for their own good or anyone else's." Leslie conceded this in a register Joni later told us was downright good-natured, especially by Leslie standards. "But I've been paying attention for a while now, and I think there's also actual ordinary. People who never wonder if this is all there is, and have never gnashed their teeth at what a raw deal this whole thing inevitably becomes at some point or another, sooner or later. You know— like you either do it all alone, or you miss them when they go?"

We like to think Pearl nodded here to show that he did know, even if Joni can't confirm it.

"And so they never make some terrible decision they can't take back, like cheating so blatantly on someone they love that it's pretty clear they're doing it mainly to get caught, or just deciding not to show up for work anymore, even though their job isn't that bad, as far as things that pay the bills go. People who live for reliable television programming and their next meal. And honestly, that might be the most interesting person of all, don't you think? I mean, can you *imagine?*"

Joni didn't hear anything for a few moments after that, and assumed they had lowered their voices, but then she caught some muffled sound she couldn't quite place, even with the door open, until she realized it was the sound of Professor Pearl laughing, something she had never heard before, in all the hours of sitting outside his door.

"Well, now," he finally said. "I bet that's one thing no one's ever accused you of, is it? Being ordinary."

Leslie thought about it for a second or two before answering, even though the answer must've been pretty clear. "That's true," she said. "But it's pretty much the only thing."

"It shows, you know," he said. "In your writing. It's highly unordinary. In a good way."

Joni was as surprised by this as she was by any other part of the conversation, knowing as well as anyone else that Professor Pearl was not in the business of handing out compliments outside of official, scheduled feedback, and even then he was sparing with them.

"Thank you, I guess?"

"Well, I mean it as a compliment, so, yes, you're welcome. I hope you'll keep writing. Not everyone does, you know, after the program. Sometimes just graduating is enough. But I hope it won't be for you, and I suspect it won't. You seem to be someone who always wants a little more. And in this way I think it'll serve you."

"Yes," she said. "More is good. And I will. Keep writing, I mean."

Joni couldn't help but notice the words Leslie chose, and paused to linger on them when she reported this part of the conversation back to us. *I will.* Not *I hope to* or *I plan to*, the way Joni might've said, had she been the one talking to Pearl.

And Leslie did keep writing, even long after all this happened.

While Professor Pearl had no small hand in that, that wasn't why Leslie had gone to his office that day, which she must've remembered at this point in the conversation. She stepped out of her slouch and back to attention to reroute Pearl's focus to what she had come to discuss with the kind of clarity and directness all the best teachers try to coach into their writers.

"Look, I bet your book is better than you think it is, and I hope I get to read it one day. And I'm grateful for our last term. However good a writer you are or aren't, you're a really good teacher. But you and I both know that if you're not going to do anything about what happened, someone else is going to have to. And we'd probably both be a little disappointed, once all is said and done here, if I didn't see to it that someone does."

All of which was another pronouncement she made good on.

Whatever wisdom Pearl might've had ready for this, Leslie didn't stay to hear it. She turned and walked out of his office without any good-bye or formal parting right past Joni, who didn't even have time to pretend to be doing anything other than eavesdropping, having been given no indication from the conversation that it was about to end.

Joni's story confirmed what we all already assumed but hadn't been able to verify just by watching the girls: that they felt some personal stake in what had happened to Jimmy. As certain as we all were that Jimmy's friendship with the girls had been real, rather than something we had magnified retroactively, the girls' conversation with Pearl was the first tangible reaction we got from them.

Having heard the story, we immediately started searching for more evidence of an off-campus friendship between Jimmy and Hannah and Leslie, which proved nearly impossible given that neither Jimmy nor Hannah had social media accounts, and that Leslie, who we only then realized hadn't accepted any of our Facebook friendship requests from the semester before, hadn't posted anything in three years. Her last post had been about a British folk band that none of us had ever heard of and her page felt almost hostile in the lack of real information it provided.

It was Jenny Ritter who finally pointed us to the only bit

of off-campus activity we've ever been able to find. When she told us about the picture and where to find it on the internet, we were surprised that she hadn't mentioned it earlier. She'd been present for at least half a dozen conversations about fruitless online searches the rest of us had made. To our indignation she said only "You never asked" in that mom voice she sometimes used, and we all silently remembered our own mothers' aversion to anything resembling gossip, regardless of the degree to which they partook of it themselves.

The picture was on a photo-sharing site that was more private than the earlier and more prominent forms of social media. You had to grant other people access to each individual album you posted. Jenny had searched for all of us there after that first June, after having had to tell us all that, no, she wasn't on Facebook, and Hannah was the only one she had been able to find. Intrigued, having assumed Hannah would be one of the savviest members of the class when it came to social media, Jenny had searched for her occasionally in the months between our first and second residencies. She got only one result, an album entitled "Jimmy, October" that Hannah posted just before Halloween. Jenny had been excited to discover the album and flattered when Hannah's avatar granted permission for her to view it, but then disappointed to discover that it contained only a single picture.

Knowing how fishy it would've looked if we all individually asked Hannah for permission to access this single-shot album, Jenny sent us her account information so that we could sign in as her. We had expected her just to send us a screenshot of the image, but it was apparently not one of the "computer tricks" her children had taught her. We felt a little guilty signing in as her at first, given how easy it would have been to just teach her ourselves how to take the screenshot, but the site was uncontroversial, we assured ourselves—mostly mom accounts, we quickly saw, which made sense, since children were the best and only reason we could think of to forgo the friendlier, more social sites the rest of us had grown up on for additional privacy. We felt a little voyeuristic as we tried not to look at the pictures Jenny herself had posted, of her husband and daughters, a feeling that dimmed a little when we saw how happy and at ease she was in all of them. We had thought her family was to blame for some of her more uptight, uncomfortable mannerisms. The burdens of a life spent taking care of others, we assumed. When we realized that something else must have accounted for them we felt a little bad for not inviting her to our more casual dorm gatherings, thinking she would be too old for them even though she was younger than most of the married accountants.

We forgot about all that when we finally clicked through to the photo of Hannah, though.

The only trace of Jimmy was in the album's title, so we assumed he had been the one to take its lone picture. In it, Hannah's sitting on the edge of a pool, surrounded by light so thick and present that it might as well have been a second person, her face both quizzical and amused in the moment before she opens her mouth to address the person behind the camera. It's such a good, active, unscripted shot that it's impossible to look at it and not see all the moments that led up to and away from it. Her open, unguarded playfulness made her unrecognizable at first glance, a new identifying mark on a face we thought we knew by then.

There are very few details to pull from the shot other than the girl and the evident joy the picture's taker gave her—not a single palm tree or license plate in the background to follow. It was so empty of anything to hang the picture on that we associate it with the month of October as much as anything else. It was not uncommon, in the years after we discovered it, for email chains between us that had sat dormant across springs and summers to be resurrected in mid-October, our own unofficial holiday stretch before the real one began.

The picture could have been taken anywhere, we know, a gap in the story that normally would have frustrated us, but that worked in our favor here, because it meant it was taken everywhere, and that the golden moment it immortalized belonged to all of us. We all remember a picture from a different place in the world.

For Tammy it was Mexico, a small, rural city in a part of the country where they don't serve drinks in coconuts or have restaurants with white tablecloths. We're not sure if she couldn't remember the name of the town or just didn't want to tell us. We had trouble picturing Tammy in any state of true repose, busy as she kept herself even during the quietest periods of the residency, when we would see her long white legs below a *New York Times* or *Wall Street Journal* spread all the way out, obscuring the entire upper half of her body. It always looked like she was too engrossed in whatever story she was reading to think to fold the paper, which was endearing unless you were sitting next to her in the auditorium. It took several follow-up questions that only Jibs would have been bold enough to ask to learn that she had taken this trip with the man she came the closest to marrying, and while we can't remember his name, either, we all remember how she wouldn't make eye contact with any of us when she said it.

For Lucas it was Hilton Head Island, where his mother took him and his siblings for the last two weeks of every summer. His father would join on the weekends, but that's not what he or any of his four brothers remembers about these trips. It was that the light stretched itself long enough that they could play in the pool of the gated community they stayed in until almost nine every night. They'd know it was time to come in only when their mother's minivan pulled into the parking lot that ran alongside the pool. They'd pretend not to notice, and so she would have to put the car in park and get out to summon them, leaving her open door pinging as she hung over the pool's gate and said, "Come home, come home, my sweet men—another night has come." He told us that that pinging sound would always make him think of the smell and sting of chlorine, skin the color of tree bark, and the taste of the greasy grilled cheese sandwiches they'd get at the snack shack down the road that left hand-shaped smudges on every-thing. After he told us that, we all felt a little bad about having rushed him through the pinging-door detail of his story about Linda and Jimmy. Linda and Jimmy's conversation had always played against the pings he had described for us when we pic-tured it, but we let them play a little louder after that.

For Bridget it was the sort of tacky spring break destina-tions that high school and college kids usually go to in clusters. Sometimes it was Panama Beach, sometimes it was Daytona. We thought this seemed a little beneath her, until we remem-bered that Penny Stanley told us Bridget had once confessed she'd never been on a group vacation and had always wanted to go on one. Bridget was always friendly enough to be sitting at the tables where the sorts of girls who went on these trips talked about them before and after they took them, but never friendly enough to be invited.

For Mimi it was Seoul, which was still the prettiest place her father had ever seen, as much as he loved America. In her mind, the picture had been taken just after or just before they hiked Namsan, which accounted for the rosiness of Hannah's cheeks. Mimi's father had been to the city only once, as a child with his own father, and if he had found beauty in the grit and noise and chaos of a city that big and dense, she loved to imagine what his face might look like, seeing it from some remove, feeling like he could have all of it at once.

Like the bits of ourselves that we started exchanging in the wake of what Tammy revealed in the cafeteria and Jimmy's death, these destinations and their origins were far more intimate than anything we had originally intended to share with one another. We knew that personal histories took a certain amount of time to impart, and that they invited the person you were imparting them to into a relationship that takes a certain amount of maintenance. We had arrived on campus six months ago determined to avoid exactly this sort of commitment to anyone, having sworn to ourselves and the people we had left at home that we were finally going to finish or revise our novels in progress, and spend the time at hand on our work alone. And while these exchanges did eat away at the time we had to implement workshop feedback into the latest drafts of our stories, or sketch out the plots of our next chapters, this is not one of the things we regret.

Despite the care we've taken here, there are still plenty of missing details of the story that only Leslie and Hannah could provide. They never have. But they probably still don't know that the pew from which they watched Simone and Pearl make their way across a snowy, frozen campus on the coldest day of that January residency is the same pew from which Margaret watched Jimmy and Hannah kiss the term before. Leslie might not even know that the kiss happened. Based on how close the girls are, we know this is unlikely, but still—it's possible. That we take comfort in being in possession of facts like this, which place us inside the story, almost part of it, makes us only a little sheepish. We don't love that we had to rely on Jiles Gardner for this piece of information, but we would've accepted it from so many less reliable, more detestable sources if we had to.

The first floor of the barn that the pew was in had a porch. It faced the same lawn that the second-story pew overlooked. That anyone would be sitting on a porch in freezing weather would feel dubious in most cases, but hardly seemed a stretch for Jiles Gardner. He smoked more than even our practical fathers and the married accountants combined, and smoking was forbidden in all campus buildings. Jiles was one class ahead of us, and British, which had made him intriguing at first until we realized that other people on campus were of such little interest to him that to pursue any sort of relationship with him would've been pathetic in its one-sidedness. He rivaled Jimmy in the amount of time he spent alone, but where Jimmy seemed afraid of other people, Jiles just didn't like them. Maybe it was because he was British, but he managed to be almost cheerful, or at least not unfriendly about it—by disliking everyone in equal measure, his dislike of each individual person felt impersonal, a given. He also served a purpose. Seeing him across campus, cupping his hands around a lit match, shielding it from the wind, or inhaling like his life depended on it before releasing everything with an almost postcoital satisfaction, was a good reminder that most writers are solitary creatures, and for good reason. And that maybe instead of meeting one another for that nine o'clock glass of wine at the student center, we should be using our free time to organize the scribbles we had made in our notebooks across the day's readings and lectures, or to untangle the ideas that had come to us in the middle of the night before like a knock on the door of a cabin you had thought was completely remote. Because in addition to being one of the least social members of the community, Jiles was universally regarded as one of its best writers.

Though he made it pretty clear he wasn't looking for friends, or even companionship, and his work made it pretty clear how dim his view of human nature was, Jiles was never unpleasant in standard, nuts-and-bolts interactions such as "Do you need a light?" or "You dropped your mitten," which was another reason most of us have fine enough feelings about him, even if he had never bothered to learn any of our names. He didn't seem at all inconvenienced, for instance, telling Mimi and Sarah what he saw from the porch that night. It was a night so cold nobody but Jiles would be out in it if they didn't have to be, which is probably the first thing that caught his attention about the two figures walking out in the dark in front of him, and the attention of the two interested pairs of eyes floating above him that he didn't yet know were there. Mimi and Sarah and Jiles were huddled outside the commons after lunch the next day when he told them this, a single cigarette between the three of them. The girls looked less orphaned without their colorful wardrobes than they had the rest of the residency, now that a male gaze was upon them, even if it was one as withering as Jiles Gardner's.

Jiles told the girls that the two figures had been walking slowly, moving the way two people do when they're walking toward a destination that matters less than their conversation, both of them struggling with the snow despite wearing boots designed for it. He said they almost didn't seem human, dark as it was, and eerie out there on a campus so empty that it felt like time and God had forgotten it, the slow stroll of their gait wrong for the context. But their voices cut right through the thin, empty air. He knew right away it was Pearl and Simone, even though, having never been in Simone's workshop, he hadn't heard her speak much. He said she was enunciating the-atrically, the way she did when she asked her postlecture ques-tions, even though she was just speaking to Pearl. This wasn't entirely surprising, especially next to the unexpected way Pearl was talking to her. He spoke so sweetly that Leslie and Hannah probably wouldn't have believed it in the face of the empathy he had tried to show them just a day or two before in regard to Simone's involvement in what happened to Jimmy, if they hadn't heard it themselves. Jiles said he couldn't be sure, but the two professors might even have been linked arm in arm.

Mimi and Sarah asked Jiles if the exchange had seemed romantic, which he seemed tickled by, and which annoyed them in turn. We always felt like sticky, wide-eyed middle schoolers to his varsity quarterback in conversations with Jiles, even though a good half of us were older than him, so we sympathized with the girls even though we suspect they used their annoyance as a sort of flirtation. He ignored their full-body eye rolls long enough to tell them that, no, he didn't imagine they were going off to the edge of the woods for a shag, and not just because it was too cold. There was some sibling quality to the exchange, or maybe a whiff of the father-daughter. It wasn't lost on us that Simone was about the same age as the four-year-old in the picture would've been by then. The similarities between them didn't go any further than that no matter how hard we tried to make them, but it's impossible to say what will make one person remind us of another.

The last thing Jiles told the girls before he turned away to light a new cigarette, which was burned halfway down to his fingers before they realized he was retreating, having told them everything he could, or would, about the night in question, was that when he had finally lost enough feeling in his fingers that he had to start walking back to his dorm, he turned back when he was only about twenty feet away. He said he couldn't say what had made him do it—he said this preemptively, knowing they would want to know. There was no noise or flash of movement he could point to. It was more of a feeling, as it so often is, that had made him look. The kind of sixth sense that feels heightened on nights and in places like this. He said when he looked back there were two faces in the second-floor window right above where he had been sitting on the porch, right about where the pew was, their faces so close to the glass that their breath left two little imperfect circles of condensation on it, and that two perfect little nose-tip dots floated above them. The glass was too thick and warped to make out who they were, but we didn't need Jiles to tell us that part even if it hadn't been.

Who else could it have been?

We've all sat in the pew that the girls must have been sitting in. We went there so often, in fact, that we immediately ruled the pew out as the place they had been hiding this whole time, as tempting as it was, because we would've seen them there long before this lonely frozen night. Either they'd been moving to various spots as their whims dictated, or they'd come out of hiding somewhere else to be at just the right place at just the right time. Or wrong, depending on how you want to look at it. We've spent enough time in the pew to know how creaky it would have been every time they so much as shifted their weight, especially on a night as empty and cold as that one, so neither of them would have moved for the entirety of the walk they witnessed, hound dog determined not to miss a word of it. Maybe they were grasping each other for solidarity, silently urging the other to hold still for just a minute longer, the way you lay a hand on someone's forearm when you want them to stop speaking so you can verify a noise you think you've heard. They were connected physically—an arm around a shoulder, heads bent together—in most of the memories we have of them, so this, especially, doesn't feel like a stretch.

Even easier to imagine is how what they saw and heard must have made them feel, and the effect it must have had on what happened next. They must have realized that for all of Pearl's compassion for Jimmy, and remorse at what had happened, Simone was going to get away with it. She already had. She was still one of his staff, someone he had vetted and presumably found impressive before approving, and they were just two of his students, like a thousand others who had passed through his classrooms by then. They must've felt angry, or at least disappointed, at Pearl. We certainly did, at first, though that's mostly passed by now. We had all read *Cactus and Dust*, so there was no letting him off on the grounds that he didn't know his way around a brutal, godless, impossible situation. In one of his scenes a man says his final words only after his head is two thirds of the way severed from his body. As violent and unflinching as his work was, though, that violence was there only so that he could reconcile it across the two hundred some pages of the book, the way all problems in novels are there to be solved, or should be. He was trying to make it right, it's difficult not to think now, which makes us remember how safe we felt on campus, at least partly because he oversaw it, even if he was going about making it right by ignoring the problem, which has almost never worked in the human history of problems.

It's difficult, too, to forget that the thickness of the glass, and the windows being painted shut, probably made the girls feel as far away from what they saw happening out on the lawn as Jibs had from that kiss. Only where it had made Jibs feel lonely, left standing outside of something she could tell even from all that distance was wonderful, it made them feel insulated from something terrible and outside of their control. Almost like what they were watching was happening far enough away that they were safe from it.

We can't think of anything else that would've given them the courage to do what they went on to do.

Despite the doggedness with which we watched the girls, we didn't look exclusively to them to tell us how to feel about what had happened. While the surprise of the news that had greeted us that first day of the term never dimmed entirely, it did evolve into something else without any help from them. Our first reaction, before even grief, had been confusion. Simone had been too harsh, maybe—maybe even harsher than we knew, in the private packet correspondence she and Jimmy exchanged—but he must have known how good he was.

The assumption behind our confusion had been that his talent, or the beauty and wisdom behind Jimmy's arrangements of words, should have been enough for him, despite whatever raw deal had made him the collection of awkward tics and strange mannerisms that he was in life. But in the blank pages of our free-write periods, and our inability to find arrangements to keep us warm in the dorm rooms that never seemed to be sufficiently heated, we started to see the flimsiness of even the arrangements we had until then held most dear. The very words that had brought us here in the first place. So that as the early, dark, cold lonely nights of January residency piled up, what Jimmy had done seemed less and less confusing.

Though even the most arrogant among us would never have gone so far as to compare our work to Jimmy's, until that point, none of us had paused in the pursuit of assembling our own perfect arrangements, no matter how steadfastly they eluded us. Like that one kid all of us had known in our home-towns who couldn't turn away from the Rubik's Cube at the end of indoor recess, we kept twisting and clicking the little plastic rows of images and plot developments and columns of pretty phrases and character traits, patrolling for repetitions and reading unfinished sentences and thoughts out loud, test-ing them on the tongue. But we found, that January—maybe even earlier, across the late nights we had spent putting the final touches on our first-term packets that we mailed out with some measure of doubt, and the knowing despair that we could've made them better—that the act of stringing words together was a dirtier, more demeaning and labor-intensive business than we had assumed when we filled out our initial applications. When it happened at all, the composition of sen-tences that made it all the way to the final drafts of our stories happened in the strictly glory-free realms of our kitchen table in the small hours of the night, or in cubicles the color of two-day-old snow after everybody else has gone home. We cap-tured stray words at red lights and scribbled them in the margins of agendas distributed at endless corporate meetings. Always, always we were on the search for more. When we did hit on something good—something we knew was good even at the time—it was better than any drug any of us had ever tried (and between the babies and the married accountants, we had tried them all). But, like all drugs, when the high wore off, we were left worse than we had been before, grasping and desperate in our neediness.

If the initial passages we loved had built a bridge between their authors and us, then our inability to put our own exquisite losses and brutal victories on paper only made us feel more alone. And while we loved our children and took pride in making it to work on time and sang in community choirs and were training for marathons and logging hours for pilot's licenses, the progress toward which felt only more measurable next to the elusiveness of our unfinished, imperfect stories, the truth is that we had all been where Jimmy was. We knew how lonely a blank page was, and that for all the company a perfectly conveyed sentiment can provide, the words just outside our grasp and the gaps they won't bridge are just as powerful.

Two months after we left campus that first June, Jordan Marcum won the kind of unwinnable case a lawyer dreams of capping his career with, finally putting away one of Chicago's most notorious criminals, a man as deft at eluding the law as he was cruel. And Jordan's second thought, after the fact that he was finally going to be able to go on a real vacation with those Ivy League kids of his before they left him to start careers and families of their own, was how much easier it was to win a case like this than to write a short story in which his professor left a single line of unchanged. Of course the law was what he should be dedicating his life to. How silly to have thought anything else. And yet it was impossible to ignore, always there in the back of his mind, that it had been reading *To Kill a Mockingbird* at the age of eleven that made him want to be a lawyer in the first place. So he kept on sending out stories that came back to him cancerous with red scrawls and cuts and *Really?* comments in the margins, each mark a reminder that he had yet to make his readers feel what his jurors had.

Those six months in between our first two residencies were the only stretch during which Melissa Raymond and Tanner Conover tried to have a proper, public courtship, before their correspondence descended into the stuff of third parties and flimsy excuses that embarrassed everybody. During that time he drank too much and she spent too much money and both of them thought they were more attractive than the other, but that they didn't deserve them. They each introduced the other to only a single friend, not wanting any additional confirmation that their relationship was a terrible idea. But neither of them could forget that night during the first residency when they made cocktails in stolen cafeteria mugs after James Wood gave a lecture that pinpointed the exact, single word choice that broke your heart in *The Prime of Miss Jean Brodie*, right there in the middle of the paragraph—right there in the middle of the *sentence*—you least expected it. And they knew that until they could channel that magic into a story of their own, they were damned to make scenes in bars and hang up on each other midconversation like seventh-graders, all for makeup sex that wasn't even that good.

We even began to understand the comfort Jenny Ritter must've taken from her word-a-day calendar and its Pablo Picasso wisdom. Each day's sentiment was trite, maybe, and a little corny, but at least its author knew what it was he wanted to say, and knew how to express it to his audience in a way that left no uncertainty about how they were supposed to feel after they read it.

So as befuddled as we were over what Jimmy did, and as despondent, and as jealous as we were of his talent (if we're being completely honest); as often as we had thought about what it might be like to trade places with him, and as senseless as we knew throwing away what he had was, never mind everything else that went with it, we also knew too well at least one of the thoughts in his mind, there at the end.

Words can fail you just like everything else.

It would've been a big night even if what happened hadn't. It was Simone's first evening reading. Each night one of the faculty read from their latest novel or memoir or poetry collection. There were only enough nights in each residency for a little fewer than half of the faculty to read, so each professor read roughly every other residency. The professors who didn't read were expected to give one of the daytime craft lectures, which examined the way writers of their choice had achieved the effects we most admired in their work. It seemed unromantic, taking apart great works like some sort of science project, but the best professors left us only in more admiration of the works they had disassembled, showing us the strings and double-sided tape responsible for their magic, not less. Each professor's reputation was at least partly influenced by how boring or insightful their craft lecture was, but even craft lectures didn't compare to readings in the degree to which we measured our professors against them. It would've been impossible to read the entire body of work of everyone who taught in the program, so these readings were often the first taste we got of a professor's work.

As much as our professor pairs might've disagreed on individual stories or rules, there is almost no creative writing program totally untouched by Gordon Lish's general philosophy of less is more, if only because he's edited a good fourth of the collective MFA community's most esteemed faculty at one point or another, as well as half the writers that our professors assigned us to read, plus he had pretty much invented making students pay way too much for one person's opinion on their writing, which, in our lowest moments, we've all silently accused the MFA of doing. He was the ghost of great novels past, especially the sort of novels we were encouraged to read and study and emulate, and we always looked for him at these readings, consciously or not. Our ears were always attuned to any number of Lishian sins that our professors were quick to point out in our own work—were there stock phrases or, God forbid, clichés? How many exclamation points were used? Or verbs of utterance? Or any word that wasn't strictly necessary in conveying a single thought or action or emotion as clearly and directly and simply as possible? And perhaps most difficult of all, had the writer managed to make you feel anything in that vast Lishian sea of efficiency and barren functionality?

New professors were given a full term to listen to faculty craft lectures and readings before delivering one of their own, so this was Simone's first public presentation of any sort. We were well acquainted with her expensive clothes and the perfume we couldn't help but love regardless of how we felt about her, and she had become infamous for her strange mix of reserve and effusiveness, her multitude of questions, and the rafter chair she always sat in, but those of us who hadn't read her novel had no idea what to expect from her work. By then, of course, what Tammy had told Bridget and Jamie had been dispersed widely throughout our class in the three days since she had told them, which only heightened our focus on Simone. We were all leaning forward in our seats by the time she started reading.

We had half expected Leslie and Hannah not to show, but they were literally front and center, in the exact middle of the fourth row of the auditorium. It's the only event we can remember Leslie showing up for early. Hannah had forgone one of her blazers for a cashmere sweater that made us want to take a nap, it looked so soft. We assumed she had borrowed it from Leslie, because it looked expensive. There weren't any runs in Leslie's stockings, a first. She had even brushed her hair for the occasion. They might've looked like girls playing dress-up if their postures and facial expressions—arranged to tell us exactly nothing—hadn't been so devoid of joy.

They weren't the only ones subverting expectations. We had thought Simone would take her usual seat and walk all the way down to the podium after she was introduced, making us wait that much longer to hear her read. As soon as we spotted her in the front row, next to Johanna Green, the short story writer who had left Pearl with ten students the semester before, and who, as the second newest faculty member, would be introducing Simone, we immediately looked up at Simone's empty chair, which we almost didn't recognize without her in it. Usually professors who were about to read were chatty with the faculty who filled the first two rows of the audience—a way to remind themselves that they were in good, supportive company and that their own authority was made stronger by the collective authority of the faculty as a whole, which had two National Book Award finalists and countless PEN awards, and the various first-novel prizes that had been popping up over the last few years. But Simone was as committed to studying the space directly in front of her as Leslie and Hannah were.

Professors often made a big fuss over how generous or appreciated their introductions were, sometimes even hugging the professor who had given it. But Simone didn't acknowledge Johanna's opening remarks with anything more than a curt nod. She also managed to bypass the second bad habit we had all come to expect from professors at these things, which was to go on for too long before reading from the book or manuscript in front of them, which is what they were there to do. Some professors were shameless, talking for almost as long as they read, often trying to be funny, or ingratiating, which always smelled a little desperate, no matter how funny they actually were, or how much their remarks endeared them to us. No matter what they actually said, it was always clear they were really just asking us to like what they were about to read, and, by extension, them.

Simone said only, "I'm going to read from my untitled novel, which is being published sometime early next year."

With these sixteen words alone Simone established several important facts that distinguished her from everyone else in the first two rows. First, that while her novel had been at least twice as successful as most of the faculty's work with the exception of maybe Pearl, she wasn't planning to rest on it. She was a novelist, not the author of one particular novel, even if it was the only one she had published. The paperback of *Girls with Outdoor Voices* had been out for less than a year—most of the readers who preceded and followed her would read from books half a decade old at least. *Was she planning to have new material ready for every faculty reading she gave?*

Second, and probably more important, by giving no

introduction to this nameless, shapeless thing—not even any context for the section she was about to read, or a joke about how she'd better hurry and come up with a title, since it was coming out so soon—she was making it clear that she gave fuck all what anyone thought of it. Either that or she just knew it was really, really good.

And it was, for the most part. Though there was little in what she read that interested us as much as her opening remarks or, for that matter, her flawless skin and silky voice, which we had plenty of time to study as she stood there under the lights. It was only in the final five minutes of Simone's reading, when she got to the final parting of the couple at the center of the material she was reading, who had been in the process of breaking up throughout, that our interest level returned to the height it had reached when Simone took the podium. The male half of the couple said, "I'll see you at the end of the world," which, from the rest of what Simone had read, clearly meant *we'll meet again*. And the woman said, "Oh, c'mon now, the end of the world is for lovers." Which it was equally clear meant *which we no longer are*.

It was just the right amount of sentiment and heartbreak for a story as emotionally removed and technically impressive as Simone's piece had been, and we were about to start admiring her for it when we were distracted by something in the front of the audience. We realized that the collective turning of heads was in response to something in the fourth row at the same time we knew it had to be Hannah. She got to her feet just as the low, involuntary moan she didn't seem to realize she was making reached its summit. She searched the space immediately around her as if disoriented, or like she was looking for someone or something to break, as if that might stop the pain she was clearly in. Leslie looked as confused as we felt, but she was up just a moment after Hannah. By the time her hand reached Hannah's shoulder, Hannah had focused her rage and panic enough to be looking directly at Simone, making no apology or explanation for her outburst, with an intensity in her gaze that demanded one instead. Half of us waited for Pearl to intervene while the other half of us prepared for Hannah to charge, though the actual, measurable response from both students and faculty alike was pure nothing. The silence of ticking clocks and dropped pins and empty forests.

Penny Stanley was sitting next to Pearl—the only professor other than Simone who sat with the general population instead of in the first two rows—and said that he only closed his eyes and dropped his head. Like he knew enough about what was happening that he didn't need to be leaning forward trying to figure it out, but not enough to intervene, or provide its solution. Lucas White turned to Robbie Myers with wide, delighted eyes and mouthed, "Dude, what the *fuck?*," which, as far as we know, were the only words exchanged for at least a full minute, silent or spoken. Jiles Gardner sat there rolling his eyes without actually having to move them, like, *Oh, here we go again with humans and their tedious drip of feelings.*

None of these reactions, or our collective lack of a reaction, were as surprising as Simone's. Once we all realized that Hannah's outburst was directed at Simone, we turned to her, expecting surprise or alarm or confusion, maybe even fear, but none of those things were anywhere on her face, which was as cool and unmoving as ever. She sat there drilling holes into Hannah with abundantly indifferent eyes, as if to say *Done yet?*

We turned back to Hannah to see how she would respond to this brick wall that Simone had put in front of her—if she would try to steer around it or just bulldoze straight through—but she and Leslie were gone.

The Empty Garden was a patch of land by the faculty housing that had been boxed in by dignified brick walls just high enough to prevent passersby from seeing what was inside. For years Fielding grad students assumed that there was some spectacular garden inside where the spoiled, unappreciative undergrads got stoned and probably screwed. We were always wondering what they got that we didn't the way the oldest, most responsible child wastes time resenting all the freedoms and privileges the baby of the family has been afforded. The year before we had arrived on campus, though, Gabe Marcus, the handsiest of the married accountants from the class above ours, realized that in the southern-facing wall of the perimeter there were grooves in the brick that served as perfect stepping-stones—almost a ladder—for hoisting yourself over the wall. We were disappointed and then delighted to discover that there was absolutely nothing inside the walls, which seemed like a metaphor for something, though we could never say what. It was an ordinary patch of grass with nothing to set it apart from the other acres of green the campus was blanketed in. If anything, it was less rich than the other lawns, given how small the patch was, and the way the walls broke up the light.

When they weren't trying to run into the girl they were both in love with, suggesting to the other an activity that would place them directly in her path without naming her, Lucas and Robbie used to get stoned in the Empty Garden, and said they always had to race Leslie and Hannah to get there first after mandatory lectures let out. They found the girls waiting there after lectures the girls had skipped, mandatory or not, talking in whispers even though there was nobody around to hear, other than the boys, who had other things to worry about anyway. Normally they would've taken the opportunity to invite the girls to combine forces—Lucas and Robbie not being the sort to miss a chance to pass an expertly rolled spliff to a pretty girl—but the girls' posture and body language and refusal to look up at them, even when the boys were close enough that it would've been impossible for anyone else to ignore them, made them turn around in pursuit of another spot.

Despite the ease with which the Empty Garden was now accessible after Gabe's discovery, most of the rest of us still considered it off-limits. Maybe we were made uneasy by how underwhelming its contents were, assuming that if there was nothing there that warranted the walls, perhaps the land had been set aside because of some unhappy event that had taken place there. It was the creepiest corner of a campus composed almost entirely of creepy corners, the kind of place that wears a history you can feel but not see or confirm with any certainty.

When we picture Hannah and Leslie there after the assembly, discussing what had made the ever-composed Hannah crumble the way she had, we picture their faces illuminated by firelight—they would never have been able to sit there long enough to discuss all the things they needed to without a fire to keep them warm. Though Hannah was probably too upset to be much help, and, between the two of them, Hannah was certainly the likelier to have any experience or ability in fire making.

Leslie, of course, would've been the one to break the silence. "You wanna tell me what *that* was about?"

"That line was Jimmy's. She stole it from him."

"How could you possibly know that?"

"I know because I read it in one of his poems."

"What, you just, like, *memorized* all of his poems?"

"That one I did."

Hannah fell silent then just long enough that Leslie probably thought that was all she was going to get out of her, and
then started reciting the poem that still doesn't have a title.

"There are truths universally, humanly known:
That beauty queens age badly, and
High school science teachers
Smell of formaldehyde.
Then there are things we're born
Not knowing and never told,
Harder but no less true:
The end of the world is for lovers
And the great wars were fought
For the poets.
The real losses,
Too bright and unmanageable
For any page,
Crouch in the small days
Of the nameless many
Who never read the works of great men."

She paused again here long enough that Leslie thought she
was done. "Jesus, Jimmy. He was dark, wasn't he?"

"That's just it, though. He could manage to make something like this funny. I mean, not *funny*, but light. He was
winking at you, too. God, how did it end?" Hannah asked,
holding a closed fist to her forehead.

"This is no more your fault
Or your father's fault
Or your father's father's fault
Than the placement of the
Stars in the sky.
But remember to say thank you
For the idling engines
And cracked soles
And attention that hasn't
Been stretched so thin that
You no longer notice
The pebbles in your shoe or
The empty toilet paper rolls
In the caked, midwestern
Gas station bathrooms
In the walks and road trips
Across this life."

"Ha!" Leslie said, confident that this really was the big finish. "I happen to know a thing or two about midwestern gas station bathrooms."

Hannah started to cry then. We might've said she wept, but she hated the word *wept*. So dramatic and fussy, almost self-indulgent. So she cried instead.

We have no way of knowing if Hannah actually cried over all this after she left the assembly—to herself, or to Leslie— but her face as she climbed over the mess of legs and backpacks, searching for the exit the way she would've in a fire, certainly made it seem likely. It was the face of someone who only just realized some horrible fact that had been true for a while. We also know that she must've been devastated enough that tears were irrelevant, the least of it. Otherwise Leslie would never have taken things as far as she did—she might've liked Jimmy, and she certainly disliked Simone, but she loved Hannah. This is the point, this point when we all saw Hannah lose it for just one second before she reapplied the blank face the two of them always wore, past which there was no return.

We like to think that Leslie let her cry that night, probably knowing that sometimes a good cry is the only way through it (despite the fact that none of us can picture Leslie crying). She's soft on the inside, though, so we also suspect she started talking after a few minutes, not trying to present a solution to the unsolvable problem but to distract Hannah from her sadness, and to cover the sound of human anguish, which Leslie had never been able to bear.

"You know what saying I always hated?"

"What?" It took Hannah a while to get even this lone word out.

"The house always wins. Everyone seems to think that I'm from somewhere big and crowded enough to have public transportation, but it's actually the opposite. There was nothing but space there, and no way to cross it. And thank God for it, by the way. I wasn't one of those small-town kids looking to get out. The space suited me fine—I'm the kind of person big enough to need a little space, you've probably noticed. And people are mean on the subway."

As if Leslie wasn't all elbows and death-ray stares once she got to the subways.

"Anyway, the one thing that came even close to filling all that space in my town was the Kentucky Kings Casino. It was probably responsible for most of the worst parts of my childhood—the poverty, and that smell you never forget once you smell it, or confuse for anything else. That stink of day-old booze on unwashed skin. But most of the happiest moments of my life—even up to now, like, counting all these MFA *kicks* we get into—so much of the good stuff happened there. I used to go with my complete drunk of an uncle—he was the king of day-old liquor on unwashed skin. He was a drunk, though, not an alcoholic."

Being Leslie, she would've clarified the distinction before Hannah had time to ask, knowing Hannah had other things on her mind: "Alcoholics are mean, drunks aren't. Anyway, he took me there every day he had enough change to make it worth getting dressed. That's where I learned Spanish. From the people who worked the food court there. Some people might think that kind of thing was cruel—taking a kid to a place like that—but the cruel thing would've been to leave me home, to make me miss out. Uncle Rick was no saint, or even a winner, but I loved him for knowing that. He didn't have much in life, but whatever he had was both of ours, which is just about the best thing you can say about a person, don't you think?"

Looking over and seeing that Hannah's face, at that moment, was still not the face of a person ready for words, Leslie would've gone on, pretending the question was rhetorical.

"Even now I still think that. I got to roll the dice every time, and none of the minimum-wage rent-a-cop security guards ever minded, because they were the closest things Rick ever had to friends. He somehow managed to make a life lesson out of every roll, even if he could never figure out how to throw milk out when it went bad, or take out the garbage when it was time. Most of the lessons from each roll contradicted one another, sometimes even within a single day, but one lesson was the same. 'The house always wins.' He said it like he didn't know it was a cliché. Like he was the first person to think of it. He probably thought he was. He wasn't the kind of person who was above taking credit for someone else's idea." She would've laughed at this to make it clear that it wasn't something she minded about him.

"He said that even on the days he came out on top. Like, 'Let's not get too proud about this, let's prepare for the rainy day.' Not that he ever put any of the money away. I thought Rick was my only living relative, but when I was fourteen, an uncle on my mom's side appeared. He had found Jesus and a lot of money at just about the same time, and decided to send me to a boarding school back east. That's what he said, 'Back east,' even though neither side of my family was ever from there in the first place."

Hannah was still crying, but silently now—just tears, and

her breathing was back under control—and she looked over at Leslie, unable to resist this new piece of herself Leslie was offering.

"Once I got into a schedule of throwing out the milk and taking out the garbage it was easy enough to remember when to go to school so my grades were good enough that they let me in. So I wasn't there when Rick died. Somehow he got it into his head to rob the casino after closing one night, and got shot clean through the temple by Sam, one of his favorite guards, who couldn't make him out in the dark even though Rick had the biggest, stupidest head you've ever seen, which was hard to forget once you'd seen it. I never would've thought the guards carried guns, looking at their budget, amateur uniforms, and I'm sure Rick figured the same, but I guess they kept a gun somewhere, at least at night. Sam and some of the other employees felt bad enough that they put some money together to throw a far nicer funeral than Uncle Rick ever could have afforded. I remember there was a sash in gold lettering across this classy white casket that was shut, thank God. Uncle Rick was ugly even with his head on. It said: 'The House Always Wins.' And at the time I loved it because it was like Rick was in on it—on all of it. He always knew they were gonna take it all in the end. And he was maybe even okay with it. So for a long time I liked that saying, but then I didn't. Because I realized, the older I got, and the further away I got from those nights at the Kentucky Kings Casino, not a thing tugging on my worry brain except that next roll, that even if Rick hadn't gone out on a kind of cosmically sick joke, he'd have died in some terrible, grotesque fashion sooner or later. And life was never going to have anything great in store for a person like Uncle Rick. You could tell from his breathing, how heavy it was, that his heart was always two ticks away from stopping. And eventually I was gonna have to figure out something else to do other than gamble away nickels and dimes and shoot the breeze with grown-ass men. So he was wrong, that whole time. About all of it. It's not the house that always wins, it's time. Especially for a person like Rick, who was built for failure and misery the way some people are built for left-handedness."

Hannah, composed enough now to speak, stayed silent for another beat or two to make sure Leslie didn't have anything else to add, knowing that Leslie would say all this only once. Finally, when she was sure that Leslie had said the last word she was going to on the subject, Hannah said, "Erotica, my ass."

Maybe it was the compliment that would've given Leslie the courage to bring his name back up.

"It would've been the same for Jimmy. You know that, don't you? That kid never had a prayer."

Leslie's eyes would've darted to Hannah's face after she said this, the way they sometimes did, searching for favor or anger, some indication by which to calibrate her next move. Her hair had probably returned to its natural, unkempt state by then.

"I don't even mean to make it personal. To make it about him, or even Uncle Rick. What I'm saying is that nothing lasts. That casino is dust and ash by now. And what's the oldest book you've ever read and truly loved? Something from the nineteenth century? Maybe the eighteenth, if you wanna stretch it? What about all the stories that came before that, and the people who loved them?"

"Is this supposed to make me feel better?"

"No, but I think there's a way to make things better. To make them right, even."

Hannah snorted skeptically, half laugh, half protest, producing a perfectly round little snot bubble out of her left nostril that probably didn't undermine her beauty even a little, not even when it popped. "What? By stopping all the clocks?"

"By making use of the time you have."

"And how do you do that?"

"You fight for the things that you love. You do what you can while you can instead of just letting the clock run out while you shake your head at what's happening."

"I'm still not sure what you're suggesting."

"Who do you think lit the match on that casino?"

"Please don't tell me you actually set it on fire?"

"No, but everybody knew the casino had an unofficial cash-only policy. They hadn't paid their taxes—at least not what they really owed—in years. And we learned all about the IRS in the AP government class at that fancy boarding school Rick let them send me to. It took one phone call."

"We already tried talking to Pearl," Hannah said, sounding a little hopeless despite Leslie's confidence. "It didn't work. You saw him with her after."

"No, I know. We leave him out of this. I have something else in mind entirely. Sometimes you have to actually light the match."

It could've gone some other way, of course. We all saw what they did, across the next June semester, but we have no way of knowing how or when they decided to do it. They arrived on campus for the next residency with the groundwork for their plan firmly in place, its intricacies and forethought apparent to us only slowly, in small gradations across those ten sunny days that both horrified and energized us, until we were as guilty as they were.

Maybe they built their plan off campus, in something as unromantic as an email, or a late-night garbled cell phone call. It's difficult to shake the image of Leslie, her back to the doors of a smudged telephone booth the likes of which became obsolete at the turn of this century, turning to make angry faces at the bum who needed the booth to conduct whatever dark business he used it for. We knew she had a gift for angry gestures she wouldn't even have to interrupt her call to make. Maybe they were in one of their rooms on campus, a bottle of four-dollar grocery store wine from town between them.

What we know is that in the hours immediately after Hannah's outburst, none of us saw either girl, and that the morning after, an email was sent to the entire student body, asking that anyone who had any information about the fire that had been set in Adam's Square—the actual name of the Empty Garden—come forward. The email also reminded us that there were certain parts of campus that MFA students were not granted access to. We were guests on this campus; we shouldn't need to be told and asked to act accordingly.

Bridget Jameson once heard Leslie refute a workshop troll's claim that her protagonist was obviously inspired by an ambulatory Larry Flynt by insisting that it was her dead uncle Rick, and Sarah Jacobs says she saw a postcard in Leslie's on-campus mailbox with a picture of the Kentucky Kings Casino on the front, sent from an address about an hour outside Louisville. When she looked up the casino she discovered that it had been closed for more than a decade, after a losing arm wrestle with the IRS. From a poem Hannah published years after all this happened, we learned that Leslie's ninth and most fiercely guarded tattoo was the line "People like to say the house always wins, but really it is time."

And last, but never least, we know Jimmy's nameless poem—by heart, all of us—the only thing he ever wrote that was published, even if it was only in the book at the center of Hannah and Leslie's final fuck-you to Simone, which they never bothered to name any more than they did the poem.

We're not trying to exaggerate, or project our own losses with time onto what happened during these residencies. It just seems like the least we can do, getting this right, pinning down all the details we can, making what happened more manageable and less frenzied, something we can contain, or at least wrap our heads around, making it, in some small but still-significant-to-us way, our own—an arrangement of words that puts these bits of gossip and strange half-events and shadows on the wall into a story that is at least as much ours as anybody else's.

There are two last things of any importance that happened before the next term, but we wouldn't know about either of them until later, to compare notes on them and secure them into their place in the story.

The first is the fact that the girls had to have gone to Simone directly before they executed their plan, likely sometime during this January term, after Simone's reading. After what happened that next June term, Simone disappeared, and resurfaced only years later, and briefly. A spattering of short stories of hers appeared in second-tier glossies and journals, though they were never published as a collection. Around that time, she gave an interview to her alumni magazine, probably one final, unconvincing attempt to make a proper comeback. When the student interviewer asked her about the scandal surrounding her time at Fielding, he must not have been expecting her to answer. She had never gone on record about it, and there didn't seem to be anything gained by doing so then. She must have become resigned to it all by then, though, because she answered the question, breeding in the interviewer a lifelong habit of asking uncomfortable questions that likely never served him as well as it had that first time. She didn't admit to anything or elaborate on what had happened, but she made an oblique defense of it. She said, "It was just words on a page. For all the fuss it created, and the mess. That's what I told the girls who led the witch hunt when they first came to me—it was just words on a page."

This is the part we really can't forgive her for.

She of all people knows what words on a page are capable of—what they've done throughout human history, and in our own lives. The lives of everyone who's ever picked up a book. What was the point of doing what we all did, otherwise—the one thing we all had in common, despite the various skill and professional levels that we did it on, which seemed to matter less the longer we wrote. This interview, when we read it years later, revindicated our own roles in that next June term. It showed us how capable Simone was of lying, this dismissal of what words on a page could do. It evaporated any lingering fears that she was more innocent than Leslie and Hannah would have us believe.

The second event of note was an off-campus reading for Fielding students that was held in a dive bar in Brooklyn between our second and third residencies, just before the city started to thaw for the spring, which both Mimi Kim and Joni Kleinman attended. The event itself wasn't remarkable—the owner of the bar was a graduate of the program, and held the reading every year. It was informal to the point of halfheartedness. Both current program students and graduates were welcome to read, and there was no scheduled order. All you had to do was show up. Those of us who did went mainly for the discounted beer—even dive bars in Brooklyn were expensive by then. None of us tried out new work, or anything we were excited about, which we saved for the glory of on-campus student readings.

The reading that March was speculation-worthy only because Leslie and Hannah appeared just as it was dwindling, just the right amount drunk for an event like this. There was a musical, fluid quality to their gaits when they blustered through the curtain that separated the rest of the bar from the back room where the reading was held, but they weren't so drunk that they would've caused a scene if everyone there didn't stop and look twice just because it was them, there. Hannah lived a good four hours away, and while we still didn't know where Leslie lived, her evident disdain for the industry people while on campus made it seem unlikely that she'd have the patience for full-time residency in Brooklyn. When we thought of Leslie and Hannah in between stretches on campus, in the Real World, we always pictured them together, even if we couldn't say exactly where, and when Mimi reported that this was in fact the case, at least that night, we felt more confident in all our other speculations about them.

Leslie looked like a drunk senior at prom—over it, but determined to make a little noise on the way out. She was wearing a highlighter-yellow silk shirt with a short sequined skirt and fishnet stockings with suede navy blue men's loafers even though there were a good three inches of snow covering the city that night. She had actually put pennies in them, a wish for each foot in the absence of anything to keep them warm. She had a crown of holly in her dirty hair. We assumed, when Mimi told us all this, that Leslie was coming from somewhere else, but now we're not so sure. Leslie has surely dressed up for less of an occasion than an offsite Fielding reading. While we were all familiar with Leslie's batty ensembles, this one seemed more appropriate in the Real World, less of a costume than it would have been on campus, and the low light in the bar softened her in a way Mimi said she hadn't seen before. Leslie was almost sweet looking, according to Mimi, despite the dark, determined roots defending their land against the bleach she used in her hair, and the brass studs on the leather bag she was carrying.

Hannah was wearing a puffy coat so outrageously cumbersome that it obscured the rest of what she was wearing. The fur of her hood framed her face like a mane, which only underscored the perfection of her features. She looked better suited for an ice-fishing expedition in Nova Scotia than a night out in Brooklyn.

The girls perched on the two most distant seats of the empty final row, and waited respectfully for the fourth-term poet to finish an ode to her pet frogs before Leslie did the most surprising thing she could have done. She got up to read, something neither she nor Hannah had done during either term on campus.

It was Joni who told us that Leslie's story was about that fussy period babies go through at six to eight weeks, when they start crying every night at the same time, outside of hunger or soiled diapers. Bridget remembers Joni herself crying when she reported this, and everyone knew that Joni and the husband she had moved to Fielding for had been trying to conceive for a while by then.

The story was a kind of explanation for those nighttime grievances of newborns. According to the story, all babies are freshly reincarnated souls—you enter the womb immediately upon death, an immediate do-over. And when you leave it a wriggling lump of flesh upon birth, you still remember your last life—the smell of the hand cream your mother couldn't really afford that she wore anyway, and the shape your father's mouth made when he noticed the smell and decided not to comment on the price. While you remembered these things, you didn't have the words to tell anybody about them. And every day your old life gets a little more hazy and feels a little more distant, and starts to fade as the new life—the things your new mother spends too much money on, and the shapes your new father's face makes when he notices them—gains focus, and you start to interact with the new world you've been born into. And it's at six weeks that these little old souls realize what's happening, that they're losing the lives they've left. And they cry at the end of each day for all that's been lost—an entire life's worth of details—knowing that when they finally concede to the gentle urging of their new parents and close their eyes for the night they'll have lost a little more of it. The color of the sky at sunrise on graduation day or the random, incoherent jumble of letters they used for every computer password. These memories, in Leslie's telling, were the one lesson any human gets before being dropped back into the middle of the world and all its cruelties and strangenesses again—a reminder of the things that would matter in the end. The things you would cling to when it was all over.

None of us knew at the time, being childless graduate students, for the most part, how universal this fussy period is in infants. We assumed Leslie was exaggerating for the sake of the story, an unavoidable habit in writers, even when we're only telling stories socially. It was only later, when we had children of our own, that we realized Leslie had been telling the truth. First Melissa, in that wintry midwestern stretch of early nights and the absence of light, and then Tanner, who married the first woman who ever responded favorably to a pickup line dropped at jury duty, with whom he would have a son. And Tammy, who never had children of her own, but filled her retirement with fostering children after she tired of writing. And Joni, finally, who gave birth to a sturdy little girl almost five years to the day of the reading. Jenny Ritter, whose kids were nearing junior high by the time we exchanged these field notes, just bobbed her head with closed, knowing eyes, too tired, or maybe empathetic, by then to point out how much earlier she had known these things than we did.

Even those of us without kids would think of Leslie's story when we heard stray notes of a baby's wail at a mall, or across a crowded restaurant, confusing our dinner dates with our private smiles at background noise most people would consider a nuisance. He's just trying to remember, we'd think, and then count our own loved ones while we still could without any effort. We saw even the most good-natured babies make this turn, however short-lived it is, which made us think of Hannah and Leslie yet again. We all leaned forward to see if we could find any trace of it in their newborn eyes—the name of the bus driver who got in trouble for telling a fourth-grader to shut up, or what the light was like on the beach where they retired with their second wife. When we saw any trace of knowingness in their looks it gave credence to every strange thing Leslie had ever said, and in our sleep-deprived new-parent comas we wondered if she had been real at all, or maybe something from another world or life herself.

The protagonist of Leslie's story was a man who had only one happy memory to take with him from his old life when he started the new: the face of a girl he had seen through the window of a bus she was riding, stopped at a red light as he pedaled past on his bike. She was carrying a bunch of grocery store daisies wrapped in cellophane, and even though she was wearing what was almost certainly a secondhand shirt and she had a ten-dollar haircut and the daisies were already starting to wilt, she was clearly happy, heading toward people who loved her, to a place that would be made incalculably better by those half-dead grocery store daisies and the smile that arrived just behind them. And he saw for one second how divorced happiness was from one's lot in life, or could be. That you could rise above your circumstances in life through the sheer power of your constitution, or a gritty resolve toward happiness. For the rest of his life, the boy would remind himself that the girl could have spent the five dollars those daisies cost toward any number of more practical but less cheerful items she was in dire need of, but hadn't. And he carried that girl and her bouquet through every other miserable year of his life.

In the early days of the boy's new life, the scarcity of happy memories from his old one didn't make him cling to it with any less stubborn resistance to the new situation he had been born into, one considerably more privileged than the one he had left. Instead he cried harder than any baby ever had for the girl, because he had spent an entire life guarding her memory, keeping it so much fresher than her flowers. He screamed his throat raw every night, knowing that once he went to sleep the girl's face would be fuzzier when he woke, and that it wouldn't be long before he forgot that the window he saw her through had been on a city bus in Detroit at the turn of the twenty-first century, or that the flowers she had been holding were daisies. He came up with all kinds of clever ways to store her memory in thoughts and details of this new life, and promised himself he would find the girl here in this life, whether she was a dog or a senator or a flower herself now.

As they are on campus, the bar readings were supposed to be capped at ten minutes. Each reading was "hosted" by a different student moderator, who was supposed to ring a bell when the reader was a minute away from their time cap, and again once their time was over. There was no protocol for what to do when a reader went over the allotted time, because no one ever had. That night at the bar, Stacy Tallecio, the Margaret Jibs of someone else's class, had been enlisted for the job of timekeeper. She had come in from Long Island, and was the color of schoolhouse brick even though it was the middle of March. Leslie didn't nod or smile when she heard the one-minute warning bell, the way most of us did. She pretended not to hear the bell even when she hit the twelve-minute mark, when Stacy got out of her seat just to the left of the microphone and leaned forward to ring it just inches from Leslie's face. Leslie finally stopped reading after fifteen minutes, just before she got to the part about whether the boy found the girl. By then even Stacy was over the gall that reading past the bell had entailed, as engrossed as everyone else in the boy's hunt, which Leslie must have sensed.

Just as she was getting to the big, juicy reunion the entire bar was waiting for, Leslie stopped reading to make room for a big, naughty laugh that advertised but didn't reveal all the things she knew that we didn't, and everyone realized she was drunker than she had initially seemed. She looked back at Hannah, still in the last row, leaning forward, as if she were hearing all this for the first time, too. If Leslie was softer off campus, Hannah was lighter—a girl with less on her mind. She gave Leslie a *what am I gonna do with you?* shake of the head, which Leslie took as a summons, and once again they were gone.

We never found out if he found her. The boy in the story. Leslie never published it, even when she started publishing stories regularly.

Mimi claims that when she met Leslie for drinks one January when she was in New York for a real reading years after all of this happened, and Mimi got drunk enough to ask about the story, Leslie denied any memory of it. She told Mimi she must be thinking of someone else, or some other story, even after Mimi kept insisting past the point of politeness. Mimi wasted no time in reaching out to the rest of us for confirmation, which we all gave her readily, even though the story wasn't ours to confirm, of course—Mimi and Joni were the ones who had told it to us. What we were really confirming was that Mimi's story hadn't changed—she remembered it the way we did from her original telling, from the hole in the left elbow of Leslie's blouse that waved at her listeners while she read, to Hannah's little school of minnow sneezes halfway through the story. What she was really asking us to confirm, we knew, was that we had been carrying the story with us all those years, too.

Once Mimi's outreach started us comparing notes again, we realized it wasn't just the existence of the story we agreed upon, or its details. But that the face of the boy on the bike we pictured was always Jimmy's, and that, while it was the more sentimental, less artful ending, in our minds he always found the girl in his new life.

June

Once again, we arrived on campus to find news waiting for us, and were relieved to discover that it was happier this time. It was apparent as soon as our airport and train shuttles and rental cars rolled up to the top of the hill the campus sat on, where, instead of finding the married accountants chucking Frisbees at one another like fraternal undergraduates, cheap beer melting in the grass not far away, we found catering vans and light installations and women with clipboards and headsets. There was money in the air.

We had known that this June would mark the twenty-year anniversary of the program's founding, and that graduates from years past would be invited to campus for certain residency events. The literature that appeared in our mailboxes between residencies chirped about the milestone with exclamation points and cheerful language that we never would've gotten away with in our fiction.

Once we had picked up our schedules and welcome packets with faculty bios and headshots, and scanned them for details about anniversary events, we saw there was more. Not only did Simone's novel now have a title, and a publication date, Professor Pearl had finally finished and sold his second novel. Because he would be going on a book tour, and because, as the flyer in our packets announcing his retirement party quoted him as having said, "I'm old," he would be stepping down as the head of the program, to serve instead as its first writer in residence after a one-year sabbatical.

We thought at first that the clouds of bustling bodies that seemed to fill even the emptiest stretches on campus could be explained by the caterers and other uniformed people who would be setting up for all the celebratory events and ensuring they ran smoothly. But it took only half a day to realize that service personnel didn't normally come dressed in blazers or glasses with five-hundred-dollar frames, or handbags made from Italian leather. Though to us our professors existed only on campus, we knew they had peers and colleagues and old friends out there in the Real World—friends who reviewed books for publication that even our practical fathers had heard of and who taught at institutions we never could have afforded, and wrote books of their own, some of which we had read in college courses and seen on the cover of the *New York Times Book Review*. Friends who would want to raise a glass to twenty years of hard work, and the start of whatever was to come next.

At first, we weren't sure how to react to these intimidating interlopers. It felt a little like someone had invited our crushes to the kickoff dance at fat camp without telling us. We were grateful, but we weren't ready yet—we had thought we'd have all summer to lose weight. Or, in our case, to purge our writing of the long list of sins that our professors reminded us of regularly, a concept that felt less absurd and heady with every packet, but still not entirely within reach. The off-campus guests weren't there to read our work, we knew, but their proximity alone felt like access to some precious, elusive opportunity, and left us feeling vulnerable to the possibility that we'd waste it.

It became impossible not to be happy after seeing Pearl, though. He displayed a physical, sprightly happiness most closely associated with puppies, happiness that was the essence of contagion. It also made us a little sad, though, seeing him direct lost first-termers to their dorms with a friendly hand on the back like the camp counselor who had taken the time to invite all those crushes. We had thought the stern gait and distant demeanor we associated with him as closely as we did his famous novel were hardwired into him rather than a function of any emotion. That he was capable of happiness of this caliber meant that he had been unhappy for as long as we'd known him, and probably far longer.

Once we decided to take his happiness as permission to

get excited about the term and the extra dose of glamour that we now saw the residencies before had been lacking, the rumors began. Jamie Brigham heard that the book editor for the *Guardian* would be there, which meant that the roster of fancy, recognizable names had dual citizenship at least. Mimi Kim said an unnamed source had told her that Simone would be named the new head of the program, which probably meant her squad of restaurateurs and B-list actors would come to campus for the announcement itself. That we all knew this was likely hopeful conjecture rather than something anyone had actually suggested to her did nothing to stop any of us from repeating it.

All the unprecedented campus activity was more than enough of an excuse for Penny to reprise her one-woman committee. It had been just long enough since she had forgotten poor Jimmy's name for her to be comfortable emailing us to suggest we reconvene to come up with a class gift for Professor Pearl. We resisted, of course, and complained, both inwardly and to one another when Tammy was out of earshot, even as we knew we'd go in the end, because it would be easier than skipping.

We were relieved when an additional piece of news kept us from having to dwell on how much time Penny's meetings were going to take. It was no more than an hour after we read her email that we learned that there were surprises waiting for us beyond those catering vans and light installations and even, eventually, an ice sculpture in the shape of Moby-Dick—Pearl's favorite book. The most shocking news we heard in our first twenty-four hours on campus wasn't that Simone had something ready to publish so quickly after her debut—no sophomore slump for her—or even that Pearl had finally finished his drawer novel so long after everyone had given up hope for it that you had to invent a new word, because *slump* didn't really get at it the way we all knew the perfect word gets at something. The thing that made us abandon our silent litany of justifications for boycotting Penny's meeting, and kept our tongues moving at rates faster than even rumors of Michiko Kakutani's attendance at the graduation ceremony, or an alleged sighting of Jeffrey Eugenides, was the news that Hannah and Leslie had signed up to volunteer as part of the orientation and welcome committee. This was a job that came with no perks or pay outside of the favor of the program administration. The girls weren't joiners; once we had understood the extent of their grief and their rage, we had counted on it only pulling them closer together, and further away from us. This new, outward-facing willingness to join the rest of the student body seemed promising, like the darkness Jimmy had left behind was finally starting to lift. What we had forgotten was that even in our first term, before what happened to Jimmy, they wouldn't have signed up for volunteer work, or anything that didn't directly strengthen their writing, or contribute to the amount of time they spent together. We wouldn't think anything of it until later, though. At the time it was only happiness that we felt.

It was June again, and thank God for that.

Though we couldn't identify which important tweedster was which—author photos lie—we didn't have to wait long for an eyeful of Leslie in the bright yellow T-shirt the orientation committee members wore, the word *volunteer* written across the chest in bold capital letters. It was the first and only T-shirt Leslie owned, as far as we knew. She managed to make it look ironic even though she actually was a volunteer, sitting next to Joni Kleinman at the table where students were supposed to pick up their dorm keys and room assignments.

We had expected, when we heard about the girls' decision to willingly take on this scut work, that they would execute it side by side, but Leslie's head was bent over something we later identified as a piece of fabric she was cross-stitching to be a decorative throw pillow, and Joni was the only other person at her table. Leslie kept calling out to Linda, the program secretary who had apparently become Leslie's cross-stich mentor while we had looked briefly away. Outside of that first cross-campus car ride with Jimmy and the pep talk she had given him, it was so rare to see Linda interact with anyone that we were more surprised at the speed and enthusiasm with which she answered Leslie's questions about how to switch thread colors and how to keep from bleeding on the fabric when you poked yourself than we were at the fact that Leslie would want to know the answers to these questions. Linda was manning a table clear on the other side of the room, and had to keep shouting her answers back to Leslie to be heard, but still managed to sound unprecedentedly cheerful. At one point Linda actually held up her finger to silence a fourth-year in the middle of a question to tell Leslie that, no, spitting on the thread to wet it wouldn't make it easier to get it through the needle. Joni made the small talk with students that Leslie and Linda wouldn't even pretend to humor with thin smiles and *uh-huh, that's nice but I really have to go* eyes, but kept looking over at Leslie's lap to laugh. She later told us that Leslie was embroidering her pillow to read "He just farted" above an arrow pointing left.

Leslie and Linda were so gripped in their cross-stitching projects that when Simone walked into the room five minutes after the key registration had closed they didn't notice her, or look up. By then Linda had come over to sit with Leslie and Joni and had taken back up her own pillow project, which was always tucked somewhere close by, and while Joni wasn't working on anything herself, she had taken up Leslie's role of question asking, which both Leslie and Linda were now answering, Leslie apparently classifying herself an expert after only a day's practice, which was probably the least surprising part of all this. They must have just been three bobbing, faceless crowns, which probably only made Simone, who had come to

complain, angrier. Joni would later tell us that Simone was ra-
diating the kind of cool anger we had long assumed radiated
around her commons conversation with Jimmy, but she had
learned better than to verbalize it by then. Her voice, when
she spoke, was all flesh-tone, elevator-music decorum.

"Um, yeah, excuse me, I just got back from my room, and
the key you guys gave me doesn't work."

Linda was the first to look up.

"Well, that's strange, honey. No one else reported having
the wrong key. So it's not that it was a swap." She picked up
Simone's key to examine it, at which point the unlikelihood of
this solving the problem was, according to Joni, clear on Simone's face. "There are extra rooms with working keys, but I
know you specially requested the room you have." She looked
down to consult her master copy of room assignments. "You're
all the way out in Lefferts, which they mostly keep empty for
these graduate residencies. It looks like you're the only one in
the building. I can put you somewhere closer to central campus if you want? Might be a little cozier and less remote anyway. It gets dark out there by the woods."

"No. Thank you," Simone said, making it clear that the
two sentiments were not attached, and the *no* was a hard one.
"I like the quiet to work. Is there any other way to get into the
room?"

Linda handed the key back to Simone lazily, at a pace that
said it was all the same to her, which it was, never mind that

the key was worthless. "I can radio security to meet you at your room. They have a master key that will get you in."

Once she finished saying this she looked back down at her cross-stitch, the matter now closed.

"Well, that would be good, but it doesn't entirely solve my problem."

That Linda was a good enough soul to teach Leslie a skill as fine-tuned as cross-stitching, but not good enough to humor two cross-stitching interruptions for a single problem she did not consider herself responsible for creating, was evident on Linda's face when she looked up. She was polite, Linda's smile said, not an idiot.

"Well, now, sugar, I suppose you could just leave the room unlocked until we can track down the spare key, or someone else reports a wrong key. You can lock the door from the inside, manually, like you do a bathroom, so you'd feel safe at night. It would just be a matter of leaving it open when you're away. So just don't leave anything of value in there."

That would've been the end of the exchange if Leslie hadn't spoken just as Simone finished opening and closing her mouth several times in a row. "I know it's not ideal, but in a place like this, with everyone as friendly as they are, what bad could possibly come of it?"

Joni said Leslie didn't look up when she said it, still apparently too invested in her cross-stitching to give the matter much thought. The funny thing, according to Joni, was that

Leslie's needle didn't move once the whole time Simone was in the room.

Penny had picked a classroom in the red barn for her meeting about our class gift, denying us the sunlight and the grass this time, perhaps hoping we would be less distracted, but really only giving us one more thing to hold against her. The dragging, pouty postures with which we all arrived at the small second-floor room on the morning after we received Penny's email—once again a disaster of exclamation points and passive aggressions—immediately fell away when we saw that it was Leslie at the front of the table where the professors usually sat. Her hands were folded crisply in front of her in a way that seemed to poke fun at the sloppy lines of her wardrobe. Our surprise turned to relief when we saw Hannah sitting just to her left, confident that if this was some sort of joke Leslie was telling at our expense Hannah wouldn't be there.

Leslie didn't begin until Lucas and Robbie arrived five minutes late. She indicated that they should shut the door behind them with a single swoosh of her wrist, a call Lucas and Robbie fell over each other in a race to answer, partly because Leslie was a pretty girl, and partly because there was no activity they were incapable of turning into a competition.

"All right," said Leslie, as soon as they were both sitting

again. "I promise I'll keep this brief. I know nobody wants to be inside on a day like this, and I think I speak for all of us when I say there are better things to be doing around here."

She paused then to give us a chance to fill the room with small, polite gestures of agreement, but we were all too shocked to move. This was by far the most number of words Leslie had ever spoken directly to us.

"Penny over here called us all together because she thinks we should give Pearl some sort of gift to commemorate his retirement." Leslie threw her head forty-five degrees in the direction Penny was sitting without making any sort of complicitous eye contact. "I think she's right. I mean, you guys have seen the schedule—everyone's making a big to-do about this being his last term and everything, and we don't want to look bad by comparison, right? So anyway, I have an idea, and rather than facing the whole too-many-cooks-in-the-kitchen problem we had with the class motto a few terms ago—no offense, Pen—I thought I'd just execute it myself with a little help from all of you."

At this use of a nickname, however clumsy and off the cuff, Penny did smile, and was immediately prettier for it. Later we would wonder if she had really reprised her committee role on her own, or if Leslie had made her do it. By then Penny was so happy to have been part of an alliance that didn't include a teacher that she wouldn't say whose idea it had been.

"The thing is, I really like Pearl," Hannah said, the first formal indication that she was part of this plan as well, though we had assumed as much. She waved a hand at Leslie. "I think we both do. I mean, you guys know how it is here—there are some really good teachers and some hacks, and you never know which type you have until well into the semester, and Pearl was one of the best that term I had him. I really think I became a better writer."

"Yeah," said Leslie. "Exactly. So we wouldn't even mind doing the extra work of putting it together. And we'd want you guys to have some representation even if we're the ones doing the heavy lifting, so I'd just need two things from you—twenty bucks and one to two thousand words of your best work."

A few hands were raised at this mention of our work, which almost always bred questions and insecurities, no matter the context, but Leslie ignored them.

"It can't be one or the other. Not because you're, like, *paying* to be part of the project, but because you're either in this or you're not, you know?"

By then we had it together enough to nod that we did in fact know what she meant, and we had no sooner given our bobbed consent than we realized Leslie was standing and heading for the door behind us. Hannah started reluctantly gathering her things to follow, ready to go, given that they had said what they came there to say, but not entirely pleased to be rushed. It seemed cruel that just as we were beginning to truly understand how noteworthy what was happening in this room was, it was ending.

"So, yeah," Leslie said. "Just PayPal or Venmo me the money—you have my email address—and send me any questions you have about the writing samples, which I'm sure you'll have. That is what people seem to like to do here—ask questions." This last part was the closest she came all morning to mentioning Simone—queen of pretentious, unanswerable questions asked from the chair on high—though none of us would make the connection until later.

Leslie was about to reach out for the doorknob to open it when Hannah put a hand on her shoulder.

"Leslie."

"Oh, yeah," Leslie said, not needing any further clarification. "And we should have a party." She said this like it was any less strange than her speaking in tongues would have been, like it was something she suggested all the time. "I mean, our time at this place is almost halfway over, and we can't leave all the fun to these invading academics and wannabes, you know? I know we haven't exactly been raging since we started here, but I have a hard time believing they know more about how to throw a party than we do. So in a few nights, let's say, I don't know, the fourth night of the residency, to get a jump on the midweek slump, let's meet at Lefferts Field at dusk."

"You don't have to bring anything," Hannah said. "We'll handle it all. We'll make it a bonfire. I think Lefferts would be a really spectacular spot for a bonfire, don't you think?"

And with that they both turned back around and left us, before we had time to ask any questions of our own.

⸻

When they tired of the boring, groundwork-laying portion of the operation and decided it was time to actually strike, they started with her chair.

They picked the welcome orientation, which might've seemed like a throwaway event, but was actually the one thing everyone went to. By that June we could have recited the orientation spiels by heart: the warning against illicit drugs that was almost insulting in the extent to which it was empty, the reminder about how many students could be present in one room before it was a fire hazard, and the hours the cafeteria would be open. But we were eager to see all the faces that we had come to campus looking for in one place. That June orientation was a particularly happy one for us third-termers. We were halfway through, a half that had girded us and prepared us, we liked to think, for what was still ahead. We had known which teachers to request for this term, and which ones to avoid. We were starting to find ways to employ the rules and prohibitions our professors reminded us of again and again without stripping our stories of what made our writing uniquely, exclusively our own. Discovering these tricks had felt a little like cheating, even though it had already occurred to some of us that this had been what our professors had hoped of us the entire time. We had at least one story that we felt confident we could include in our final graduation thesis, which required a hundred pages of polished, professor-approved fiction.

We'd had some of this acquired wisdom that second term, in January, but there was some strange, supernatural benediction from the weather that January residencies lacked. We weren't sure if it was our imagination, or if the sun really had already kissed us in the one half-day we had spent romping through what now felt like our own personal corner of Vermont. That first morning of the welcome orientation, we were starting to smile the kinds of smiles that give you crow's-feet and make your cheeks look round in pictures.

We were too busy waving to one another across the auditorium, or, if you were Lucas and Robbie, making half-perverse gestures to the girls they were after that term, to notice that Hannah and Leslie were sitting in Simone's chair. Like all of the others in the auditorium, it was a small, hard chair, uncomfortable even when occupied by only one person, despite the elevated status and sanction that Simone's repeated use of it had bestowed. They each sat balanced on the edge of one half of the chair like the two-headed monster they were.

Simone's reaction, at first sight of them, could not have been any more dramatic if they actually had been some grotesque fairy-tale creature. When she was about five feet away from them, she looked up from the stack of papers she had been riffling through and pulled back physically when she saw that her throne had been breached. Even those of us close enough to see her look of horror knew she wasn't going to say anything. She couldn't. She was supposed to be one of the nice ones, after all. She couldn't possibly mind finding somewhere else to sit just this once. Seats weren't officially assigned. Everyone else sat in a different spot each night. It was a wonder someone hadn't taken it unknowingly sooner. She couldn't begrudge two students, whom she was there to serve, really, a place to sit. She took a seat one level and two rows farther down—squarely in their line of sight—offering herself as prey as surely as the black mouse who runs out across the snowy field in front of an owl's favorite tree.

They waited until Linda took the podium to introduce the new head chef of the cafeteria to begin. The noises they made were an unmistakable nod to Simone's verbal acknowledgments of the points and beautiful lines that speakers and readers made and read each night. Coming from where they did, it was that much easier to place where we had heard these noises before. We all *mmm-hmmmm*ed and *ahhhh*ed throughout the presentations the auditorium saw—it was a common MFA courtesy, at least at Fielding—but Simone was a woman who liked to be heard above the crowd. Leslie and Hannah's version of it was no more discreet than Simone's, but there was something hard in their imitation. Something violent. It almost sounded involuntary, compulsive, but the extent to which they were in sync betrayed how premeditated it must have been. It was aggressive enough that while the rest of us didn't dare look back and risk encouraging them, making ourselves complicit or, worse, descending into laughter we'd never regain control of, we did silently elbow one another with wide eyes and tight, closemouthed smiles that didn't hide the real, bursting levels of naughty joy we felt. Only Simone looked back. It was clear she couldn't help it. We almost felt sorry for her, looking as small and ordinary as she did down in her less prominent, mortal seat, turning up to face whatever this was.

They were relentless in their noisemaking. They *ooh*ed when the student activities director announced that yoga had been added to this term's list of classes available during free periods, and *mmmmm*ed when the president of the graduating class got up to say a few words about the graduates' class gift. Sometimes it was in unison and sometimes their hums leapt out in solos that almost sounded louder than their combined force. Other than a few pointed looks from nearby faculty members, no one reprimanded them, and we were reminded once again how powerful plain old human audacity can be. It's hard to reprimand someone for doing something so strange that it hasn't been expressly forbidden. That Jo Ann Beard was in the third row of the auditorium and Geoff Dyer was two chairs away from the girls incited these faculty members' anger, making their pointed looks sharper as the orientation wore on, but also made that anger completely agency-less. They couldn't afford to make any more of a scene than the girls already were.

Simone looked back and up at them every time, too

startled for her looks to be challenging. She forgot, each time, that her reputation required that she smile at them, so that the gesture was clearly empty by the time she thought to make it. The third time Simone looked back, Leslie actually waved. It wasn't difficult to see that Simone was rattled, trying hard to keep her gaze straight ahead but helpless to stop herself, like the jilted lover who spots her ex in the wild with the woman he's upgraded to—breezy, *I'm over it* body language with *I'm already crying about this on the inside* eyes.

She should've tried harder. She should've bit her lip and squared her shoulders and lied. It was really over that first day, when they realized they had her. It's almost disappointing how easy it was.

We get it, though. This isn't the undergrad program or summer camp that it sometimes feels like. Even the babies among us are old enough to have lost people and walked out on places we could never return to and said things we couldn't take back, no matter how good or bad each of us is or was at translating these things into words on a page. We've all felt things so strongly that no part of our bodies will lie about it, even if it might be better if they could.

We know, too, that feeling Simone must've had that last time she turned around and saw that Leslie and Hannah were both staring at the dead center of her back without betraying any of the emotion she was, their pretty faces slack. We had all felt our stomach pits bloom at the first indication that the price for some random, lonely sin that we thought had been overlooked or forgotten would be larger than the amount we had budgeted.

We knew that sometimes the world would let you take without giving anything back and that other times, well—other times the world had something entirely different in mind.

On the third day of the residency, there was a cocktail party at dusk to celebrate Pearl's forthcoming book, and to wish him well in retirement. Everyone was there, even Jiles Gardner, who rarely made it to anything but workshop. It was one of those slow, sunset-cocktail affairs at which the dropping sun promises to keep pace with your drinking, and you can't seem to turn around without someone topping off your glass, the kind of event more common at five-hundred-dollar-a-night hotels than on campus lawns. Being part of the student body this residency, we were starting to discover, was better even than being one of the spoiled, entitled undergrads. Certainly there was more champagne. Even the middle child has a wedding day.

We tried to rise to the occasion. Patrick Stanbury stood talking to Carter, who was holding a tray of champagne flutes. The impossibly tall figure Patrick cut was even harder not to notice now that he wore a pressed collared shirt that hung on him with the formality of a three-piece suit and only made us love him more. Carter kept reaching over to try to button Patrick's top button to hide the top of the lettering on the T-shirt beneath, putting his champagne charges in a precarious position that would have worried us if we didn't feel confident that there was plenty more of it. Tammy kept walking up and down the length of the food table, grabbing generous portions from the towers of shrimp the pink of baby-girl nurseries and circles of cheese so richly stinky you could smell them from feet away. She stopped only to ask people if they had tried this or that with half-masticated wads of whatever it was still in her mouth. Jibs stood at the periphery, trying not to reveal how delighted she was to be at an event like this, complaint beyond even her.

At the center of it all was Leslie, her Cyndi Lauper hair as blond as it had ever been, in a silk slip dress the color of a fresh head wound. That her last shampoo job was on at least its third day and that she had paired the dress with purple hightops might've made people less familiar with Leslie think the dress was an afterthought, something she just had lying around. We knew her well enough to notice that the dress still had the folds from the box it had been shipped to campus in from whatever high-end department store it had been summoned. We kept looking over at her, waiting for her to do something to undermine the glamour of it all, like stick a cocktail shrimp in the clutch that even Tammy recognized as expensive. That Hannah, with whom she had arrived, was circulating separately, making friendly, noncommittal chit-chat with the rest of us, only made us more unnerved. Though we had little actual evidence to confirm it, we liked to think that Hannah often kept Leslie from going beyond the limits she was constantly testing.

Leslie had just said something to the non-Carter champagne waiter that made him laugh and hand her a second glass of champagne when Professor Pearl approached her, so she had two glasses to raise toward him in greeting. The waiter took a step back to let them talk.

"Leslie," he said, nodding. "You look well."

"Well, free champagne looks good on everybody," she said. "Speaking of which. Here." She held out one of her flutes to him, which he declined with a smile.

"No. Thank you. I prefer something a little stronger, but only after dark."

"I respect that," she said. "But it's probably bad luck not to drink at your own party, unless it's to celebrate your AA anniversary. Though I'm guessing that's not the kind of thing you'd worry about."

"No," he said. "I think I'll rest easy on that front. Although I'm not completely without concerns this evening."

At this, we suspended our chewing and dress rustling and champagne sipping.

So. He knew something was up. He probably didn't know what it was, but Leslie's name on a volunteer sign-up sheet and her assembly murmurings were hard to ignore, even she had to know. Only Pearl would use an occasion like this to press the issue, probably hoping the champagne would help, or maybe looking for a distraction from a spotlight that was blinding.

"What can I do to help?" she asked. She said it completely free of sass or petulance or irony, so that it almost sounded like she was really offering her services in earnest.

"I've noticed that certain unwanted attention has been paid to some of the faculty by some of the students." He said this with a look so direct and piercing, it left no uncertainty about the students in question.

Leslie bought herself some time by finishing one of her champagnes in two thick sips, an improbably graceful, swan-like gesture that she capped with a smile that drew all of us closer still. Hannah stepped away from the small circle she had formed with Tanner and Melissa, where she had generously made a joke at her own expense to fill an awkward silence between them just before everyone stopped talking. She took a few tentative steps toward where Pearl and Leslie stood but then stopped, satisfied just to be close enough to intervene if she needed to.

"I hope you're not implying it's me," Leslie said.

Pearl stayed silent, making it clear that he didn't consider this an answer.

The party had fallen silent enough, waiting for Leslie's

response, that we could hear children laughing somewhere on the edge of campus, out of sight.

"Professor Pearl, I'm not here to cause trouble," Leslie finally said, just after the last laugh had faded to nothing. "I'm here to drink as much free champagne as humanly possible."

"Suit yourself," he said. "But even the highest bar tab at the nicest restaurant is a hell of a lot lower than what this place charges these days. So I hope you'll reconsider before your last residency." He started to turn away from her.

She let her body collapse in frustration that he was ruining a perfectly good joke. Hannah opened her mouth to say something but Leslie spoke before she could, leaving Hannah's mouth dangling, the only awkward, half-intentional gesture any of us can remember on her.

"Okay. Fine," Leslie said. "I'm here to write the *best* thesis that this school has ever seen." She closed her eyes on the word *best*, like she was savoring something delicious.

Pearl paused, but still didn't turn all the way back toward her, appeased but not completely satisfied with this addendum. "Well, all right, then," he said, before he started to walk away.

She almost looked disappointed that he hadn't tried to talk her out of whatever she was planning with any more conviction, or even acknowledged more openly that he saw what they were doing. Leslie still liked Pearl, we knew, even after the betrayal she had witnessed from the barn the semester before. Maybe not in the same way she liked Hannah, or even

Jimmy, but she respected him, and she was maybe even more like him than the others in certain ways. She could smell on him the exact sort of wisdom she most needed. She had a sort of wild, dangerous intelligence that was often at the root of the trouble she got into, and she saw in him a similar intelligence, a certain way of looking at the world, that had settled in him in a way that it had not quite settled in her, and in a way that she probably hoped it might one day, despite a confidence that was as wild as her intelligence. If there was anyone who might've inspired her to change course, it was him, despite her normal distaste and disregard for most forms of authority.

She waited until he was a good twenty feet away from her before finishing the second champagne and flagging down the waiter she had been laughing with to take both empty glasses away. It was only after she had dismissed him with her chin, his disappointment at not getting another opportunity to flirt with her as pronounced as the smudged fingerprints on the flutes he was holding, that she turned toward Pearl's retreating figure. On the distant horizon of the direction he was heading, we saw a fugitive balloon floating up into the sky, and hoped the laughing children we still hadn't seen had thought enough to make a wish before they let it go.

We kept waiting for Hannah to do something to fix this with the sort of grace only she was capable of—for her to bring everyone back together and make it all right. But while she was still turned to Leslie and Pearl the way the rest of us were, her mouth was firmly closed by then. We see now that while Leslie might have been acting largely on Hannah and Jimmy's behalf, there are acts and words and turns in the story that belonged solely to Leslie—that she was doing simply because she needed to do them—and Hannah knew Leslie well enough to know this.

When Leslie called Pearl's name to summon him back he stopped and bowed his head, almost like he was praying.

"Aren't you going to wish me luck?" Leslie asked.

At this, he turned to face her.

"And why would you need that?" he asked.

"You know. On writing the best thesis this school has ever seen? You won't be here when I graduate. So this is probably it. Your last chance." She meant it playfully, we knew, but it came out wounded, like that middle child on her wedding day, waiting for a compliment from a withholding father.

He smiled at her, a smile more amused than happy, and not big enough to hide the kind of sadness that shows in the eyes, even from twenty feet away. "I wish you way more than luck."

Fielding was a place where word choice matters. It's the kind of thing people notice more than what you're wearing or how long it's been since your last shower. Maybe they notice, but they're less likely to judge you on those things than they are by what you say, or write. Just as Joni had remembered Leslie's exact word choice in Pearl's office, Leslie would always remember the exact seven words Professor Pearl used, saying good-bye and setting her loose that day. Not just *I wish you more than luck* or *I wish you far more than luck*. Pearl had a rule against modifiers and informalities that might be defended as colloquialisms—the only rules he held you to every time. But he knew, it was clear to Leslie that day, that the rules for writing were different from the rules for life. Sometimes more was more, and you had to let someone know how much you really meant something.

She would always love him a little for that *way*.

She didn't let it show that afternoon, though. She retreated to the discreet half embrace Hannah had waiting for her, then mingled with the remaining crowd with a friendly, extroverted relish that hung far less naturally on her than the gash-colored dress did. We pretended not to notice that for every third person she talked to, she looked up to search the crowd for Pearl, turning back to her companion of the moment only after she had successfully located him, the way we imagined the laughing children tracked that fugitive balloon until it had completely vanished from the sky. We assumed she was planning to talk to him again, to leave things on less wistful a note. She became looser—more fluid in her hand movements and bigger in her laugh—with every person she talked to. In our most generous interpretation of the day's events, each person she talked to increased her goodwill toward the place, as did each glass of champagne, all of which she wanted to pass on to him.

As the final act of the sun's descent began, reminding everyone that this party would have an end, she went just outside the glowing orb the revelers made to smoke a cigarette with Jiles against the horizon. It was an activity he preferred to engage in alone, but she was apparently the one person he didn't seem to think was one long running joke. And though she returned to the party in a fit of champagne-and-nicotine giggles, and both she and Jiles smiled the smile of people who know where the after party would be, we all saw her shoulders slump when she looked around and found that, in a move only he could make inoffensive, Professor Pearl had left his own party twenty minutes before it was scheduled to end.

We all woke up the morning after the cocktail party with hangover melancholy, and while we knew these feelings were standard morning-after stuff, we also knew it wasn't just the alcohol. We were also a little blue that the party had come and gone, and that we had nearly reached the halfway point of the residency. Now that we knew firsthand how much better Junes were than Januarys, we knew that we'd have to wait another year to see the campus in its full glory again, and by then we'd be graduating.

We were also starting to understand how singular this particular residency was, with all its glamorous touches and extra events. We might not have been the ones the program was trying to impress, but the effect it had was uncontainable, and floated freely around the campus and through our open windows. The program normally tried to keep the writing process and the concept of craft—what we were there to learn—separate from the publishing industry. They warned us over and over against the danger of focusing too much on what would become of our work at the expense of making that work as good as it could possibly be. As different as they all were from one another, every faculty member had a horror story about publishing something before it was ready to be read. They all assured us that the only thing worse than not being published was publishing something too early, and having to see anything less than your best work with your name on it for years after you had put it out into the world. They made publication seem like such a distant notion that it had nothing to do with what we were doing here, which was of course maddening even if we knew on some level that what they were saying was true. But here, now, people were coming from the city, where books were bought and fixed and made into real, tangible *things* that sat on bookstore shelves and made their way into people's homes to give them the sort of solace and joy and confusion and anxiety and good company that the books on our own shelves had given us. These people worked in the shiny upper levels of the skyscrapers most of us had seen only on postcards and television shows and movies. They knew the exact coordinates of the Random House building and what the cafeteria there served. They weren't here to celebrate us, fine, or even acknowledge us, but with all these spectacled people who looked far too pale for June among us, the fact that publication was a real thing seemed impossible to deny. This was all becoming clearer and clearer to us as the residency bore on and the champagne flutes and speeches mounted, but so, too, was the fact that this residency would be the only one of its kind. We were trying to figure out how to make last the unnameable feeling we all later pinpointed as hope when we remembered that the girls' bonfire was scheduled for that night. Without saying anything to one another, we all realized that the only thing more elusive and titillating than the idea of publication was the idea of the kind of party Leslie would throw if she ever threw one or, more to the point, decided we were worth inviting.

She didn't disappoint us.

We all went as one group, partly out of excitement, none of us wanting to arrive a minute later than anyone else, and partly out of skepticism, or an unwillingness to be the only one to show up for a party that wasn't actually being thrown. Leslie hadn't sent a follow-up email about the bonfire, or mentioned so much as a word about it to any of us who had seen her in the hours just before it. None of us wanted to arrive alone only to discover that of course the field where she had told us to meet was empty. She hadn't been serious, or it had been a stray thought she had sent out into the world as soon as it occurred to her, never to think about it again once it moved from her brain to her mouth to our ears. We might've emailed Hannah to confirm, but there was no set of feelings on the planet we less wanted to hurt than Hannah's, and given how reliable and kind she'd always been, it felt wrong to question something she'd told us directly.

Lefferts Field was the last man-maintained patch of land on campus before the woods that surrounded campus began. It was more of a clearing than a field, big enough for Lefferts Cottage, the most remote housing building on campus, and a semicircular patch of flat, uninterrupted grass that sat in front of it. Clusters of trees surrounded the building on all sides so that it looked a little like the building and the clearing had predated the forest, which was slowly but steadily migrating forward to swallow the building whole, even if the opposite was true. Admissions to the school grew every year, to both the graduate and undergraduate programs, and it was only a matter of time before more trees were cleared to make room for new buildings, and new patches of grass for students to sun themselves on.

Because we all went together, we all saw what the girls had turned Lefferts Field into at exactly the same time.

They'd somehow dragged colorful couches and retro lamps and organized it all so that the field looked like a rich man's living room or a cocktail bar in Paris. It was impossible to tell, without closer inspection, which parts of the gentlemen's parlor in front of us were natural, and which they had paid some lonely soul to help them lug halfway across the campus. What at first appeared to be a rug was actually a blanket of wildflowers, we realized only as we walked across it and felt the petals tickle the soles of our feet. By the time they lit the colorful

Christmas lights they had strung throughout the trees that lined the perimeter of the clearing, we would've believed the light they produced was from fairies living in the trees. We noticed the giant stack of weathered books sitting just to the left of the flower rug only when Jamie Brigham kneeled to look through them and Leslie, who had been standing uncharacteristically silent next to Hannah in the middle of the clearing, shouted "Stop" with such urgency that he dropped an ancient-looking copy of *The Comfort of Strangers* so that it landed wide open and facedown on top of the pile.

Hannah gave Leslie a look that made her soften her message before any of us could react to it.

"Sorry—I just don't want anyone to get the wrong book. They were chosen with such care by this one," she said, popping her head in Hannah's direction. "You know how she can be."

Hannah smiled a smile full of the preternatural patience and Zen Leslie must've required of her often, but didn't say anything.

"So, anyway, here's the deal," Leslie went on, not the sort to have patience for even patient smiles when she was as moved or energized by an idea or activity as she was by this one. "There's a book here for everyone—either a book we think you'd like, or a book we think you embody, or an author we think reminds us of your writing. The intended recipient's name is written on the title page."

We all started fidgeting at once, each of us eyeing the pile for our favorite classics, already starting to get defensive that a certain title we spotted might be associated with us at the same time we felt indignant that others might be associated with someone else in the class. Leslie saw our restlessness and, firm in her resolve to make us behave the way she wanted us to, started talking louder and faster.

"Only open books you think might be intended for you. This is a guessing game, not a race to see who can open the most books in a certain amount of time, wearing out the spines of these books that were, quite frankly, kind of expensive, at least some of them." She looked at Lucas when she said this, which the rest of us thought was fair, but to which he gave her *What the fuck, me?* eyes that she ignored. "And for the love of God, if you pick up a book that was intended for someone else, do *not* tip them off and ruin the fun for them. No one likes that guy."

When she didn't say anything after this, giving no explicit indication that the hunt should begin, it was Hannah we all looked at, knowing, somehow, that while Leslie was the face of whatever this was, and maybe even the brain, Hannah was the heart. She didn't seem surprised by the attention, or that she was the one we came to. She nodded, and we all lunged at once.

They both watched us stumbling around like the loving parents of toddlers at an Easter egg hunt, but couldn't have reacted more differently to our incorrect guesses, of which of course there were many. Leslie delighted in our wrongheaded notions about ourselves, and how far off the mark we inevitably were. When Patrick Stanbury picked up *The Basketball Diaries* she cackled a cackle we had never heard before, equal parts affection and wickedness before she said, "Uh, yeah, right. We're at the graduate level here, P. It's gonna be a *little* harder than that." She relished in stumping us every time, never flagging in her evident joy even as we slowed in the pace at which we opened books, more pointed now in every guess.

Hannah was the patient, encouraging parent whom you go to at midnight the night before the big math test, when you're out of time and you're still getting the wrong answer to a problem after a hundred different approaches to solving it. She gave us clues without even making us ask for them, clues that weren't condescending or insulting—clues that didn't give away the answer, implying that we would never land on it ourselves, but that flipped the contexts and settings of our brains so that the answers descended independently of her, little gifts from heaven. When Tanner Conover picked up *Romeo and Juliet*, looking across the book pile at Melissa with something we might've called love if we didn't know any better, she was gentle in her suggestion that he think about the masculinity of his prose, saying nothing to hint that whatever existed between him and Melissa, it was lesser or more ordinary than what Shakespeare had been trying to capture. Watching them together, trading off their responses to our guesses, careful that none of us went too long in our hunt without some sort of loving attention, be it playful or doting, without even making eye contact with each other, we saw, suddenly, why they made so much sense together.

It was shocking, in the end, how well they knew us. Not a single one of us left that clearing, or looks back on the day, with even a hint of resentment, or that crippling feeling of being misunderstood, even in the art form we had undertaken to help clarify to the world what we felt and thought. Though we did all later confess that we were secretly afraid that we would be the only ones for whom there wasn't a book. We just couldn't imagine that Hannah or Leslie had thought about us long enough to have any idea what we read or who we wrote like. It was a fear that gripped each of us until the very moment we saw our names on the title pages of books that rose in our estimation the moment we saw ourselves in them.

Even now, knowing what we do, it's flattering to think of this day—of the amount of time they must have put into it, both immediately before, buying the books, many of which were rare or expensive first editions, and all the days before it, to have any idea of something as personal as which authors we loved, or might. It's still irresistible, the idea that we meant anything to them, given how much they meant to us. How much they mean to us still.

None of it had anything to do with us.

Because they were on the volunteer committee, Leslie and Hannah knew Simone's room was in Lefferts Cottage in the middle of Lefferts Field, and that she was the only person to have a room in the otherwise empty residence hall. There were rumors that Simone had requested the empty building so that there would be room for all her city guests, who were scheduled to arrive for the residency's final events and feting. This gossip gave only more credibility to other rumors, about the announcements those final events would hold, but only the girls had any insight into housing matters. Leslie waited until it was just dark enough that we needed the Christmas lights to do more than set a tone to suggest that we get to work on the bonfire. She said this like she had just then thought of the idea, her voice uncharacteristically breezy. Simone wrote to classical music—she recommended it to all her workshops, claiming it had lent itself to the timelessness of her work—so she wouldn't have heard our merrymaking, but there would be no missing a fire the magnitude of which the girls had planned.

Buoyed as we were by the books tucked in our bags, and still feeling misty-eyed about the generosity of what Leslie and Hannah had planned for us and maybe even feeling a little guilty that we might have misjudged them, we set about the task with relish equal to the one Leslie had shown at our incorrect guesses. We were so busy lugging wood, ignoring the splinters that inevitably jammed their way up under nails, and the smears of dirt and bark that were starting to stain the only set of party clothes we had packed for the entire residency, that the long list of rules we were breaking didn't immediately occur to us. We didn't think about the notice we had all read in the handbook, and which had been read to us at each of the three welcome orientations we had now attended, about how matches and candles and lighters were prohibited in any of the living residences, and that smoking was a strictly outdoor business everywhere on campus. We tried not to let our minds get too close to the surprisingly fierce language the administration had used in their email about the bonfire Leslie and Hannah had lit anonymously in Adam's Square at the end of the residency before—the administration normally treated us like a favorite, prized student, respect and admiration apparent in their syntaxes and tone, which had been absent enough in this one particular dispatch that we all should have remembered it six months later. We tried hardest of all not to think of the two senior undergraduates who died in a fire that had been started by a joint someone had tossed in the bushes outside the main residence hall back when the school was still a women's college, even though we all loved the ghost stories that the incident had borne.

In far less time than it had taken us to correctly identify the books intended for us, we had gathered a pile of wood so towering only a dozen people or more could've built it, and would ignite a bonfire of comparable magnitude. We had all been dragging our kindling finds to Leslie's feet, which she encouraged by not moving from her spot once we started bringing them to her, and it was only once we had finished and stepped back to admire our work that we saw how close to the building the pile really was. When Jenny Ritter, who had spent a not insignificant portion of the last six years of her life reminding actual children not to play with matches, wondered out loud what the rest of us had been thinking—if the pile wasn't *too* close to the building, and should be moved—Leslie made a pish-posh *nonsense* noise.

She raised her hands dramatically overhead, as if trying to distract us from our worries, or wave them away. She looked like a third-grade teacher on a field trip, eager to regain the attention and control of her class. "All right, guys," she said, pulling one oversize match from the front pocket of her overalls, "who wants to do the honors?"

Despite the handbook warnings and the dead girls and the January email that had felt like it was scolding us as much as it was scolding Hannah and Leslie, we all raised our hands without hesitation, both instinctively and fully committed. When Leslie took a full five seconds to scan all our faces, making it clear she wasn't choosing at random, before extending the match to Margaret Jibs, we might've been a little hurt, or even started to doubt that she knew us as well as the books had made us think, given how unworthy a recipient she had chosen for what suddenly seemed like an honor. Now that we knew the girls had been paying more attention to us than we had ever dared to hope, we wanted to know what it was they had seen. This was the night we started to think of ourselves as characters in the story they were telling, however peripheral. And we were eager to know what roles they had planned for us.

But there wasn't time for that yet. Jibs made quick work of the task she had been selected for, and the pile went up in flames with such angry velocity and blinding magnitude that we would later wonder if Leslie had doused the wood in the field with lighter fluid before we arrived, though even the most convinced theorists would concede they hadn't smelled anything.

Later, Mimi would say that when the face first appeared in the window, she assumed it was another surprise that Leslie had conjured just for us. Some whimsical, half-real, half-pretend creature that only Leslie's brain was capable of creating.

Though Mimi's thought hadn't occurred to us, we recognized the feeling she was talking about—excitement and anticipation, maybe even a little bit of wonder—and remembered having it, out there on the edge of where the campus met the woods, even if only for a moment before anxiety replaced it. It didn't take long to see that the face in the glass was very much human, and very angry. Or agitated, at the very least, stimulated to the highest degree of unhappiness even if the face didn't yet know what precise form that unhappiness should take—fear or anger or sadness. We all pinpointed whom the face belonged to before it had time to express its decision.

Simone.

We all turned and ran at the same time. We ran in such a blinding, desperate state of panic that we didn't notice anything other than the heavy thud of our hearts and the dryness of our mouths. It was all we could do just to watch for debris in front of us, and stay on our feet. It was only later, when we were safely in the lounge of the third-term dorm building most of us were staying in—too scared of being fingered for the crime we had just unwillingly committed even to show our faces in the student center—that Jordan commented how strange it was, the last thing he had seen in the clearing. Loath as he was to do anything to jeopardize his good standing with the faculty, Jordan was also a good enough guy that he stayed behind to make sure the rest of us got away safely before taking off at the sprint he was capable of, the all-American titles of his college career resurfacing all these years later, ghosts every bit as present as the dead girls. So he was the last one to flee the scene. He made us press him on what he had seen that was so strange, of course.

"Leslie went in the opposite direction of the rest of us, closer to the window Simone was looking out of instead of as far away as she could possibly get." Jordan ran his hands through his hair as he said this—a tic he'd had as long as we'd known him—even though they were covered with dirt and ash, his normally pristine nails black. We all took a moment to wonder how the fact that his hands were literally dirty should be worked into the story later.

None of us believed him. Jenny Ritter said even her six-year-old would know better than that, and Tammy said that while Leslie was probably crazy enough to get off on an insanity defense, she wasn't dumb enough to come right out and tattle on herself for so expellable an offense. But Jordan said he saw it as clear as his hand in front of his face. He said Leslie walked up to the window until her face was so close to it her lipstick might've left marks on the glass if she had been wearing any. He said she was mouthing something. Two lone words, again and again. He said that at first Simone ignored her, looking past her, at all the fleeing people, curious, and probably alarmed, at whatever they were running from. He said at first he couldn't make out what Leslie was saying, and that it was only when Simone started freaking out that he realized what it was. We couldn't imagine any two-word combination stronger than *fuck you*, and Simone wasn't the type to get worked up about something even as aggressive as that, and we said as much.

"No," Jordan said. "'*Get out.*'"

It was so far off from what we were imagining Leslie chanting by then, over and over, that at first we thought Jordan meant *Oh, get out of here, no one would put up with someone saying* fuck you *to them. Certainly it would have warranted the reaction I saw.* When his words were met with only blank, noncomputing faces, he clarified.

"That's what she was saying, again and again. 'Get out.' With her mouth only, not with actual words, and Simone thought she meant to get out of the building, I think. Because it was on fire. She started to panic because she thought Leslie was telling her she needed to get out, and quickly."

Apparently Simone tried to open the window, but, like so many of the other ancient windows across campus, it was painted shut, which is when Simone really became unhinged, according to Jordan.

"Has anybody read her novel?" Penny asked. "Simone's, I mean."

Penny so rarely spoke when she hadn't been the one to organize the event she was speaking at that we all flipped our heads in her direction as quickly as if she'd just handed over some missing piece of the story that explained Leslie's actions, which we were still a few moments away from realizing that she had.

"You're the only one who reads the books of the faculty members they *don't* have," said Jibs in a voice so snooty it reminded us of how we had felt when Leslie picked her to light the match.

"It's about a small town that's just had a string of fires," said Penny, impressing us by ignoring Jibs.

"Uh, *no*, it isn't." Robbie took no small pleasure in this correction. "It's about a bunch of blond chicks getting stabbed while they run through the forest in slow motion."

"That's the movie," Penny said, still undeterred. "They aren't stabbed in the book. They die in fires someone started intentionally. I mean, it's still young girls, and they're still the ones who narrate the story. The dead girls, I mean, from the grave. But in the book, it's fire."

Without Penny or anybody else having to say it, we knew that this meant fire was high on the list of things that kept Simone up at night. We all wrote about our biggest fears in our work, inevitably—sometimes intentionally and sometimes against all efforts to the contrary.

It's why none of Hannah's protagonists would ever have mothers, and Leslie's characters might eventually fuck in the parts of her stories past the samples she gave us to workshop, again and again, and in detail that made even the married accountants among us blush, but none of them would ever be in love, even when they said they were. The same reason that the wayward sons and daughters in Pearl's novel never did make it home. We also knew that Leslie knew as much about what made people write the things they wrote about as anyone, and that Penny was probably not the only one in our class to have read Simone's novel.

"I don't know about all that," said Jordan, who was eager to get to the end of his story, used to juries who weren't allowed to interrupt him. "But I know that Simone worked herself into a complete fury, looking this way and that for who knows what. She looked like a woman who had lost her mind and didn't know which way to run after it. It was a good few head turns before I turned to see that she was finally making her way toward the door."

Jordan said the last time he stopped in his pursuit of the rest of us to turn around, Simone had made it out to the clearing—past the door that she couldn't lock, and the eight lonely rooms that stood empty between her and the closest exit, past the plaid couch and baby grand piano of the common room. By the time she got far enough outside to see that the flames had been part of a planned—and controlled—fire, she was as agitated as she had been on the other side of the window, still searching frantically for some invisible person or thing for clarification, but now because she couldn't understand why Leslie had made her think she was in danger, or where she had gone. The fire was out by then, so thoroughly doused that not a single spark or ember still burned. And Leslie was gone, so completely disappeared into thin air without a trace that even Jordan hadn't seen where she went.

By now Simone must have been really starting to panic, because she wasn't at the next evening's event. Though it wasn't held expressly in her honor, her book was part of the general elevated buzz of the term, and our campus guests were certainly expecting her, if not eager to talk to her. She would normally rather be caught reading a mass market erotica novel than keep these people waiting, we knew. Just as we knew they started the event late because they were waiting for her to arrive. Pearl kept looking off in the direction of Lefferts, then back at the gathering crowd. It didn't occur to us until much later that it was also the direction of the housing for visiting guests, and that it might have been his daughter he was hoping to spot on the horizon. Guests had been arriving steadily for the last day or two. We didn't know much more about his daughter than we had that first term—we would eventually learn her name was Ana—but it did seem like Pearl spent this term waiting for some happening or arrival outside of Leslie and Hannah's machinations. But who's to say what hopes each person pins on their fugitive balloons as they ascend. Everyone knows if you say them out loud, they won't come true.

Pearl finally gave the *okay* nod for the program to commence at fifteen past the hour.

None of us knew what to expect of the event, which was held out on the main lawn. It was listed in our schedules as simply "20 Years: A Look Back." When we were still out on the distant edge of the lawn it became clear that we were going to be watching something—a giant movie screen had been put in the center of the lawn, drive-in-movie-theater style, with white wedding ceremony chairs where the cars would've gone. Maybe it was the absence of a bar table to the right or left of the screen, or maybe it was the formality of the chairs' arrangement when we'd been looking forward to idle chitchat with one another, rather than another presentation that would demand the silence and mental isolation that our days were already so full of. But we realized, seeing the screen, that we were starting to feel antsy at the festivities we were awash in instead of anticipatory, restless instead of eager. We were reminded that there was a danger of staying too long at the party.

Once everyone was settled and the sea of chairs was completely full, with a row or two of people standing behind it, Pearl gave one last anxious look toward Simone's residence building out on the wilds of campus. Seeing not even a trace of a distant figure approaching, or any indication that there might be one soon, he signaled to the two undergrads who tended the AV needs above and beyond the grasp of a bunch of writers, and the screen jumped to life.

It started as a montage of program graduates' accolades—grainy black-and-white photos of writers from their dust jackets next to compilations of praise for their master works, and action shots of graduates with other noted writers, in one case even President Clinton. There were shots of graduates holding up their National Book Award finalist medals, and other, lesser trophies, and even tabloid-esque pictures of authors at the Hollywood premieres of the movies that had been adapted from their books. It was a little self-satisfied, we all recognized, and maybe a little desperate in its aim to impress the better-dressed, more professional-looking members of the crowd, but even though none of our books would be featured in the video because none of us had so much as a first draft of a novel, it revived us, lending more effervescence than even the priciest champagne could have, giving us more evidence that good things came of the course we were on. That people who had been where we were had ended up exactly where we wanted to go. We took comfort in the perfectly straight lines of wooden soldiers that the chairs we were sitting in made. There was order here, and logic—A led to B. Do the work and end up where these people had.

We were all so busy imagining what the review excerpts about our own work would say when it was us illuminating the empty lawns of Vermont, and what we would wear for our own author photos, and whether we would smile in them or not, that we didn't notice right away when the video shifted its focus from accolades to memorials.

We were three ghosts in before they flashed one that we all recognized—one of the founding poets of the program, who had won the Pulitzer just before ceding to the cancer she had been battling for years without telling anyone—tipping us off to what this portion of the montage would contain. We had barely had enough time to adjust our postures and resting faces accordingly, somber now instead of buoyed and hopeful, when Jimmy dropped in. He appeared on the screen so much bigger than he ever had in life, at the very moment that we had forgotten about him, or stopped equating whatever it was the girls were up to directly with his absence. He looked like a normal boy in his picture. It made us remember that so many of his haunted qualities were in the way he carried himself. That he had been born just like any of us, and that it was but for the grace of God or whatever else the world ran on that we hadn't ended up like him.

We were so surprised to see Jimmy's face that we didn't immediately think to look over at the girls, as if they had somehow been responsible for it. They seemed to us, by then, capable of anything. It was clear when we finally did look at Hannah that the picture was as much a surprise to her as it was to us. The thing we remember about that night was not that seventeen Fielding alums' books had received rave reviews in the *New York Times Book Review* or that eight of them had been optioned by major Hollywood studios, or that two of our alums had been MacArthur "geniuses" in the last ten years. But Hannah's face when we looked over.

She was just so happy to see him again.

There can't have been too many pictures of Jimmy in the world—he wasn't on Facebook or any of the other social media platforms, and a Google image search of his name didn't turn up any pictures that were actually of him. Even Hannah's album named after him had been a picture of her. It was probably the first time Hannah had seen him since the last. We might've expected tears, or anger, or the furtiveness we had come to associate with the girls since January, but there was none of it. It was a face wide open. And when we feel guilty now about all that happened—when we're tempted to think of it all as a series of vengeful acts or anger or sadness turned to poison the way it will often turn—we're quick to remember Hannah's face at that moment. There was something good in the middle of all this, too—that thing a human face does when it recognizes some rare or sacred thing its owner has been so long without that they thought it might be gone forever. Maybe it's hope. Maybe it's relief. Maybe it's love. But whatever it was, it was there on Hannah's face that night, and surely wrapped up in all that happened before and after it.

The moment couldn't have lasted more than five seconds. As quickly and unexpectedly as he had arrived, Jimmy vanished, and was replaced by a Tribeca firefighter who had graduated from the program two years before dying at Ground Zero; his widow would write a *New York Times* bestselling memoir about him. Leslie *tsk*ed loudly when Jimmy's photo faded out, as if someone had committed some social faux pas or interrupted some important point she had been in the process of making. We knew this meant she had been glad to see him, too.

Two dead alums later, the video's music turned an upbeat corner, signaling its entry into candid shots that were meant to be intimate and goofy, and we all shifted in our seats and adjusted the hems of our skirts and the knots of our ties one last time. Tanner and Melissa sank into each other contentedly despite having bickered publicly all week, and Bridget Jameson turned and smiled when Tammy exclaimed happily at a picture of herself roasting a hot dog at The End of the World next to a trio of stray cats. Patrick Stanbury looked over his shoulder to nod at Carter, two seats down, acknowledging that he, too, was hoping for a shot of the two of them playing basketball at dusk. We all perched forward even more eagerly than we had during the accolades portion of the video, the better to identify our own faces among the floating images, happy at the possibility that we might hold a spot in this night, and in the history of this place.

Simone's missing key never turned up, of course. Missing things turn up only when they've been misplaced, not stolen. Simone must've known better than anyone that the more nefarious the reason for a thing disappearing, the less likely that it will ever reappear, which had probably been keeping her up in the small hours of the night by then, out there on one of the most remote edges of an already desolate, haunted place, a burned-out hole in the ground outside her window.

It's impossible to say whether Leslie and Hannah chose to make use of their hot property on the day they did because of the looming storm that everyone was talking about—one that was supposed to be so big and unrelenting that even a bunch of writers felt okay doing something as ordinary as talking about the weather. Maybe it was just luck. Throughout that entire June term it did seem like if the gods were out there, they were watching, making things just a little easier for the girls to do what they did, and a little more impossible for Simone to dodge it with any grace. But maybe we only remember it that way.

It was almost four by the time Simone got in the shower the afternoon after the memorial, an act less fugitive than it would have been for anybody else, given that she was maybe the only person on campus who showered every day. It was the beginning of that quiet stretch before dinner, quieter than usual that afternoon, since the storm had sent everybody into their rooms. The thunder was still distant rumbling by the time she had turned the hot water off and the mirror had started to bead, but the sky was gray enough that we all minded the warning implicit in the rumblings. In our own dorm rooms across campus, we closed our doors behind us and rifled through our things for granola bars and jars of peanut butter that would sustain us if even the hundred-yard walk to the cafeteria became unpassable. There would've been no one out—on campus or in the dormitory hallways—to take Simone's towel from where it hung between the door to her shower stall and the door to the communal bathroom. But when she reached for it, still humming whatever private tune she hummed under her breath as she rinsed the last of the expensive conditioner out of her expensive haircut, it was gone all the same. She probably kept reaching, her perfectly manicured grasp becoming more and more frantic before it drooped in acceptance of the fact that the towel really wasn't there.

We don't know if she pulled down the shower curtain she probably still wishes had been more opaque to fashion it into the clumsy toga she eventually wore for her journey across campus right away. We don't know if she already had it when she made that first dash back down the hall to her room, or if she did it naked, counting on the door she had left open being unlocked, which it wasn't, of course. Lefferts Cottage was likely as empty that afternoon as it always was, so maybe she just made a run for it, but that doesn't seem in keeping with the guarded, private woman we remember. We don't know if she was literally naked, or if she only felt like she was, when she pulled down the two sheets of paper that had been taped up to her unbreachable door: a page of poetry that Jimmy had sent her in one of his workshop packets and a Xeroxed page from her forthcoming book—the two uncomfortably similar lines from the two very different pieces of writing underlined in the exact same shade of red.

We don't know if she realized at only that moment what she had done—if what had felt like inspiration revealed itself to be something darker, or if all she felt, other than the breeze of the still empty hallway, was pure, physical panic at having been caught.

What we do know is that when she returned to the bathroom to cover herself she found two more sheets with a different set of matching lines underlined in that menacing shade of red she was probably really starting to hate by then. By the time she had the shower curtain wrapped around her as secure as possible using only the materials she could find in the bathroom, the sheets of paper were everywhere, leaving a trail even someone as confident and unflusterable a person as Simone would have no choice but to follow.

We all love the part of the story that comes next, and not only because everyone loves that moment in any story when it starts to look like the good guys might actually have a chance, underdogs though they may be. Even better when it's a true story, and it starts to look like it might be that one in a hundred times that David actually fells Goliath, which he so rarely does in real life. We still counted Hannah and Leslie as the good guys, even if they were the only ones who broke any rules or acted with any overt malice.

We still think of them that way now, and hope we're telling this story in a way that makes you see it that way, too.

We also love this part because we were all there to watch it. The quad that Simone scampered across after she left her lonely Lefferts hideaway is the quad that our third-term housing clustered around, which was part of the point. For this to be as humiliating as they intended it to be, Leslie and Hannah needed witnesses. Which means we're not only the keepers or tellers of this turn in the story. We're part of it. They could've made the trail that forced her out of her self-made seclusion lead anywhere. We like to think leading her from Lefferts all the way to us was no mistake, and that both girls, different as they were, were too savvy and meticulous in everything they did for that to be an accident.

We had seen other pieces of all this firsthand, of course—Hannah's outburst at Simone's reading, their big exit from the first graduation party in the student center. But it had felt then like we were reading their most private thoughts, hand-scrawled across journal pages. Even the bonfire staring contest had ultimately been between Leslie and Simone alone. But here, now, it felt like they were inviting us in, telling us a story they had written just for us.

We all remember what we were doing when we looked out to see Simone's tiny figure stumbling its way across the path the blowing papers dictated. Melissa Raymond was pacing back and forth across her dorm room in tiny steps that didn't suit her agitation, but were all the size of the room could accommodate, talking on the phone with her off-campus boyfriend, who had a lot of questions about the number and duration of times she had seen Tanner Conover that day, and the day before, for that matter. When she looked up and out at the quad she said "I have to go" in a voice so firm and certain that her boyfriend knew it was in response to something bigger and more important than her affair with Tanner ever would be. He didn't even object when she hung up on him without another word, but did call back later to find out what in the world had happened or what she had seen. Mimi and Sarah looked up from the fashion magazines they had hiked into town to buy. The pages were so glossy and shiny compared to everything else on campus, they didn't mind that all the issues on sale at the one grocery store in town were a month out of date, and that both of them had already flipped through sticky, dog-eared copies of the magazines in the nail salons and dentists offices of the cities they lived in in the Real World. When Mimi realized that the fluttering motion in the far upper-right-hand corner of her vision was not the flipping of magazine pages, she looked up. Neither of the girls said anything after she said "Hey" to get Sarah's attention and directed her with a nod toward the quad, and the strange, beautiful woman who was streaking across it. At almost the exact same moment, they turned back to each other and smiled, happy to know that their real lives would sometimes offer sights as stunning as the Kenyan model in platform shoes with cockatoos on her head in the *Vogue* that sat between them. Bridget Jameson looked up for only a minute from the workshop piece she was reading for the fifth time—the kindest, most diligent workshopper among us. Though she wouldn't report it to us, we knew she was reading it again not because it was so good, or inspiring, but because it was so bad, and she wanted to come up with a real, genuine compliment to give the writer at the following day's workshop, even if she had to take the story apart to find it. She turned back to the workshop piece after only a few moments—she had less than two free hours before the story was being workshopped, not counting the seven hours she had budgeted for sleep—and didn't have time to waste. As brief as the interruption was, though, we knew she would always associate Simone's trek with the story, and the tiny kernel of grace she would eventually find in it.

We didn't know, watching Simone bob and weave with clumsiness we wouldn't have believed a woman like her to be capable of, without seeing it for ourselves, what it was that she so desperately wanted to collect every last trace of. Only that she was desperate to a physical degree. If she hadn't been such a modern, technologically minded person, consulting her laptop for notes on students' work during workshop, we might've thought it was the sole copy of the novel everyone was in such fits to read. What we must've known, on some primal, instinctual level, even if it wasn't one of the things we murmured to one another after we left the privacy of our individual rooms to gather in the stairwell that provided a clearer view of the quad, was that Leslie and Hannah were behind this. And even further away, and dimmer in our collective consciousness, was the knowledge that they were too smart to surrender her only copy of something valuable enough that Simone would completely strip her dignity over it. It was a futile, beaten-before-you-start hunt, which made it only more disgraceful, and made us keep looking long after we knew we should turn away, and kept even the kindest and most noble among us—the Bridget Jamesons and Jamie Brighams, the Tammys and Jordan Marcums—from making even the emptiest gesture of assistance.

By the time we had congregated, the rain had gathered speed, the drops so big and close together they were one sheet of falling water, and the thunder was upon us, just over our shoulders instead of out on the horizon. One of the things we all loved most about Fielding was that there was very little between us and nature. We romped to lectures through fields of wildflowers and ate our meals with the sun on our faces, the grass convening with the backs of our thighs. Unfortunately, the same proximity was true of thunderstorms. We were *in* it, even huddled safely together in the stairwell.

"She needs to come in, like, now," Lucas said, his voice hanging low with worry, no joke to lighten the gravity of the situation. Robbie didn't jump in with his usual chorus of agreement, but turned instead to Sarah Jacobs, his face searching for some sort of comfort there.

"The lightning's getting closer," Jordan said, shaking his head in fatherly disapproval, still not making any sort of move to call Simone inside.

"Should we call Pearl?" Bridget asked. "I mean, I think he'd want to know about something like this."

"I mean, I think *everyone's* gonna know about it pretty soon," Jibs said, nodding down to the very public quad Simone was still moving slowly across."

"You guys don't think Hannah and Leslie would—"

But we never got to hear the first question Mimi ever asked instead of answered, because just then, we saw Simone spot the last speck of white paper on the quad before her, wedged into the lowest branch of the first tree signaling the end of the quad's wide-open stretch. She froze like the gazelle at the watering hole who realizes he isn't the only one who comes here for sustenance, contemplating whether to make a run for it or fold. We all knew what she was going to do before she leapt, every trace of her awkward lobster crawl gone, shed for the impossibly long arcs of an Olympian's valedictory gait. We saw, in the steady, unwavering line she made, the same determination that had finished two novels in four years.

Until the very moment the lightning hit the thickest branch of the tree the sheet was nestled in, we all felt confident she was going to get it.

We felt the force with which the branch smacked her crown as squarely as if it were hitting the person standing closest to each of us, even from as high up as we were, and across all that rain. She crumpled as if she were no more durable than the lone sheet of paper she had been after, the pages she had managed to retrieve still tucked tightly, firmly under her arm. Still her secret and burden alone, at least for another day.

The branch didn't kill her.

After Jordan called for help and went sprinting out onto the quad to look for a pulse that he immediately signaled up to us he was able to find. And the local paramedics came huffing and puffing across campus to arrive at their first real emergency in some time, judging from the labored paces they kept. After even Lucas and Robbie looked away from the moment the paramedics actually lifted her body onto the stretcher and the curtain that was never good enough to begin with fully betrayed her, and the all-student email canceling her workshop the following day, we all collapsed back into our rooms to see what would happen next.

Simone was back on campus for Leslie's big finish a few days later. By then even the most diligent students among us were attending workshops and lectures in body only, our minds assembling and reassembling the pieces of this story. Even Bridget had missed a mandatory craft lecture. We didn't feel guilty, though, or worry that we might not be getting the education we had paid for, because we were learning more than any workshop or lecture could've taught us. What Leslie and Hannah were executing was meticulously plotted, and revealed as many dark secrets of the human heart as the best Ian McEwan novel. It feels next to impossible to capture all that on the page, but maybe it always does. Maybe that's what writing is. What we want to make sure is clear, though, is that any shortcomings here are ours, and not the girls'. You can't blame a protagonist for a flaw in the plot—to them it's only life, messy and imperfect, and maybe better and truer for it.

It was a perfect day. We never would've dreamed of being late for what we had been called upon to do that morning, and not only because Leslie wasn't someone you kept waiting, afraid she might change her mind about showing you whatever it was she had called you over to see. It was a day so too-good-to-be-true that any excuse for tardiness would've immediately given itself away as false, no matter who delivered it, or how true it happened to be. It was the sort of day on which it felt like only good things could happen. Car accidents and heart attacks and even the far smaller bits of unluckiness that might delay you felt as foreign a concept, in weather like this, and in so beautiful a place, as the children's laughter had at a writing residency.

Standing in one tight cluster of third-years that morning, unified, finally, and for the first time, in the way that Penny had been trying to unify us since almost the beginning, and probably looking like a pack of traveling evangelicals to anybody who didn't know better, we practically glowed. In the white book-handing-out outfits Leslie had instructed us to wear, even Jenny Ritter's mom haircut looked fresh.

She had given us our orders in her Leslie way, leaving little room for uncertainty, the afternoon before, when we had all gathered for our second and final meeting about our class gift. Once again, the email instructing us on time and place came from Penny's account, but as soon as we arrived at the barn classroom it was clear that Leslie was still the one in charge.

Either Leslie or Penny had arranged the room so that there was the exact right number of chairs for us around the wooden table old enough to have hosted student protests in the sixties and seventies, and the first coed classes the college had ever offered. There was one bound, unmarked book in front of each chair, including the one where Leslie sat. She was flipping through her copy like it was the new Neiman Marcus catalog, breezily, but not uninterested. She waited until we were all seated before looking up at us.

"Okay, guys, on a scale of one to ten, how surprised are you that I came through on the class gift, which, obviously, is what's in front of you?"

Her smile was so winning, as she said this, that we were all tempted to try to produce a number, just because she'd asked for one. She held up a hand, two thoughts ahead of us as always.

"Don't answer that. The point is that our books are ready, and I think you guys are going to like what's here. And not only your own work." She smiled naughtily at that last possibility. "Here's the thing, though, it's not for the faint of heart, so I wanted to give you a chance to read what's here before you decide whether you're in or out. No one's name is on the book, so it's not too late."

At that point our eyes were divided between the books themselves and Leslie's face; the half of us who turned our gazes to the latter searched for some indication of what we would find inside the books. It never occurred to us to just open them without express permission from her.

"Well??" she said, disbelieving our hesitation. "Open them!"

What was on the page was Jimmy, plain and simple, although the combined effect of the crisscrossing phrases and lines and lone words in bold were anything but. It was his poem from the illicit second-term bonfire, yes, and other poems like it, and the Xeroxed pages of an early copy of Simone's novel with its offending passages underlined—we still haven't made any guesses as to how Leslie managed to get that—but also lines from his papers on the poets he read and wrote his mandatory packet papers on, and every combination of all those things again, and again. It was the sum of these things in every conceivable order they could've fallen in, so that in the end it was just a tornado of words you could practically feel migrating across each page that you turned to, falling into the shape of a boy we had once known.

Hannah was the one who had created and compiled what was actually in the books, that much was clear from the grip with which she held her own copy of it to her chest in the corner of the classroom where she stood, just behind Leslie's left shoulder. We hadn't noticed her there when we walked in, eager as we were to know what had been placed in front of us, and mesmerized as we were by Leslie's almost military presence. But in the few moments of silence after Bridget Jameson began weeping silently and Patrick Stanbury closed his eyes and rested the book against his forehead, and Melissa and Tanner looked for each other's hands under the table, even though they hadn't exchanged more than twelve words since their latest standoff, it occurred to all of us at almost the exact same moment that only Hannah could have made what this was. We all started looking for her at once, and there she was.

From the magnitude of Leslie's voice and gait and personality, from the strangeness of her workshop stories—legendary by then—and all the things she said and did that no other real live person we knew would ever do, it might have been easy or tempting to finger her as the mastermind or driving force behind their plan, but the book was at the center of it, to be sure, and that was pure Hannah. Only someone who loved him could've done what she did with Jimmy's words.

She'd cut them out and arranged them like flowers. She pasted them down—to keep them, or hold them—to make them stay. But each time she finished one layer she would start another, the words in a slightly different order, and wore the layers like armor from the fact that he wasn't actually there anymore. She had taken his best lines—the ones you knew were true as soon as you heard them—and scattered them throughout her own work, and then ours. Not plagiarism, memoriam. Not a shred of unoriginality, but elegy.

It was even more than that, we knew. If Jimmy's suicide was evidence of the limitations of writing and storytelling and the gaps they can bridge and the wounds they can mend or make manageable, here was evidence of just how much those things *could* do. We heard Jimmy's voice on the page in a way we'd never been able to in life, and it was impossible to drown out or play over, clear and permanent as it was, fixed for all eternity. It was maybe the only existing antidote for what Simone had done; the solution to the unsolvable human problem that was as much Jimmy's Goliath as Simone had been.

We hadn't known that he had given them to Hannah, his words. That when he sent his packets to Simone, he sent them to Hannah, too. We didn't celebrate one another's birthdays unless the party was at The End of the World and attended one another's weddings only through Facebook. We kept our new story ideas and our theses on Henry James to ourselves, and lost one another to the days that passed steadily toward packet deadlines. So it didn't occur to us that they might have been keeping track of each other during those four months between the end of our first June residency and Jimmy's death, from afar, the way the air traffic controllers track the red dots of planes in the sky.

But that must have been how she knew he was gone. His words stopped coming every month.

We're not going to pretend that we didn't keep flipping after the last of his words to look for our own writing. It was there, or some better version of it was, and we realized later that for all her hubris and all the craft lectures she had skipped, Leslie must have been keeping at least one eye and ear open while pretending to walk around with headphones playing music at impolite levels or sleeping through seminars, or at least borrowed notes from someone later, because she had learned a thing or two while she was at Fielding. Enough to tweak our works in progress in the ways our professors had been urging us to do. She had just gone ahead and done it without asking us for our permission or making suggestions that would help us do it ourselves—an impatient and unbending but brilliant editor. We never looked for or received confirmation that she was the one who had edited our pieces for the book, but we knew it the same way that we knew the Jimmy magic was Hannah's.

Though we don't have a single picture of Leslie or Hannah on campus, and between all fourteen of us, no one can produce the T-shirt from that first term, or even remember what motto we finally agreed on, every single one of us still has our book. It's partly nostalgia, yes, and partly because it contained the versions of our stories in progress that we would ultimately build into fuller, complete pieces that would end up in our theses, but also because what was inside of it was just that good.

We were still completely engrossed in what we had been given, still dabbing our eyes as surreptitiously as we could and trying to remember the last time we had each seen Jimmy, when Leslie stood up to make her exit.

"So anyway, you guys take as much time as you need to think it over, and anyone who wants to distribute our gift can meet at the flagpole tomorrow morning at ten. And, you know, look halfway presentable. This is a gift to a faculty member, not a fraternity party." We were too eager to get back to the books to be offended at the idea of Leslie giving us wardrobe or etiquette advice.

Maybe it was because of their history as hall mates, and the dance they'd had to do around Leslie's bathroom routine, that Jibs felt comfortable asking the one question still left unanswered by the books, which most of us had forgotten about until she asked.

"But what about the picture?"

"What picture?" Leslie asked, showing no evident distress at being the one in pursuit of information, for once.

"The one Jimmy took of Hannah by the pool."

"Oh," Leslie said. "Loveland, Colorado. But it wasn't Jimmy who took the picture, it was me. Jimmy was next to me, but he couldn't work an iPhone for shit."

We couldn't believe Leslie would end up in a place so unglamorous, never mind all the hopes we'd held for the picture. When we all started to press her for information at the same time, more gingerly than she would've pressed us, she said, "They have the best tortillas in the country," shrugging like it was the most obvious fact in the world. "You can live on tortillas for almost nothing."

"But why not Denver or Boulder or even Fort Collins?" Mimi asked.

"Don't get me started on the fucking yuppies there," Leslie said. "Do I look like I'm the type of person who can be bothered to spend two hundred dollars on leggings?"

Not even Lucas or Mimi were bold enough to say that, yes, of course she did. She must've been able to see how disappointed we were in the silence that settled in lieu of anyone pointing this out to her. Because she went on.

"Jesus, here's the thing you need to realize if your writing's ever going to be any good."

We wanted to be good too badly to be wounded at any suggestion that we weren't already, and leaned forward to hear what it was we needed to know. Seeing how much better she had already made our writing, we would've done just about anything she told us to do by then.

"Not everything interesting happens in New York or L.A. or Paris. If you're with the right people, Loveland can be the most interesting place in the world." We realized as she was saying this that she had already proven it true. Because none of us would ever meet anyone half as interesting as this strange girl we had met in an unremarkable corner of Vermont.

"I mean, I hate to break it to you guys, but sometimes being original means being uncool. Do you know how many novels have been set in those fashionable places everyone wants to go to, and all the other hipster paradises around the world? And do you know how many novels have been written about Loveland?"

"So is that what you were doing there?" Jamie Brigham asked. "Writing a novel?"

We tried not to be hurt when Hannah crept silently past us to the door and left the room.

"I mean, we got in enough shit to fill one," Leslie said, not acknowledging Hannah's exit in any way. "Or at least a really robust short story. But, no. We were there because it was one place to be. I have a second cousin who was managing a mostly empty apartment complex there, and I was able to arrange a deal. You wouldn't believe how cheap it was. And the tortillas, of course. Jimmy was only there a few weeks. We tried to get him to stay longer, but he said he had shit to tend to."

We tried not to linger too long, imagining all the things that probably entailed.

"We didn't hear from him after that, which I guess isn't surprising. The guy didn't even have a cell phone. They wrote to each other for a while after he left, though—Hannah and Jimmy—which is just the sort of outdated weirdo thing those loons would do."

We thought this might be the end of what she had to tell us about the picture, and were relieved when she went on.

"The apartment complex was kind of out in the middle of nowhere, on the edge of town. I mean, it was a real dump, but the mountains and the sky around there are so pretty that even a second-rate cockroach fest like this place couldn't ruin it. And it kind of felt like we were surrounded. By the mountains, I mean. Like they separated us from the rest of the world and anything that happened there. We spent the days watching movies. Jimmy had never seen anything. Like, he might have *actually* never seen a full movie from start to finish in his entire life. But, man, he took to them. We watched it all. *The Terminator. Star Wars. Indiana Jones. The Godfather* movies. They both had a thing for musicals, which I can take or leave, so we watched a lot of those, too—*Newsies* and *West Side Story*. You know, she's kind of a scholar, so Hannah made us watch some of the classics, too, which were a snooze, but Jimmy liked even those. We watched maybe every great story that's ever been told on the screen. Hannah has this theory that to be a good storyteller you have to study stories in other formats, too—songs and poems and movies. So the great thing was we didn't even feel guilty, how much time we spent watching. And then we'd smoke at the pool at dusk—well, I would, mostly, but I got Hannah to smoke a full cigarette once, don't let her tell you any different. After that we'd make an epic dinner every night before we sat down to write. At first we tried to all write in the same room, but Hannah vetoed that pretty quickly, because I may or may not do this thing where I tap my pen in sync with the rhythm of the lines I'm trying out before I write them down, and she likes to write like it's her job. So she took the kitchen while I took one of the bedrooms. She always has to be sitting in a hard chair to write, while I like to get comfortable. Jimmy took the bathroom, God love him."

Jibs opened her mouth here, to which Leslie held up her hand before Jibs even took a breath to begin.

"I have no idea why. He was a strange kid, you know that. There was a second bedroom he could've taken instead. Anyway, there was a real nice long, flat stretch of land that runs parallel to the complex and at night sometimes guys from town would race their motorcycles down it. Revving their engines, making a big spectacle. Mostly it was fine, but this one night they were really going for it. Shouting and carrying on in between runs. We thought it might be a Saturday, the way they were going on. We had completely lost track of the days. For a while we all just waited for it to pass, all in our own separate rooms. But then Hannah came into the bedroom with her head in her hands, and I thought she was gonna lose her damn mind, and—"

"I was so mad, I really was." Hannah said this from the doorway. We hadn't noticed that she had returned. She was smiling at the memory, nodding her head to confirm that it had really happened the way Leslie was telling it. "I was on the verge of something smart, I could feel it! And they just wouldn't stop, and I could feel it all, being lost. And that stuff doesn't always come back."

"No, it does not," Leslie agreed.

"I started jumping on the bed you were on to keep myself from going crazy. You know, just jumping my crazy out, which of course scared poor Jimmy. Those goddamned springs were so loud. He came running. And he was so relieved to see that it was just me. Do you remember that?"

Leslie nodded. "I remember you came into that bedroom like a complete madwoman. I was so glad to learn that I wasn't the only crazy one between us. And the fact that he ran toward you instead of away from you, as scared as he must've been from all the noise you were making . . . Well, I probably don't have to tell you he wouldn't have done that for me or anybody else."

"I decided that we all needed to get out of that apartment, so I just started running. Down the stairs and out the door. And I'll always love you both for following me right away. For not having to think about it for even a second. At first I was just going to give the guys out there a scare, screaming and carrying on in the middle of mostly empty nothing—they couldn't have seen a spectacle like the one I gave them very often. I thought it would at least startle them, but they loved it. They raised their beers and whooped, glad to have another wild creature to howl at the moon with them. And you and Jimmy both howled back. I still can't believe he howled."

"I wouldn't believe it either if I hadn't heard it myself," said Leslie.

"And at first it was just the three of us and the guys with the bikes, and then it was the three of us and the empty apartment lot, the asphalt and the yellow lines the only proof that any human being had been out there anytime lately. But we kept running, howling whenever it would occur to one of us, happy the bikers had given us something back for what they had taken. And I just kept waiting for one of you to stop, but neither of you did."

"Which is no small thing when you smoke a pack of cigarettes a day."

Hannah shook her head at this in disapproval, but she was smiling.

"It felt like we ran all night," she said. "And we were completely breathless when we stopped, covered in sweat, and we had wasted almost an entire night of writing. But he was happy for a second there, I swear to God he was."

"I think that's right," Leslie said.

It occurred to us only then that they might not have talked about this with each other yet.

"You're leaving out the best part," Leslie said.

"Discretion, Leslie," Hannah said, but again, it was clear she didn't really mind.

"Nah."

"And then without having to say anything we all turned toward the pool in between the parking lot and the apartments," Hannah conceded. "And we ran even faster than we had been toward it, and all jumped in at the same time."

"Buck-ass naked," Leslie clarified.

"Not all of us," Hannah said. "Jimmy and I kept at least a few things to the imagination."

"Wimps. That poor boy didn't even know how to do a

cannonball." Leslie turned back to the rest of us. "Don't worry, though, I taught him."

"He was gone a few days later, and I left the week after that. I lied to you and said my leave from work was up, but I'm pretty sure you knew I was lying."

"Yeah," said Leslie. "You're not very good at it."

"It just didn't really work the same without him."

And it was impossible, when she said this last part, not to feel sorry for her, as beautiful as she was, and as poised, too full of fire and her own supply of Leslie brass and guts to need our pity or anything else. Because we saw how much she missed him, despite how spectacularly she had called him back in the books we were all holding.

"Anyway, I hope you'll all come tomorrow," Hannah said, turning to us.

Every single one of us went, of course.

We assembled in the center of campus the next day, at the spot just between the library and the bookstore where the flagpole stood, and where anyone who needed to travel from almost any one point of campus to any other would have to pass. We must've looked out of place in the formal ensembles Leslie had told us to put on for the occasion. Leslie herself was wearing a billowy white dress that looked like a nightgown Emily Dickinson might've worn in her self-imposed isolation if it had been designed by Alexander McQueen.

Anything more expensive than off-brand dormitory hous-ing soap was considered a luxury to us during residency, but we had all managed to get our hands on an iron, or a hanger we could put next to a steaming shower. Everyone's outfit was crisp. Even Patrick Stanbury looked like someone's mother had had five minutes with him. The girls had finally brought us into the plan directly, and told us what to do and why it was important that we do it instead of just making sure we were there to witness whatever it was they were doing, and this was part of what made us stand up straighter and comb our hair and create the first ever shower line the program has probably ever seen. But we also did these things partly because we had spent the twenty-four hours since the girls had gathered us into the barn marveling again and again, over and over, to both ourselves and one another, at what they had made from Jimmy's words.

When we first started handing out books like Mardi Gras revelers distributing beads it was a festive, celebratory morning. A ceremony that unfolded in bits and parts we couldn't plan, not knowing who would be walking by when, but fluid at every turn. Recipients thanked us for the books with smiles that were clearly genuine. Even the cafeteria workers and the random students and the Lindas of cross-stitch mastery, whose preferences and opinions on the books we spoke about in precious, elevated terms we never got to know, seemed happy to be handed what we gave them. When Johanna Green, the short story writer who had abandoned Professor Pearl that first term in order to tend to her orphanhood, accepted her copy, she *ooh*ed like it was an early review copy of Jonathan Franzen's next novel, which we appreciated. The books were bound in plain black cloth with no text or type on the cover, which seemed only to increase the intrigue in the people we handed copies to. In a rare moment of uncertainty, Tammy turned to Hannah when Jude Morgan approached, unsure if he was worthy of so coveted a good, and Hannah urged her on with an *of course* scooch forward of the chin—like all great texts, this one was for everyone.

We might've been starting to sag a little by the time the one-hour mark came and went, but we kept our top buttons buttoned, and not even Jibs complained. By the two-hour mark, though, it was really starting to get hot, and it seemed intentional that Simone was one of the few people on campus who hadn't walked by. Maybe she was less vulnerable to this attack than we thought.

We had started to lose hope, but none of us had admitted it out loud yet. Patrick was sitting on the curb trying fruitlessly to arrange his body gracefully, as clearly consumed by the heat as a panting dog, though he kept his tongue in his mouth and his head between his knees the way athletes do. Lucas and Robbie were playing kick the can like the grown children they were. Bridget Jameson had pulled a tattered paperback copy of a Camus novel in its original French and started reading it—we weren't sure which novel it was, none of us versed in Camus's mother tongue. Those of us who hadn't found anything to pass the time with watched the bead of sweat at Bridget's temple that grew with every page she turned and waited for it to fall.

It was Leslie who saw her first, of course. She didn't say anything—we knew the moment was upon us only when she walked over to Jibs, who was leaning against a telephone pole in a slouch that left little doubt about the extent of her agitation, to hand her a copy of the book, and said, "You do this one," giving no indication what made this one different, or even that anything did. When we looked over and saw who was approaching, it made us each think that maybe the earlier honor of lighting the match hadn't been random after all. And that in Jibs Leslie saw something of a wounded bird—or even a broken egg not unlike the unnamed narrator of Hannah's first, beloved story—a tinny little voice that wasn't afraid to say whatever it felt or thought whenever it felt or thought it where the rest of us saw only a nuisance. We realized that maybe Jimmy hadn't been the first person Leslie would look after and defend, even if by questionable means, even if she did the looking after too late, and probably wouldn't be the last.

We didn't have too long to consider this thought. Simone was now close enough that we could read the expression on her face, which gave exactly nothing away. Her normally untouched skin was a collage of purple clouds and exclamation marks of scrapes, calling attention to her for all the reasons she would've hated. Only Hannah gave her the kindness of looking down as she approached.

It's tempting to come up with some clever way to say she looked at us the way you speak to telemarketers when they call during dinner or the good part of a show, but the truth is she couldn't be bothered to rise to nearly that level of passion. She simply walked by us, holding up her hand in a hostile *thanks, but no thanks* gesture that didn't require her to take her eyes off the phone she was clutching in her other hand. We all turned to Leslie, of course, who was patting Margaret in a motherly, comforting way, or the pantomime of the way she'd seen other mothers do it—a seventh-grader playing the mother in a school play.

"Don't worry," she said, once Simone was out of earshot. "I have plans for that one." She turned to the rest of us then, making it clear that what she was saying was meant for all of us, not just Jibs, however dignified her role was to be in all this. "Thank you all for your help. This next part I've got."

Simone had a western-facing corner office on the second floor of the most distant classroom building on campus. Its walls were so white you could almost feel the light bouncing off of them when you closed your eyes. They weren't eggshell white or taupe, just pure, blank slate white. That Simone hadn't hung a single picture or postcard or book jacket, even her own, made them seem even more impossibly pure and saturated. When the sun set, the office filled with light as surely and tangibly and physically as it would have with people if Simone ever had visitors, which she almost never did. The effect was something like a thousand tiny points of light converging in the center of a blizzard, something good where you least expected it, which of course was all wrong for Simone.

One of our favorite images from this story, real or imagined, remembered or constructed, is Leslie making her way toward all that light in her Emily Dickinson dress. She waited just enough time after Simone had rebuffed us before setting off toward her office. Simone would have just settled into the chair she had had shipped from her favorite furniture designer's studio in Brooklyn. She would've just shaken the last of the fading stills on the backs of her eyelids of a good third of the student body hawking books of unknown origin at her like Bible salesmen. Leslie walked without any urgency—she would get there on her own time—but with the steady gait of someone who knows exactly where they're going.

The image we have begins with a wide angle, zoomed completely out, and looks a little like a video game maze with an avatar that is mostly gauzy white nightgown dress and rock-and-roll sex hair and an end zone that is mostly just flashing rays of light, promising every association from heaven to gold. Leslie kept the book behind her the whole way, always positioning her entire body between it and Simone, safe and out of sight until the exact right moment.

The focus narrows slowly as Leslie makes her way across

the field with wildflowers in front of the music building and on past the Empty Garden, where the burned remains of her January fire still probably sat, and continues to narrow until you can see things like her disastrous eye makeup—smudged as always—but eyes as white and pure as Simone's office walls, unblemished by even a single red vein, clear and alert and completely seeing. If Leslie didn't have the perfect shoe to pair with an outfit, she went without, calluses and rusty nails to hell, and since this dress floated outside of time or season, it had no footwear companion. She had painted her toenails the color of eggplant, but the polish was chipped, revealing the pink of toenails cleaner and better manicured than we would have guessed of Leslie, the pink of a baby fresh from the bath.

Arriving at the end of her maze, Leslie didn't knock on Simone's open door, but arranged herself lazily, comfortably against her door frame, so that when Simone looked up, she was simply there, no lightning or fire in her pocket this time, but something better. How long she had been there, Simone had no way of knowing.

While Leslie found Simone's insistence on having this office childish and distasteful, she had to admit that the campus laid itself out magnificently on the other side of all Simone's windows. Facing her head-on and from only a few feet away, Leslie saw that Simone's bruises had the swollen, tender look they take on after a day or two, which must have made her look small in front of so much uninterrupted space.

Leslie began, as she always did, without any preamble.

"Did you go to public school, Simone?" We imagine her asking this as casually as if she were braiding Simone's hair at a sleepover party. "You seem like the kind of person who went to public school for a year and then always called herself a public school kid at cocktail parties because of it. You know, for, like, the cred?"

"I'm sorry, why do you care where I went to school?" Simone was learning—you couldn't pet the animals on this ride.

"Not that there's anything wrong with private school. I went to Catholic boarding school myself. You hear *boarding school* and you think *fancy*, probably, right? And mine was expensive, to be sure, but it was run by nuns, so it was hard knocks, too, you know? *Austere* is the word I think they would use for it."

"I see your semester with Professor Pearl has imparted the importance of word choice to you. I'm sure he'd be proud."

If this was meant to soften Leslie with its flattery or scare her with its mention of Pearl, it had neither of its desired effects. Leslie didn't even bother to bat it away with a response before she went on.

"They taught us all sorts of things there with their tough love. They taught us to cross our feet at the ankles and always sneeze into the V of our arms. To never wear navy blue with black, or stockings with runs. It sounds more like finishing school, I know, but they taught us some things that stuck, too. You know, things that still seem to matter, all these years later."

"Okay."

That was all Simone would give her, Leslie would tell us later. She was still trying to figure out the rules here, or maybe locate the speediest exit.

"They taught us to protect the weak, and always have appreciation—gratitude—for the miracles constantly at work around us. Grace, I think it was called."

"Well, you're just full of information, aren't you?"

"No," said Leslie, still ignoring her. "Not grace. Wonder." And it's here that something must have narrowed just enough in Leslie's eyes that Simone knew this wasn't a ride that ended with fluorescent exit signs, and Simone tried something else.

"Wonder?" she said, like she might've said the word *genocide*, or *colonoscopy*. "What the hell does that mean?"

"That's what they called it—the feeling you were supposed to have for the unstoppable, magical forces of good at work in our lives. You know, for David Bowie, and banana pudding from Magnolia—the West Village in its entirety, really—and freshly painted yellow walls. For the first sip of your favorite wine after a twelve-hour day, or Shelley Duvall's sweaters in *The Shining*. And those few weeks in late April and early May when cherry blossoms come to the end of their bloom and it rains flower petals, and there are blankets of pink and white everywhere. Or—here's one you'd appreciate: reading the last line of a perfectly written book. The kind of line you never saw coming but know, as soon as you read it, is the only line the book could've ended with. I mean, those aren't the miracles the nuns would've used as examples—those are mine. But we all have to find our own miracles in this armpit life, right? You don't really seem like a drinker, do you? It's no good for the skin. And you're probably more of a Springsteen girl than Bowie."

Simone would neither confirm nor deny, no longer pretending to be complicit in whatever this was.

"*Anyway*, I didn't come here to bore you, I just came here to give you a copy of this."

Leslie had started her speech in the frame of Simone's doorway, and had been inching steadily closer. By now she was leaning against the edge of the desk Simone sat behind, close enough to hand the object she had been hiding behind her back to Simone upon its big reveal. It was the same book we had been giving out on the lawn, only this one was leather bound, and had Simone's name embossed in gold. Simone only blinked at it.

"If there's one thing graduate students appreciate, it's free things," Leslie said. "So I'm happy to tell you that when you make a hundred copies of something, they give you one embossed in gold for free. I knew right away the gold one should be yours."

"And why's that?" Simone finally asked, probably relieved to finally be at the part of this exchange where someone handed her the bill.

"Well, since you're the star of the book, of course."

And here, finally, with this line, Leslie got the reaction she'd been aiming for all along.

"I don't want it," Simone said, completely terrified now, staring at the book Leslie was still holding out to her like it had the time and date and means of her death written inside it.

"Oh, I think you do," Leslie said, close enough by now that Simone must've been able to feel Leslie's breath on her face. "You seem like the kind of person who likes to see her name in print, and there's quite a bit of it here." She placed the book gingerly on top of the pile of student manuscripts that sat in the center of Simone's desk before she turned to go.

Leslie was pretty much already gone, having turned left out of Simone's office with only the tail of her white dress flapping behind her, when she popped back in like a human after-thought. She leaned only her head and shoulders into the doorway, letting the rest of her body hang outside its frame, promising that whatever she had come back to say was only a postscript.

"I almost forgot the best part about this. I paid for *three* copies of the leather-bound version—only one was free, which you can imagine was a bit of a pinch on my graduate student budget, but I think it will be worth it. I sent one to your agent and one to your editor, along with Xeroxes of Jimmy's pack-ets. Maybe I should drop a few copies off at Lefferts, too, now that I think of it—all your guests must be here by now."

Simone's "*No!*" to this was the most impassioned word or

gesture that Leslie or any of us would ever get from her, and her last word on all of this, disappointingly brief coming from a woman of so many words.

"Jimmy wasn't only sending his packets to you, thank God. He sent them to Hannah, too. You probably haven't given her much thought, but she's the girl I'm always skulking around with. Anyway, he loved her and she loved him, and he showed her by giving her his words and she showed him by reading them right away. Like, the very second they arrived. I bet you always waited a day or two to open your students' packets, huh? There was always some party or opening to go to, right? It's a shame they're probably not going to let you teach here anymore, because you're going to have a lot more time. No more parties."

Leslie was so happy by this point, the smile she gave Simone was almost genuine.

"I don't want to blur the point by going on too long. The point *is* that they were each other's wonder, and he hadn't had a whole lot of it in his life. So little, in fact, that even the word got him excited. But I bet you knew that better than anyone, having read so much of his work, which I still think is the best way to get to know somebody. And just to tie it all back in with the nuns, pretty much the one thing they and I would agree on is that there's no greater sin in all the world than to steal someone's wonder."

Leslie looked out beyond Simone, maybe to whatever would come after all this was finished. She was in no rush for final words. When she finally turned back to the room, the cost of her visit must have been all over Simone's face.

"What's the matter, Simone?" she asked, seeing Simone's despondency, and noting that she looked almost as desperate as Jimmy had been that day she and Hannah went to his room after his disastrous workshop. "It's just words on a page, right?"

By the time Leslie finally left for good, her question trailing just after the hem of her dress, Simone's mouth was a perfectly round, dumbfoundedly gaping O, and the sun had started its descent. How long it took the O to shrink into a tight line of pinched, resigned lips, and the degree to which its shrink kept pace with the wilting sun and anything else that transpired in the last burst of sunlight in a room that collects it, is something no one can tell you. Leslie had skipped back down the hallway and out across the lawn back to Hannah and the rest of us by then.

Maybe it was a bit too tidy, the way Leslie left Simone perfectly, completely defeated—destroyed, even—not to mention the speed with which Simone was subsequently dispatched from the program after that. After a closed-door meeting with Pearl early the next morning that not even Joni Kleinman knows the contents of, she left campus immediately. Her second book was discreetly canceled by the publisher. She never did make that comeback, even after the alumni magazine interview and the short story publications. She tried to write for TV for a while, for pilots that never saw the air. The last any of us heard, she was living quietly in New York, one of countless other artistic souls there who know their work to be underrated. Even her first, celebrated novel is out of print.

She had cautioned us against this very kind of neat, bow-wrapped ending in the same workshop in which she eviscerated Jimmy's poems, we never did forget. It was the clearest warning any of us had ever been issued and the most directly we had ever been instructed on what our fiction should aim to achieve, by someone whose opinion we surely courted at the time. And no matter how terrible a person she was, and how spectacularly her career combusted after these events, it was hard to argue with her storytelling or her line-by-line skill. Maybe Leslie was used to ignoring instructions like this and blazing right ahead, but not the rest of us. So it's no small thing, our decision to end things this way, in what we all consider to be the closest thing to an official record of these events.

But we know better by now. From our time in the program, yes, but also from the books we read and loved both before and after that, and the parts we have figured out about the books we're still planning to write. From the very things we saw across these three residencies we've reported to you, and all the countless other things that Hannah and Leslie and Jimmy showed us.

Fiction is meant to achieve all kinds of things.

Everything After

We hope you'll forgive us for taking liberties that must be clear to you by now, and plugging in the holes with the sometimes mismatched materials we had at hand. We like to think we're a creative body, capable together of what we could never do alone. We inevitably got some parts wrong, but so what if we did? Maybe it's for the best. *No live organism can continue for long to exist sanely under conditions of absolute reality; even larks and katydids are supposed, by some, to dream.* That isn't us, of course. It was Shirley Jackson first, and then Leslie, who got it tattooed on her forearm the first semester she taught at Fielding, bringing the tattoo count to ten. We like to think her decision to commit to the sentiment so permanently means she wouldn't mind these liberties that we mention.

Here's another one for you: *A story was nothing more than a lie you got away with,* or maybe *Tell a lie long enough and it will turn to truth.* Both are from Yaa Gyasi, a very successful, highly paid MFA graduate, we'd like both you and our practical fathers to know.

We all lost touch after graduation, of course. But after Sarah Jacobs married Robbie Myers, who we were all shocked to learn wasn't already married, and the girl both Robbie and Lucas White were in love with came to the wedding and he felt, upon seeing her in a gold sequin dress that must have been custom-made, absolutely nothing. After Melissa Raymond had a second child with the husband she became more faithful to over time instead of less, and finally shook Tanner Conover for good. And the small stir that Patrick Stanbury caused when he emailed to tell us that, paging through a celebrity rag someone had left in the seat pocket in front of him on the flight to a coaching interview at a D-3 school in Pittsburgh, he had spotted an item about the pop star whose heart had been broken by one Jiles Gardner, now an acclaimed British novelist. We started exchanging bits of news with one another.

By then we all had tidy little stacks of rejections wishing us luck in our writing endeavors, right next to regrets about being unable to publish us. Though this was a very different kind of luck from the luck Pearl had wished Leslie, that line, which might've stung otherwise, deceptively cheerful and optimistic as it was, made us think of him, and the program, and

Leslie and Jimmy and Hannah, and one another, too. Which made us grateful to him for having said it all over again.

Once we got the marriages and divorces and babies and publications out of the way, we turned our attention to finally sorting through and pinning together what happened those first three terms we were all together. It was incredible, the things we all remembered the same, and the things we remembered differently, and the things that each of us had seen and heard alone without thinking to tell the rest of us. Most incredible of all, maybe, was how much time we were willing to spend trying to figure out which overheard conversations and which after-hours meeting of two spotted across campus were the most important, and which parts of each varying account had the most credibility, and the methods we used to determine this.

Bridget Jameson is the one who finally suggested we write it all down. To elevate it above petty gossip or whispers, yes, but also because the one thing we all have in common, she reminded us, is that we're all writers. She was tireless in her answering and gathering of our emails. She picked up more late-night calls than any of the rest of us probably would have, and patiently mediated the squabbles that inevitably erupted between us. When it came time to actually start writing the story, once we had the facts and the timeline down, we were prepared to just let her tell it, but, being Bridget, she refused, insisting the story wouldn't be complete—wouldn't even make sense—without the exact piece each of us had contributed. We finally agreed on the communal *we* simply because it was clear to us, by the time the story was ready to be set to paper, that she was right.

Without any one of us, the whole thing falls apart.

Leslie and Hannah are the only two classmates who weren't consulted. Bridget managed even to track down Jamie Brigham, whom she had stayed friendly with even after he dropped out of the program after our third term, the milk incident something of an inside joke between them by then. We had thought the timing of his departure might mean what happened on campus that second June had been a factor in it, but we learned he had left when his wife became pregnant with twins before either of them had planned on parenthood. He was living in Paris by the time Bridget emailed him, and happy to contribute what he could remember even if it was less than he would've liked, given that two more children had followed the twins in rapid succession.

At the outset we plotted how best to get in touch with the girls but stopped when we realized that any answers they could give us would be akin to reading the CliffsNotes to a novel we were meant to savor. Or maybe we just couldn't bear to hear them tell us no. Though they weren't directly included in the project doesn't mean, of course, that they lost the intrigue they had held for us, or that we stopped collecting the small bits of information about them any one of us was able to find and report back to the rest of us.

We never saw Hannah again after that third residency. Leslie saw her off at the train station the day after we distributed our class gift. She didn't return to campus for the next residency or even for our graduation, not even to celebrate with Leslie. She was done with the program. She didn't need it, we knew, after reading what she had done with Jimmy's work. She had only come that second June for Jimmy, and she would leave and do whatever came next for herself. It felt good to read what she had made, because we realized that part of why she had given so little of herself to us wasn't snobbery, or timidness, or even Leslie. She had been there to work, and now she was done. That she would've given any piece of herself that could've been working to Jimmy only showed how much she really did love him, or could've, given half the chance.

She published only one novel, a five-hundred-page sweeping family saga that spans Boston and Mumbai, which was a finalist for the Pulitzer. Determined as she had been to get Jimmy's poetry the praise it deserves, it surprised no one when she gave up her urban planning work to become a critic for the *New York Review of Books*.

Leslie borrowed Linda's Honda to take Hannah to the station that last residency Hannah was part of, but insisted on dropping Hannah off right as the train was pulling out, because she refused to miss Professor Pearl's final lecture on melodrama in contemporary fiction. She started a standing ovation before he finished his last line and then started

running for the car, where Hannah was already nestled between her bags, sunglasses on at dusk.

She took her time seeing Hannah off despite the rush
leading up to it. She held her hand up to the outside window
of Hannah's seat. Hannah wouldn't hold her own hand up to
it, not willing to aid and abet so uncharacteristically sentimental a gesture on Leslie's part. This did nothing to deter
Leslie. She kept her hand up until the train started moving,
and even after, walking slowly, calmly, looking straight ahead.
She stayed until well after the train was out of sight, until she
saw the kind of Vermont dark that Jimmy had seen that first
night, after falling asleep on the train. Then she walked back
to the car to turn her headlights on—two lone beams to cut
through all that dark—and drove back the way she had come.

Professor Pearl didn't retire after all. How could he, after
his most prestigious professor left in disgrace, jeopardizing the
program's legacy? He took a year off as planned to promote his
second book. His daughter got the dedication—*For Ana,
always*—but the first acknowledgment in the back went "To
Leslie, who believes in miracles." It outsold *Cactus and Dust* in
a month. His first decision in his new, old role when he returned to campus was to hire Leslie to the faculty to teach
genre-bending writing. Literary sci-fi and mystery and, yes,
erotica. Because some things—sometimes the best things—
can't be put in any one box, and are everything and nothing we
can name or imagine at once. He pushed her start date back a
year, so that anyone who had been a student on campus with

her would graduate by the time she took her post, but she said yes immediately. Her student reviews were so unanimously positive her first two years in the position that she was asked to stay on full time, as a professor in the undergrad English program as well.

She planned to stay only for a few semesters. Wanderers have trouble staying put, after a certain amount of wandering, even when they've wandered somewhere good. She learned halfway through her second term as an associate professor that she was going to have a baby boy, though she didn't know he was a boy until he arrived, because Leslie likes to keep even herself guessing sometimes. No one has ever gotten the name of the father out of her. It's not that she stays silent on the subject, but that she has a different answer for everybody who asks.

At first, having learned she was pregnant, she stayed on only because she needed the insurance. But after Fielding's lone ob-gyn held up the squirming, almost-too-alive tiny human, who was furious at the indignity of birth, and announced it was a boy. And after Leslie looked at him with a tilted head and eyes so tired she struggled to keep them open long enough to determine what he should be called with a level or certainty only Leslie is capable of. And after deciding that this Jimmy would get the home—home in a permanent, physical, doormat-in-front-of-a-door kind of way—that the last one didn't, she resolved to stay for good without telling anyone, and simply began to do the things that lend themselves to tenure with Leslie relish. This created friends and enemies, of course, neither of which Leslie had been a stranger to, and adoring students and long nights of reading and writing and drinking syrupy wine out of plastic cups. And publications and reviews good and bad, and favorite students Leslie never took too many pains to hide were her favorite—they were the weak and meek and broken and strange ones, always—and to whom she would tell the sort of incredible, over-the-top, unbelievable tales that only Leslie is capable of telling, only she tells them so well you start to believe they might be true. And it was very rarely a raw deal for her, at least the way it had been the first fifteen years of her life, or as raw as she had thought it would become again, at some point or another, sooner or later.

She kept teaching even after the kinds of successes other teachers often retired after to write full time. She's published stories in *The New Yorker* and *Harper's*. Her second novel was a bestseller and her third was optioned by Sofia Coppola. We have yet to find a single sex scene in any of them. We all eagerly await the fourth, not least because we think this might be the one.

Hannah is the last of the Hannah-Jimmy-Leslie trio to take up the role of living ghost. The whispers these days have her coming to campus once or twice a year to see Leslie, whom she hasn't managed to shake after all these years. She came alone at first, then with her timid, handsome husband, a law professor who fills a white-shoe firm's pro bono quotient, helping the weak in slightly more aboveboard fashion than

Leslie, and finally with their two daughters. She doesn't make herself any more available, or even visible, when she's on campus these days than she did when she was a student here, but there are rare sightings reported by undergrads and MFA students alike. It's hard not to wonder what she felt, seeing Jimmy's namesake for the first time, or what the women themselves whisper about these days.

But those are different stories.

Acknowledgments

I owe huge thanks to my editor, Laura Perciasepe, and my agent, Monika Woods, both of whom made this book much better than the one I originally wrote, and made what could be a daunting process good fun at every turn. Thank you to the entire Riverhead team for sprinkling their book magic on my work, especially Shailyn Tavella, Geoff Kloske, Jynne Martin, Kate Stark, Lydia Hirt, Mary Stone, and Delia Taylor.

Thank you to my publishing fairy godmothers, Deborah Garrison, Ann Close, Gillian Blake, and Maggie Richards, for teaching me invaluable lessons about storytelling (and life). And to my work wives Katie Freeman, Josie Kals, Sarah Bowlin, Leslie Brandon, and Serena Jones, thank you for reminding me again and again how fun the work of telling stories really is, and how lucky we are to get to do it.

I was fortunate enough to get to pursue a low-residency MFA at Bennington College, and I'm grateful to both my professors and classmates there. Few things have been more inspiring to me as a writer than the passion I found on Bennington's campus, and I hope that's apparent on these pages. Special thanks to Louise Munson and Sarah Fuss for making my time there so magical. To MFA students there and everywhere, past, present, and future: keep writing.

Thank you to my Brooklyn and Kenyon families for being so insanely supportive of my work, and for making their moms buy my book. Special thanks to Ben Wasserstein and Julia Turner for their support of my work (and reliably good company).

Thank you to my family family—of all things I'm glad to have done or be, being a Zancan and a ZML will always top the list. Thank you especially to my parents and siblings, and Emma, one of my own greatest sources of wonder, who I love getting to watch grow up even from far away. And to Ben, who combed through numerous drafts of this novel with me, and humored even my most insane queries about it—there's no travel companion I'd rather have for this adventure we're on, and I can't wait to learn how the rest of our story unfolds.